A New Zepher

By

David Munson

For information contact: David Munson

www.davidmunsonbooks.com

Book Cover design by Jodi L. Cox

DEDICATION

This book is dedicated to every friend I have made along this adventure. Every kind and encouraging word that has helped to fuel my imagination to give life to the world of Ellspire. A special thanks to my loving family and supportive friends. It is also dedicated to any fellow dreamer who has been told to give up. Life is not always about winning, sometimes it is all about finishing the race.

A special thanks to my parents for all the sacrifices they had to make to get me where I am today, this project has only been possible through un-relenting support from my mother and the dedication that was taught to me by my father.

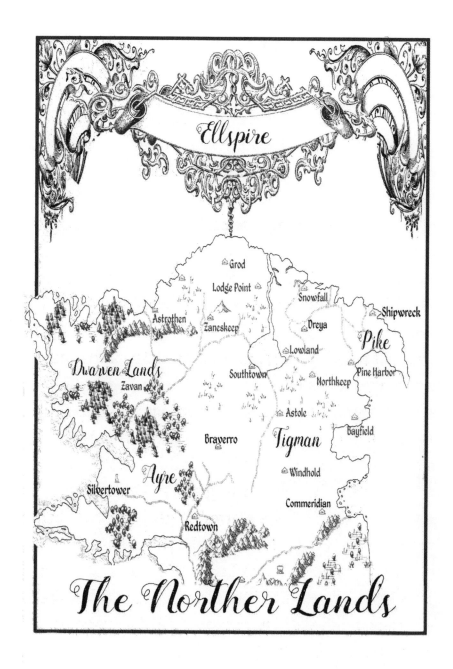

CHAPTER 1

ASTOLE

The next morning was cold, and Jadeance was having the hardest time getting out of his blankets. No matter how hard he tried, he simply couldn't open his eyes. Jadeance could hear Brie's voice, and somewhere he could feel her shaking him, but it seemed as if his mind had been placed in a fog that he simply couldn't escape from. He didn't even feel her pulling his top off. He did however, feel the ice cold skillet she placed on his newly exposed back. That cleared the fog from his mind instantly! He jumped free of her, screaming and swearing like a cornered badger. As he started to get his senses back, he could see Tannis rolling on the ground laughing hysterically, and Brie was kneeling at the end of his blankets holding the skillet as a weapon. "What the hell are you doing?" he screamed, his heart racing.

Tannis began to laugh even harder.

"I'm so sorry! We have been trying to wake you for almost an hour," Brie replied.

"But I...," Jadeance stuttered.

"We tried everything. Please don't hate me, but we have to go."

He looked over at Tannis, who was laughing so hard his face had turned red. "Are you done? You look like an idiot."

"You screamed like a girl!" Tannis roared.

Jadeance jumped for Tannis; however he was tied up in his blankets and fell hard on his face. Jadeance was struggling to free himself when Brie tackled him. She was surprisingly strong, and he was bound up in his blankets. Brie had quite effectively pinned him to the ground.

"What are you doing?" Jadeance yelled.

"I'm not going to let you up until you forgive me, and we can get back on the road."

He looked into her eyes and his anger slowly dissolved, however his embarrassment doubled. "I'll think about it if you get off me."

"Don't you like it?" Brie laughed.

"No I don't, now move."

Brie laughed and kissed him a few times before jumping up. Jadeance couldn't stop blushing. He freed himself and started throwing things at Tannis. The rest of the morning Jadeance rode in silence. He looked over at Brie and Tannis, feeling just a little picked on. He couldn't help being so tired. It was exhausting trying to use Magic. His sword jabbed him as he moved back towards the pack horse and he began to swear. He didn't like it very much, it was heavy and uncomfortable. At first the thought of having a sword was exciting, yet after days of painful jabbing and long nights spent learning to use it, the appeal had completely worn off. He didn't feel much like a soldier. He looked down at it again and sighed. The sooner this was all over with, the sooner he could return to Wagstaff. Seeing a traveler's life, he started to think that an innkeeper just might be a better fit for him after all.

They traveled into the afternoon. Then as the sun started to set, they came over the crest of a hill, and there was the fishing village of Astole, set on the banks of the Toor River. To Jadeance it seemed huge. The river stretched as far his eyes could see. He had never seen a river so large. Astole itself was easily twice the size of Windhold. But it was built differently than any town or village Jadeance had ever seen before. Instead of going out from the center of town like Windhold, Astole was built up the river long and narrow.

"Astole," Vel said with some relief.

"Where to now?" Tannis asked.

"To the Serpent Head Inn," Vel replied. "It is the largest in town. Food is not great, but it will do."

As they rode into town there were people everywhere, moving around shouting. It had an unpleasant smell of dead fish.

"Does the whole town stink like this?" Jadeance inquired.

Vel smiled slightly, "No, the main loading docks are just down that street. That is where most of the smell comes from."

"If that's what a river boat smells like, I hope I never have to set foot in one," Jadeance said aloud.

Tannis began to laugh. "You used to want to come here and be a fisherman, don't you remember?"

"Just keep quiet you," Jadeance threatened.

They moved through the town for what seemed like hours. There were trader's tables and people moving about in numbers Jadeance had never before imagined. Through the masses there were groups of hooded men moving about, who bore a strange green emblem on the breast. Jadeance had never seen anything like it before, and he did not care too again. He did not know why, but these men scared him. Shaking himself, Jadeance looked around. "This place just keeps going on and on, how big is this town?"

"It is quite large," Vel replied. "We are

nearing the inn."

"Is it just me, or are there a lot of men wearing the same black outfit?" Tannis asked.

"Everyone seems to be afraid of them," Brie added.

"I did notice that. There is a strange evil in the air," Vel replied looking at a group of four men walking down the street. Everyone seemed to melt and give way leaving a clear path.

"Why are they acting like that? It feels very unfriendly here," Jadeance said.

"They are afraid," Vel replied. "We must be cautious, do not speak to anyone unless they speak first. Something is not right here." Vel stopped in front of a large inn. It had large carved serpent on the doors. "This is it, be cautious and stay close." They got off their mounts, and Jadeance handed the reins over to the stable master and followed Tannis inside. The inn was large and open, the tables were lopsided and in poor repair. What candles did burn were small and gave a dull glow that left the room in a dull haze. The tables that were not scratched up were covered in dirty dishes, and there seemed to be an unnecessary amount of pipe smoke in the air. An older balding man approached them. He was normal sized with light brown hair and a neatly trimmed beard. He was neatly dressed, and despite his age he carried himself as if he were young, walking with a grace and elegance Jadeance had never seen before.

"Vel-Imein, you made it safely," the stranger said with a smile. "Things are getting bad here, and I feared the worst."

Vel fell to his knee. "Magistrate Atrius," he said with deep respect.

"Stand up old friend," the old man replied quickly. "We have much to discuss. These must be the children." He looked them over. "We had better do our introductions at the table."

Jadeance followed them to a large table off to one side of the inn. They all sat down. Jadeance was looking forward to a good meal and some rest.

"Ahh, this is much better," the old man said, and then he looked around at them again. "My name is Atrius. That is all you need know for now. There are unfriendly ears about." He looked at Vel. "Where is Balseer?"

"We were attacked not two days ago. A tracker with considerable power ambushed us. We were able to defeat him, however Balseer was gravely wounded. He left a trail for anyone who might be tracking us."

Atrius let out a deep sigh.

"He fought with great honor," Vel replied lightly.

"You seem troubled," Atrius replied with a sad voice.

"I never truly believed in him," Vel said.

"You have old prejudices. His heart was on our side."

Vel grunted, "Well he made the path clear."

Atrius flagged down the inn keeper. "I need you to tell the cook to prepare dinner tonight for twenty men. You'll need to have several kegs of ale ready." He handed the inn keeper a hand full of coins. "That ought to cover it."

"My lord," the man replied slightly embarrassed. "Your table won't sit so many. More importantly, you will have trouble if you bring so many men in here."

"Oh, don't worry about the table. It's plenty big enough. I'm not really going to have twenty men joining me tonight."

"But you just ordered."

"Ahh," Atrius interrupted with a slight grin. "I have ordered food for twenty men, yes. However, it is my great misfortune to have men coming who eat far more than they should. Not to worry, they will eat it up for you. Now, the trouble you were mentioning... is it?" he pointed at the small group of men who were in the same black suits they had seen out in the town.

The inn keeper looked away quickly and nodded. "They don't like competition. Well I guess you could say they don't like much of anything at all, except young girls, that is." And then he looked at Brie. "Keep her hidden. They came in after you, so they haven't noticed her yet. Pray that they don't." With that he left with the coins in hand.

"What is all that about?" Tannis asked.

"Oh, you are not the only travelers I expect tonight," Atrius said with a smile.

Vel also smiled slightly. "It will be good to see them all again."

"Who is coming?" Brie asked.

"Oh I don't want to spoil it for you. This should be a night long remembered." Atrius said with a smile.

"What does that mean?" Tannis asked.

"Well, they are not what most people consider to be normal. More importantly, this is a special gathering that has been long foretold." Then he smiled, "they are certainly an interesting group. You'll get the idea, but now on to more exciting things. You see, now you know who I am, and I believe it's time for you to return the favor. You are the eldest, he who bears the birthright, and the first of the new and great bloodline."

"If you say so," Tannis replied slowly. "My name is Tannis. This is my brother Jadeance."

"Can it be? He who bears the will and power of the Divines? The one for whom the world shall all know?" Atrius said his face filling with excitement.

Tannises eyebrows shot up. "What are you talking about?"

"Nothing at all, please continue," Atrius replied, his face set with excitement.

Tannis looked confused. "This is Brie, a good family friend. She is somewhat attached to Jade here."

"She who bears the sight and wisdom of the ages," Atrius said still smiling.

"What is going on?" Jadeance asked.

"Nothing to worry about, young man. In fact, the world has much less to worry about now that this day has finally come."

"I do not know if the day has truly come or not," Vel replied. "I do not think he is going to come. Nobody even knows where he is."

"I do," a stranger said as he sat himself next to Atrius. Vel started to stand up. The stranger simply waved his hand at him.

"Don't be a fool," the stranger said. "You have to stop bowing every time we meet."

"It is customary in my country to rise up."

"Please Vel," he interrupted. "You have explained it to me already. I don't like ceremonies. 'It's good to see you again' will suffice." Then he looked around the table, grinning at the confused faces. "I'm not going to lie, I love surprising people like this. Confusion is a wonder to behold."

Atrius shook his head, "You're ever the joker, and this is Grand Master Wurwick, an old fool with a quick wit. Currently First Chair of the Great Circle of the Wizards of the Silver Tower."

"Formerly, my dear fellow," Wurwick replied with a smile. "I have decided to come out of retirement."

"What do you mean?" Atrius asked puzzled.

"That is a game for later," Wurwick replied with a smile and a lift of his eyebrows.

Wurwick seemed to be very old. He had a long grey beard that was well maintained. His long grey hair was partly covered by a moth eaten hat. His blue eyes were a strong contrast to the silvery gray in his beard. He carried a beautiful staff of finely carved wood that had a man smoking a pipe depicted on it with more detail than Jadeance could believe. The man seemed alive, his beard and hair seemed to flow as if a real man had been placed inside the staff, and now that is where he resides.

"That is a beautiful staff," Brie said in wonder.

"Oh this?" Wurwick replied with a little laugh. "I have been working on it for so long now I can hardly remember why I started. Not that it matters." He smiled fondly at it, "It's the journey you take that counts."

The inn keeper returned and brought ale and bread to them. "Is there any particular time you will be eating?"

Atrius smiled. "Not for at least an hour or better."

The inn keeper shook his head. "Just let me know."

The men dressed in black robes moved to a table not too far from their own table, and one of them locked his eyes on Brie and started poking the others at his table.

"I don't like the looks of that," Atrius said.

"What do we do?" Tannis asked.

"We hope they stay there," Atrius replied.

Four of the men stood up and walked over to their table. With a smile, one of them reached over and knocked over Wurwick's drink. "Sorry about that, old man. It seems as if accidents have a way of happing around here lately. That's why we're here. You see, we are here to help. You seem like a nice old man, so I'll tell you what. You give me that girl there and I'll see to it that no real bad accidents happen to you tonight."

"Fascinating," Wurwick replied. "Who could have predicted this could happen so fast?"

"Thank you for your very gracious offer," Atrius replied. "You seem to be such a brave man to ensure our safety like that. Truth is, the girl is kind of a simpleton and is always getting in her own way. It's tragic really. I can tell you that she won't be able to make you as happy as you wish." Then Atrius snapped his fingers as if he had just had a good idea. "Tell you what; I'll give you this coin purse." Atrius tossed a small purse on the table, it made a jingling noise as it landed. "You take the money, have a few drinks on me, then you can give us the same protection and everyone is happy."

The man looked at him and began to laugh. "You're a shrewd one, indeed. I think I'll take your gold and your girl, and you can be glad I didn't slit your throat for speaking to a Hoyrrl."

Vel stood up.

"I think it's time for you to go back to your table before there is a bad accident," Atrius said sitting upright in his chair. "My friend here is a highly trained Ulmich warrior. Why take the risk of facing him? Take the money and go back to where it is you have come from."

"How dare you!" As the man raged, drawing his sword, the whole inn fell as silent as a grave yard at midnight. "You think one off colored fool has the strength to oppose the Hoyrrl?"

Then the Inn's main door opened and a man nearly as tall as Vel walked in. He was elaborately armored, and he had curly blond hair that was well groomed. On his back he carried two large jeweled swords. In fact, everywhere Jadeance looked on this new warrior he found the hilt of a knife. The newcomer walked right into the group of men.

"Am I interrupting something important?" he asked the man with the sword.

The man took a step back. He was much shorter than the new man, and had to look up to threaten him. "This is none of your business, stranger. Now leave before you are also marked."

The tall stranger looked over at Vel, "You're going to fight him, are you? I don't think you brought enough men. But then, I am an incurable optimist. I think I'll watch."

"Do you not have ears?" the robed man yelled. Leave this place before death befalls you all!"

"I can't leave," the stranger replied seriously. "You're blocking my seat, and I haven't had a drink yet."

Then the door opened again, and Jadeance wasn't really prepared for what walked through the door. He was utterly a giant. He was taller than the first man, but what was so shocking was the fact that he was nearly as wide as the double door. He had thick arms that rippled with mussels. On his back he wore the largest axe Jadeance had ever seen. The axe head seemed to be the same size as a full grown wolf. He

wore thick plated armor on his chest and arms. He
had a long blond beard, and his long blond hair came
out the back of his helmet into a long ponytail. He
walked up to the group and stood next to the man
who had entered first.

"Cyres, what the devil is going on here?" the large
man boomed.

"Well it seems like this group of hearty fellows
wants to fight Vel."

"Oh," the giant replied. He looked over to Vel,
"he is out numbered." The giant mused. "Maybe we
should help him."

"Come now Barvik he doesn't need the help."

"No, but it might be considered rude just
to watch."

The robed men started to back away.

"Oh come now, you seemed to be willing for a
good fight a moment ago. Now the numbers are a
bit more even, you all began to turn green and flee?
Why don't you stick around, there must be one of you
worth a good fight."

"That's enough both of you," a new voice said.
Jadeance had his eyes so fixed on the giant he didn't
even notice the next to enter. He was the tallest so
far. He wasn't nearly as massive as Barvik, but he
was heavy set. He had a medium sized black beard
and serious features. He also wore thick plated

armor, however his armor was trimmed in a red metal Jadeance had never seen before, and he wore a red cape that was elaborately decorated. It was easy to see that he wasn't a normal soldier.

Both of the large men looked as if they had seen a ghost, and they immediately fell to their knees, and bowed with deep respect. Vel let out a shocked noise, and also made his way to him, bowing also. The large man smiled a gesture that was pained for there was a deep sadness in that smile. "Rise old friends, and let us sit for a time." Then he looked at the shocked group of robed men. "You will be leaving now." He said sharply. "And you will be leaving your weapons here."

The robed man looked at him for a moment, but then Barvik stepped forward and took the sword from his hands. "There, see how easy that was?" The other men were disarmed and quickly fled.

"Don't you think that's going to come back to bite us?" Atrius asked with raised eye brows.

The big man shrugged. "It might. But you were already in trouble when I arrived, so there's nothing for it."

Atrius shrugged, and then he looked around the table. "We were doing introductions were we not? This is Kainan, a great leader and dear friend."

"Leader of the past," Kainan replied quickly as

he sat down.

"No. You lead again today," Atrius said. "You must push your way past all of this, my old friend. We never lost our hope and faith in you and your abilities." Then he smiled, "Continuing on, the big one here is known as Barvik. He has a bad attitude, and has a tendency to pick unnecessary fights."

"It's good for the blood." The big man shrugged. "I had a good one going there, too." He threw a regretful glance at Kainan.

Atrius shook his head. "Yes, it's too bad you weren't able to disembowel anyone today, but keep your head held high because there is always tomorrow," Atrius replied sarcastically.

"Yes," the big man cheered. "I think I can drink to that."

"You can drink to anything," Cyres said with a laugh.

"And this, not to be forgotten is Cyres. A man on a mission to know every woman, married or not, in the world."

"Women get lonely," Cyres shrugged. "I'm just doing what I can."

"Yes, and corrupting them as you go," Atrius replied with a look of disapproval.

"Well, of course it's going to sound bad if you say it like that," Cyres replied with a hurt look on his face. "I just spread my love around, that's all."

"Can we drink to that?" Barvik nearly pleaded.

Atrius sighed, "I was hoping to hold off the serious drinking until later, but I don't think I'm going to have much luck."

"But Atrius, it is later. I haven't had a drink since yesterday," Barvik complained."

"Yes, I feel so bad for you," Atrius replied shaking his head.

"Where the blazes is that disgusting little thief, Samous?" Barvik asked as he looked around.

"I don't expect him until tomorrow morning," Atrius replied. "Now then," Atrius said looking towards Brie, "I must beg your forgiveness, my lady. The 'simpleton' comment was merely a diversion. Not fact."

Brie smiled at him, "its ok. I knew what you were doing."

"Yes, it was a bit exciting there for a minute," Wurwick replied, still drying off the front of his green robe.

"I'm surprised you didn't turn him into a toad," Atrius replied.

"That is pure folly," Wurwick replied with a scowl. "Wizards don't turn anything into toads! Stupid myth that is humorless at best."

"You can't prove that," Cyres said leaning

forward. "Have you seen every spell that has ever been cast?"

Wurwick looked at him with an angry face. "Perhaps you might want me to experiment. You might look good as a toad."

Cyres smiled, "Come now, old friend. You wouldn't turn me into a toad, now would you?"

"No, but I might just dissolve your hair," Wurwick replied with a grin. "You would never get another girl without those golden curls you so love."

Cyres's hands flew to his hair. "Don't you ever say a thing like that again! Crazy old bungler, that's going too far, that is."

"Come now, you can hardly tell it's been years in between our last meeting and this," Atrius said with a grin.

Jadeance couldn't take his eyes off of Wurwick. He had been told over and over he wasn't to use Magic because it was dangerous, and he needed a good teacher. Wurwick, seeming to feel Jadeance's eyes on him, smiled slightly as he closed his eyes.

"Yes, I am a real wizard, and yes I can help you," Wurwick voice sounded in Jadeance's mind. "We don't yet know how you obtained this power, or what it will lead to. Now, don't speak out loud. Instead, think your responses in your head. When was the first time you felt the burn?"

"How did you know it made my hands burn?" Jadeance asked, thinking in his head.

Wurwick laughed, "Your body isn't used to having the elements run through it. It burns us all the first few times. It will also burn you if you try to do something too big, or something your body isn't used to. Using Magic is much like using a muscle. The first day you spend on a plow in the field it hurts, you blister and get sore. The same holds true with Magic. That first time I used Magic, I was unconscious for nearly a week."

"Yes," Jadeance agreed. "It seems to be getting better now though."

"It will, but you must exercise it. Help it to grow. This is where it gets dangerous. Just because you're able to manipulate the elements doesn't mean you can do anything. Some are more powerful than others. For some, simply raising a pale full of water from a river causes extreme pressure and they need to sleep for days. Some can turn the sky red and not even break a sweat. You must be cautious while we are finding your limits. If you push too far too fast, you will hurt yourself, just like pulling a muscle. If you do too much, you can tear a muscle. There are some things you just can't fix. If you go too far, you will either kill yourself, or maybe cripple a part of your body."

"I didn't know that," Jadeance confessed.

"I will help you safely find your limits, but you must swear to do exactly as I say and never question it. You will now serve me, and perform the greatest kind of apprenticeship known to this world. I will give you this night to think it over. If you agree, we will form a Zepher."

"What is a Zepher?" Jadeance asked.

"It is a binding Magical contract that is unbreakable. To do so would destroy us both. I will swear to empower you with all the knowledge that I possess. You will swear to serve me and no other, to obey my every command without question or complaint. To keep and stay with me until you are ready to face the Great Council alone. This must be done without question, no matter the sacrifice."

"What sacrifice will I have to make?" Jadeance asked.

Wurwick opened his eyes and looked at Brie. "It is not always clear to us what we must sacrifice, but I can tell you that a family is hard maintained when you are training."

"Well, how long will this..., well what I mean to ask is...?"

"How long?" Wurwick interrupted with a laugh. "I don't know. It all depends on how fast you learn and grow. It could be two years, or it could be fifty years.

Having said that, I must tell you that if it takes you fifty years, I'm going to be extremely put out."

Jadeance thought about it for a minute. "I will need some time."

"I know that boy, that's why I gave you until tomorrow to decide. Now, I'm going to have a drink." And with that, Wurwick's voice left.

Jadeance looked over at Brie. She, of course, was looking at him already. She didn't speak, she just slid her hand into his and nestled into him. Jadeance could tell she knew more about what was going on than he did. He sighed and looked down, not knowing what to do. He looked around the table. Everyone was laughing and drinking, talking amongst themselves. Everyone that is, except Kainan. He sat listening, holding a mug, and saying very little. There seemed to be a sadness about him that ran deep into his very soul. It seemed to mark him, a sadness that seemed as evident as was a scar or a bad burn. Jadeance wondered what had happened that had hurt him so. Soon, the food started to arrive, and Jadeance watched in awe at how much the giant Barvik was able to eat. Notwithstanding the fact the Vel was taller than anyone in Windhold; he seemed almost small next to the other three men, Barvik, Kainan, and Cyres. They ate and drank deep into the night. As Jadeance began to nod off, Brie nudged him.

"Come on, let's go to bed." Offering his goodbyes, Jadeance made his way upstairs with Tannis and Brie close behind him.

The next morning Jadeance and Tannis were awakened by Wurwick pounding on their door. "Get up you two, breakfast is getting cold. You didn't drink that much."

"We're coming," Tannis replied, as he began dragging himself out of bed. "Come on, Jade get up."

Jadeance felt strange. He was getting his strength back, but it was unlike him to sleep in. He was usually up early to run. As he pulled his boots on, he remembered how much he missed his morning runs.

"Tannis, if I didn't come home for a while do you think it would upset Uncle Keldon and Aunt Suena?"

"I don't know," Tannis replied carefully. "Why wouldn't you come home?"

"Wurwick wants me to become his apprentice. He says he can make me control myself and push me to my full power."

"That's great Jade," Tannis replied.

"Well it is, and it isn't," Jadeance replied, looking out the window. "You see, it is a total commitment. I must do as he says and go where he goes. I won't be able to go home with you all after this is over."

"How long will you serve him?" Tannis asked.

"I don't know, years I guess. He said it depends

upon how fast I learn."

Tannis looked out the window for a moment. "Jade, all of us that love you know that this is something you need to do. We will be waiting for you when you get back."

Jadeance looked at him, not willing to say anything.

"Have you told her yet?" Tannis asked.

Jadeance looked away, "No, not yet."

"I don't know that you need to worry so much, Jade. Brie is very understanding, you'll see. Now, we had better get down there and get some breakfast."

When they arrived downstairs, everyone was sitting at a large table, talking and eating. There was a new man sitting next to Atrius. He was a small man, not much taller than Jadeance, with a thin, yet muscular frame. He had short, flaming red hair, and a medium length, well-trimmed beard and long, thin, pointy ears. His skin was slightly paler than most, with an odd reddish look. Jadeance wondered what type of fellow this new stranger was. His clothes were dark and he, unlike all the others they had met the night before, was wearing no armor. He looked at them as they approached, his eyes moving quickly from face to face. Jadeance could tell that he was far more intelligent than most, and he seemed to study them in only an instant.

"Ah, there we are now," Atrius said as Jadeance and Tannis approached. "You have made it. We thought that you were planning on sleeping the day away."

"Well, it was the first time sleeping in a real bed since we left home, and probably the last time for a while," Jadeance replied quickly. "I was just trying to savor it."

"Ha," laughed the new comer. "I think I'm going to like that one."

"Boys, this is Samous. He is a liar, thief and trained assassin. Did I miss anything?" Atrius asked, looking at the red haired man.

"Yes," Samous replied, "you did." He looked at Tannis and Jadeance and said, "I am also an all-around, good natured, happy fellow."

Atrius shook his head, "You never stop do you?"

Samous smiled, "Why, what ever would you be talking about?"

Jadeance sat down next to Brie. He knew he needed to talk to her, but he didn't want to do it in front of everyone. He began to eat, trying to think about what to say.

Brie looked at him and gave him an understanding smile. "Stop worrying, Jade. I already know what you are going to say."

"Wurwick told you?"

"No," Brie replied. "I have my own ways of seeing things." Then she looked into his eyes. "Just tell me one thing. Tell me that I am waiting for something. Tell me that no matter what, you and I stay together. I don't want to wait for something that I will never have. Tell me how you really feel."

Jadeance felt his ears turning red. "You know how I feel, Brie."

"How could I know?" Brie protested. "You have never told me."

Jadeance lowered his head in defeat. "All right Brie, I guess I owe you. I do love you and I don't want to lose you. I promise that I will always come back for you." Then feeling completely embarrassed, Jadeance looked around slightly. "Are you happy now?"

Brie smiled and kissed him. "Yes and I love you too. I will always be here waiting for you. Don't worry about me. Just don't hurt yourself."

"Hurt myself?" he responded, a little shocked.

"Yes," she replied. "You have a way. Call it luck if you wish. Just promise me you will be safe."

"I will," he promised, and then he looked at his plate. "Hurt myself...I don't hurt myself."

"You mean it was someone else who ran under the biggest boar ever to be seen? It was someone else who climbed a tree, and was knocked a half mile away? It was someone else who..."

"Ok, ok. I will be more careful," he interrupted, blushing slightly.

She smiled, "Thank you, Jade. You should stop arguing with women. It does you no good."

He went to open his mouth again, but his words fell short when Tannis, who had been listening, started laughing.

"She has you again, little brother."

"Just shut up, you!" Jadeance flared.

"Eat up, all of you!" Atrius said. "We will be leaving very soon. There are unfriendly eyes in this town." Then he turned to Samous, "Did you get everything?"

"Yes, we are ready."

"Where are we going?" Tannis asked.

Kainan looked at him. "Eighteen years ago, there was a rumor that an ancient object of unspeakable power had been found; something that had been lost to time itself. Many believed that it was a lie. Many more believed that it had been destroyed. Still, there were some who believed that it could be used to turn the balance of power and to free the enemy that had been held captive for so long. Murios Ker has long dreamt of returning to enslave and punish this world, together with the High Council of Kings and the Inner Circle of Wizards. It was decided that this object was to be found and hidden under our protection. Several of the world's top and most elite were gathered together to find it and bring it to safety. This group spent uncounted days seeking it out. When it was discovered there was a mighty battle, for the agents of darkness also sought it for their design. After the battle it was brought back to Astrothen by those who had survived. There, that great council decided where the object was to be hidden. It was soon delivered and sealed, and the men who were present formed a special Zepher. We do not know how the Trolls found it, or how they broke the encoding on the Zepher seal. But we do know that the Trolls now have the knowledge to break the Zepher itself. To prevent this, we must travel to Astrothen. I cannot tell you more here, but I do know that it has been decided that the object must have a new home."

"I thought you couldn't break a Zepher," Samous said in confusion.

"Well no, you see, there are ways to break it, several ways actually. And each of them means death to us all. It is definitely time to move it to a safer place," Wurwick replied as he repacked his pipe.

"Where do me and Jade fit into all this?" Tannis asked.

"I cannot tell you that now. You must trust me, and know that you are needed to lift the Zepher safely. That is why you have been brought to us. The

Trolls also know you can break it, and that is why they are trying to get at you. When this is over, you will be safe again and will be able to return to your lives," Kainan replied.

"If we survive, that is," Tannis joked with a smile. "So far we haven't been very popular."

Kainan dropped to a knee, which made Jadeance and Tannis feel very uncomfortable.

"I swear to you here and now, to keep you both safe. I will lay down my own life before I see any harm befall you."

"I could never doubt you," Tannis replied shocked. "I don't know that my life is a fair trade for yours."

"That is where you are wrong. Many of the great men who have preceded me demand no less. There is a debt to be paid," Kainan said seriously.

"What debt is there to be paid?" Tannis asked curiously.

Kainan looked to Barvik and Cyres, who both looked at the ground. "Now is not the time. All you need know is that you are in good hands."

"Speaking of time," Samous interjected, "we must be on our way. The east wind blows cold, and a dark evil is in the air."

CHAPTER 2

THE ZEPHER.

Jadeance made his way out the door to where the horses were ready and waiting. Jadeance noticed something on his horse as he moved closer. It was a whole new set of packs. There was also a strange looking sword and a long smooth staff strapped to the saddle.

"Well boy, we stand at the greatest crossroads of your young life and it is time for you to make a decision. So what is your answer?"

Jadeance turned to see Wurwick standing right behind him.

"Will you join our ranks, and become an ambassador of light? Swearing an oath to the inner circle itself? This is a life of privilege and duty few can even imagine. Greatness or death will be your eternal companion."

Jadeance looked to Tannis, then to Brie. Both were

giving him a look of approval.

"I will serve you," Jadeance replied simply.

"This is the last time I will ask," Wurwick replied. "Remember there is no backing down, no turning away. I demand a total commitment. Are you sure? Are you ready? Will you serve with all your heart has to offer?"

"Yes," Jadeance replied with confidence, feeling the excitement filling him.

Wurwick took his staff and held the tip of it just above Jadeance's head. The staff burst out with a bright green light that filled and surrounded Jadeance with a warm feeling, as if he had just been wrapped in a large blanket. At the bright flash, Jadeance covered his eyes to shield them from the intense light. It was a moment frozen in time, as if time itself slowed, and Jadeance felt himself being infused with a power not his own. "Swear it, Jadeance. Swear to hold not only to me, but to the light itself. The Divines grant us power, and in turn we serve all of mankind here on this earth, protecting them from the untold fears most can only see in their worst nightmares. Swear to hold to the love of life that brought you here, for you and your family, for your old life and for your new life as a Magi." Wurwick's voice sounded in his mind, and there was a power in his words that Jadeance could feel.

"I swear," Jadeance said, his words seeming to echo in the vaults of his mind as if they could be heard thousands of miles away. Jadeance felt a rush of voices streaming through his veins, a hollowing sensation as if he could feel the excitement of countless numbers of faceless people cheering. It was a feeling that Jadeance would remember with a perfect clarity until the very end of his days.

"And I swear to give you all I possess. Everything I have, I will show unto you. I will mold you into a power that this world hasn't seen in an age. You will become a powerful tool in the hands of the Divines, a force for the armies of darkness to fear." When Jadeance opened his eyes, the light had faded. He looked down and all of his cloths had been changed. He now wore a deep blue robe that ran to the ground. It had a thick cloak running down the back with a thick hood. At his side was the sword from his saddle. Drawing the sword, it seemed to have little to no weight at all. It was about four and a half feet long. The blade was tapered and surprisingly thin, ending in a sharp point. There were intricate designs engraven upon the surface of the blade and also upon the hilt. Jadeance had never seen anything so fine in his life.

"This is Tyuru, a great Elvin blade of old. It has not seen hand nor battle in over eight hundred years.

Only recently recovered, it is a gift to you from an old friend."

"Who?" Jadeance asked in wonder.

"None other than Meshire the Wise," Wurwick replied. "Keep it well and keep it safe and it shall do the same for you. Now grab your staff, boy."

Jadeance looked at his horse. The staff was still on his saddle. He started to walk towards it when Wurwick's staff stopped him.

"You may not leave this spot," Wurwick said, pointing with his staff.

"But...," Jadeance began to complain.

"No!" Wurwick replied harshly. "There are no 'buts'. You must grow. Never question my orders, it may get you killed. You must take the words 'but' and 'why', and forget you ever learned them. They will not help you here. Now, that staff boy, get it."

Jadeance was filled with anger. He wanted to fire back at his new instructor. Tightening his jaw, he took another look at the horse. He could see the staff. Taking a deep breath, he reached out his hand and thought of what he needed to do. "Come here!" he demanded. And with a slight 'pop', there it was in his hand. As he held it, he could feel a power deep within the staff, almost as if it was just as alive as he was. He looked at it in wonder.

"This staff is bound to you. It cannot be destroyed

unless you are destroyed. It holds the key to your element. Use it, and it will open up a completely new world to your eyes."

"What does that mean?" Jadeance asked.

"That is one of your first lessons, and I wouldn't want to spoil it for you. Now, touch your staff with mine and the Zepher will be complete."

Jadeance stretched out his staff towards Wurwick's, and when the staffs touched, time once again stood still.

"From this time on, you will call me Master. I shall be your Master until you also become a true Master and go forth on your own," Wurwick said, firmly.

Then, it was over and Wurwick was walking towards his horse. Jadeance turned to see everyone kneeling before him.

"We have truly beheld the beginning of a new era today," Atrius said. "A day I greatly feared that I would not live to see."

"May we all live to see his destiny fulfilled," Vel said standing and moving towards his horse.

Brie ran up and hugged Jadeance tightly. "You look good," She told him. "You will be turning people into toads before you know it."

"We do not turn people into toads!" Wurwick yelled. "That is pure nonsense."

Brie smiled at him. "Cyres told me to say that," she giggled.

Jadeance mounted his horse and fell in besides Tannis.

"Do I look ridiculous?" Jadeance asked.

"No, not at all," Tannis replied with a straight face. "You look like a wizard, that's all."

"What do wizards look like?" Jadeance asked. "Is that like when you see a monk you know it, no matter where you see him? Will I forever be judged like that?"

"Well, the staff kinda gives you away" Tannis replied with a smile. "Wurwick gets away with it because he is so old. You, not so much."

Jadeance fell silent then he heard Wurwick speaking inside his mind.

"Keep your staff close, boy. It will feed your energy. You will find that it gives you a significant boost. It also feeds your body when you are hurt or wounded."

"What do you mean?" Jadeance asked.

"When you use Magic, you are manipulating the elements that hold and bind this world together. Or you move them, you might say. At any rate, that can be very stressing to your body. You feel tired and in extreme cases you may pass out. It all comes from a loss of energy. Your staff will feed you, so you won't feel as tired. When you use Magic from now on, try to use your staff as much as possible. You need to get to know it. It is very much like an extension of you. You will find it to be your closest companion. It has a will of its own. You can't force it, you must work with it. You will get the idea. It will keep you safe in the same way a good friend would. And in time, you will come to understand how it thinks and what it wants."

"My staff thinks?" Jadeance asked looking down at it.

"In a way, yes it does. It is infused with living elements, just as you are. It is different certainly, however it follows some of the same rules that we do. Life, all life, never dies, it simply changes. When a man dies, his body changes, he feeds the soil, but the soul lives on. The elements of life never die. It's these elements that are the key to everything we do. You'll get the idea."

"So is it safe for me to use my Magic now?" Jadeance asked.

"Yes, now you will have guidance. I can protect you and stop you from doing anything too foolish."

"Won't it draw people to us?" Jadeance asked, thinking of the awful encounter that had cost Balseer so much.

"It might, and if it does you must leave them to me. You are not strong enough to repel an attack from an evil source. It can be very dangerous."

Jadeance was looking around as they rode. Everyone seemed to be looking at them in fear. Jadeance thought this was strange, because when they entered the town nobody seemed to care, or even notice them at all. They turned onto the main road leading out of town. Jadeance looked around and saw the street was completely empty; there were no sounds at all. He was wondering where all the people had gone when he heard an arrow buzzing towards him. With a quick flash, the arrow burst into a thousand pieces. Jadeance looked up in time to see a group of men appear on a rooftop, wearing the same dark robes as the men from the inn. They drew their bows and released. The bow strings made a peculiar whistling noise as they released their arrows. Wurwick raised his staff, and with a flash of green light, he sent the arrow storm back on the men who had loosed it. Then there were shouts and the sound of men running. Dozens of men burst out of several houses, all of them wearing the black robes they had been seeing.

Jadeance felt panic crush upon him. Atrius started shooting arrows, as Barvik, Cyres, and Kainan charged forward. Vel charged a small group trying to get at Atrius. Tannis drew his sword and pulled in close to Brie, who had also drawn a bow and was losing arrows as fast as she could. Jadeance grabbed for his sword when Wurwick yelled at him, "Your staff boy! Use your staff!" A man was trying to get to Vel's back side while he was fending off another. Jadeance pointed his staff at him, letting his excitement flow. A bright blue ball of light burst from the end of his staff, crashing into the man and knocked him into an alleyway nearby. He then leveled another man trying to run towards Tannis. It didn't take the attacking force long to realize they were out matched, and call for a hasty retreat. Jadeance looked up to see a Troll standing on the top of a building, screaming with frustration. The Troll leveled a horrible looking staff at Vel and a bright spark jumped towards him. Wurwick stopped the deadly blow midflight. Jadeance looked up at the Troll who was now sending a great wall of fire down upon Wurwick. Jadeance began to feel a deep hatred burning inside him. Vel had saved his life, and it was clear that this Troll had been the cause of this attack. Jadeance raised his staff and yelled "fire." A powerful blast of bright blue fire knocked the Troll to his knees. The flames swirled around him for an instant. A dark staff emerged from the flames pointed directly at Jadeance. Before Jadeance even had time to blink, Wurwick sent him sailing towards the ground with a sharp burst of light. The Troll landed with a thud.

Jadeance looked around. Everyone was checking for injuries and cleaning their weapons. Tannis and Brie were making their way to where Jadeance was, when the energy started to drain from him. He slipped off his saddle, unconscious.

When Jadeance awoke, he was lying on his back. The sky was a deep blue and there were light clouds moving slowly past him. He felt at peace. The field he was lying in was soft, and the warmth from the sun seemed to calm him. He stared at the clouds for a time, trying to decide if he should get up or try to fall asleep again. He could hear his friends nearby. With a sigh, he stretched and sat up. They were sitting in a large field. Bright flowers dotted the ground, and a light breeze seemed to pull them from one side to another. For a moment it almost seemed as if the field itself was dancing. Looking around, he spotted Tannis who was training with Vel and Cyres. It was an odd sight. Cyres and Vel were a good bit taller than Tannis. Brie was sitting by the fire, cooking with Atrius and Samous. Wurwick was sitting by himself smoking a pipe. Feeling eyes upon him, he looked over to Jadeance.

"Come here boy," Wurwick said.

Jadeance got to his feet, and looked for his staff. It was lying near his horse. Jadeance stretched out his hand and the staff obediently came to him. The staff felt strange in his hand. It was defiantly no ordinary piece of wood. Looking at it a bit closer, he noticed it was made from the same red wood that furnished Wagstaff. For some reason, that made him feel like home wasn't so far away.

"I do believe that is what Meshire had in mind when he made it," Wurwick said as Jadeance sat down next to him.

Jadeance looked at Wurwick confused, "How did you know what I was thinking?"

Wurwick smiled, "I can't teach you all my tricks in one day, my boy. How do you feel?"

"I feel better than I have in a long time," Jadeance replied. "Did you do something to give me my strength back?" Jadeance asked.

"No," Wurwick replied. "Your staff did. You will come to find that your staff can do a great many things. That is going to be your most important lesson."

"My staff?," Jadeance asked, puzzled.

"Yes. You see, your staff is like a mountain range, of sorts. Many mountain ranges look similar. However, no two are alike. They have secrets, places of great beauty and places of great danger. Each staff has a personality, just like you and me. You must learn it. Study your staff. Listen to it, and see if you can't learn to hear its subtle hints. Now, you have a great will inside of you. There is no changing that. It seems to come out most as a bad temper." Jadeance blushed. "You must learn to keep your head when you are angry. That was a very dangerous thing you did, attacking that shaman like you did."

Jadeance looked confused, "But why?"

Wurwick smiled. "He was much stronger than you can realize. I want you to use your gift as often as you can, but understand you need to learn good judgment. By attacking him, you left yourself open for a return attack. He would have easily destroyed you. Let's keep your attacking to small things like game and trees. Things that can't attack you back, for now anyway."

"Ok, but why would I attack game?"

"You will learn to use your sword, and use it well might I add. That sword will serve you well. However, there will be no need for you to ever touch a bow again. You will do all your hunting with your staff. You will undoubtedly completely destroy the first few things you see, but that's why you practice. You must be able to be gentle and fierce. This is not a light undertaking. Soon enough, you will get the idea. As for now it looks as if lunch is ready, and I'm starved."

"What's our road?" Samous asked Kainan as Jadeance sat next to Brie.

The big man looked to the sky, "This isn't my journey. This journey belongs to Atrius."

"We need to get this over right now." Atrius said with some heat. "You are the one meant to lead. It is to you that we look. I'll not have you second guessing yourself. Its time you put yourself together and find the soldier you lost. Too much is riding on this. I won't pretend to understand what you have gone through. You know more than most that it has never been about the soldier, it has always been the cause. We fight for what we love. We fight for what we believe in. We fight for a cause that is greater than our own, to help the world around us rise to new heights. I love you far too much too see you give up all you are, all that you have done, for a pain that can never be healed. Wounds and scars are bound to happen and though they leave their mark upon us, we must never let a scar define who we are and how we live."

Kainan looked hurt. "You don't understand. The man you seek was destroyed long ago."

"Then take what you have left and build a new one." Atrius fell to one knee. "I, Atrius of Astrothen, pledged my loyalty to your leadership over twenty years ago and my oath holds true to this day."

"But what you ask is,"

"You have always been my captain," Barvik

interrupted, taking a knee next to Atrius.

"I would be lost without your guidance," Cyres said, kneeling also.

"We all need you. It's time for you to bury your demons and arise anew. Your old life may be but a distant memory, but look around. There is a new life to be made. You will be the one to lead the leader, you have read it yourself." Wurwick replied.

Kainan seemed to be struggling with an unknown force. Finally he turned his back on them. "We will take the great east road to Braverro." Jadeance caught a brief glimpse of Kainan starring at Tannis as he walked close to Cyres and Vel.

Jadeance moved closer to Atrius, "Who is the leader that Kainan is supposed to lead?"

Atrius smiled, not taking his eyes off Tannis. "Only the future can tell us that."

That of course, was an answer that Jadeance didn't particularly believe. Shaking the question from his mind, he sat down next to Brie and Wurwick. "How long does it take to get to Braverro?" Jadeance asked Wurwick.

"Some three, maybe four weeks, assuming the weather holds," Wurwick replied.

Jadeance took a deep sigh. "I think I am going to grow tired of horses long before we reach Astrothen."

Brie smiled. "I think we all will."

CHAPTER 3

TRAINING BEGINS

After they had finished their lunch, the group got back on the road and continued on towards Braverro. Tannis rode past Jadeance and fell in next to Cyres. They were fast becoming friends. Cyres had joined Vel in teaching Tannis how to use his sword. In fact, they had been teaching him a great many things surrounding what it means to be an honorable soldier. Cyres had been showing Tannis shadow drills to do while riding. Jadeance watched as they rode side by side, their swords moving in unison.

"It's important to find a good teacher," Wurwick said, looking over to Jadeance. "You see, a good teacher can be as hard to find as a shadow in the very depths of the darkest night. Just because you know your way around a sword doesn't mean you can teach what you know. Even if you are a good teacher, finding the right way to teach can be just as difficult.

Tannis has truly found a good teacher. Which, if you ask me, is quite remarkable considering that Cyres lacks everything that you would consider to be a moral role model."

"How do you know that he is going to be such a good teacher?" Jadeance asked.

"My boy, you will find there are few things that I don't know," Wurwick replied with a grin. "Just look at them! You will find that some people have been destined to meet since the very beginnings of time."

"Were we destined?" Jadeance asked.

"We might have been. That is a question that you will have to find out on your own." Wurwick replied.

"Are we going to visit the Silver Tower?" Samous interrupted hopefully.

"I rather doubt it," Wurwick replied. "There is far too much at stake here to be making side trips."

Samous grunted as he searched the horizon.

"What are you looking for?" Barvik asked.

"Anything unusual," Samous replied.

"Ha," the huge man laughed. "You are always looking for trouble."

Samous's face took on an irritated look. "I don't like surprises. We are in a certain amount of danger. Trolls can move great distances."

"Trolls? Come on man, you can't be afraid of a Troll," Barvik replied.

"Well, one might not be such a bad thing," Samous replied. "Find a thousand and we could find ourselves in a pinch."

Barvik grunted. "That won't happen."

"Well if it's all the same to you, I'll keep my eyes open anyway." Samous replied.

"Why are you asking about the silver tower?" Wurwick asked curiously.

"What? Oh, there is a certain scholar there. I've been meaning to get back to see her for quite some time," Samous replied, a smile slowly creeping upon his face.

"Samous!" Wurwick said with a hint of heat. "The scholars there are not for your personal pleasure. They are serving a very important...,"

"Take it easy, old man," Samous interrupted with a smile. "She is just a friend. Anyway, she doesn't have much for company besides dusty scrolls and..."

"I don't want to hear another word of this," Wurwick replied, cutting him short. "I'm going to talk with Kainan." Wurwick pushed his horse forward, and left Jadeance to listen to Samous and Barvik laughing.

They stopped for the night in a huge open field. The wind was blowing the miles of open grass in a way that it almost seemed as if it were an ocean, with wave after wave rolling out of sight. It took them several hours to get camp set up and dinner cooked. Afterward, people began grouping together. Tannis was practicing with Cyres and Vel. Kainan, Barvik, Samous and Atrius sat around the fire listening to Brie play her lute. Wurwick pulled Jadeance aside to work on his Magic.

"All right my boy its time you started to focus your will in a new way. For attacking or hunting, you will need to be able to launch attacks with a certain amount of accuracy." Wurwick walked a good distance away and formed a bright green ball of energy. He weaved it out of the air with an apparent ease that set Jadeance's mind afire with wonder. With a smile and a toss, Wurwick sent the ball sailing high into the air. "There now, my boy. There is your target, so destroy it," Wurwick instructed.

"What should I hit it with?" Jadeance asked.

"I don't care," Wurwick replied. "On second thought, use anything you want except fire. No fire with all this grass here you see."

Jadeance thought about it for a moment. It wasn't the easiest thing he had tried to do. For the most part, every time he had tried to use his Magic it had been on impulse. Looking at Wurwick's target, he sent a blast of bright blue energy forcing the green target back twenty yards or so. With a quick flicker, it returned to where it had been floating.

"No good," Wurwick replied. "That's too general. You need to focus it on a central location, harness all that power on a single point. Try again."

Holding his staff out in front of him, he stared intently at the center of the floating ball. Releasing his energy, another bright blue blast of energy flew towards the target; however he only managed to push the target again.

"Closer," Wurwick replied with a grin. "Try again!," he laughed as he filled his pipe.

They practiced until Jadeance was nearly exhausted. When Wurwick said that it was time to stop, Jadeance sank gratefully to his knees. He was sweating profusely.

"You are doing well," Wurwick told him. "It is important that we build up your strength. We will work on it more tomorrow."

Jadeance nodded, his body was trembling from exhaustion. Not trusting himself to walk he sat back, allowing the wind to cool him off. He wasn't sitting for very long before Brie made her way to his side. She helped him to his feet, and walked slowly back to where everyone was sitting. After sitting him down, she fetched him a water skin. He drank gratefully. Brie hummed lightly to herself as she sat down next to Jadeance. He found her to be all around comforting, and he was grateful to have her help.

"Thank you," he said to her, offering her a drink.

"No thank you, you need it more than I do," Brie replied.

"What do you mean?" Jadeance asked. "It's not like we're going to run out."

She smiled at him. "Soon we will be entering the Great Red Woods. It can be difficult to find good water in there."

Jadeance looked over to Wurwick. "I'm sure we'll be just fine Brie."

"How goes your training, lad?" Atrius asked Jadeance.

Jadeance looked over. "Tiring, very tiring."

"Practice hard child, practice hard," Atrius said with a smile.

"Why do you ask?" Tannis asked.

"No reason," Atrius replied. "Education is the most important thing a youth can do."

Tannis turned his head slightly, as if he were about to say something, however he let it slide.

"The proper question should be, how is your training going?" Samous added with a laugh. "Jade has a proper teacher, after all."

Cyres fixed Samous with a hard stare. "What would you know of teachers? Every time you go to the Silver Towers, you make the teachers put down their books."

Samous coughed uncomfortably, looking over at Wurwick. "Maybe we shouldn't talk about teachers after all."

"Indeed not," Wurwick replied, as he lowered his pipe.

Kainan stood up. "We have a long road ahead of us; we had all better get some sleep. I'll take first watch."

"Right," Barvik replied. "I'll relieve you at midnight." Kainan nodded and made his way over to the horses.

Jadeance laid down next to Brie and Tannis. The two of them were talking quietly, but all Jadeance could think about was sleep. He fell asleep almost as quickly as he laid his head down. His sleep was filled with strange glimpses of his past, images of running through the forests and fields surrounding Windhold.

Jadeance was awakened early by Vel. "Come on, time to get up," Vel said as he shook Jadeance.

Jadeance shook his head and rolled out of his blankets. He looked over at Tannis, who was belting on his sword, and a strange thought occurred to him. "Will we ever be able to go back to just Jade and Tannis?" Jadeance asked.

Tannis looked down, "I don't know Jade. Things will turn out ok, you will see."

Jadeance was in a somber mood as they made

their way back to the road. Winter was coming on and the ground had started to freeze at night. It didn't help that they were steadily heading north. He rode in silence, watching the hours drag by. His eyes fell on his staff. It was a deep red wood. Nearly as tall as he was, it fit him well. It looked as if it had been polished by the angelic hands of Chronicles themselves. They were a strange group of Priestesses that were completely devoted to the Divines, and they were known for the unbelievable finery they made in semblance of the Divines. He could see his reflection quiet clearly. The staff itself had no distinguishing head piece like Wurwick's staff did; instead it came to rounded top as if it were waiting for someone to finish it. He peered into its shiny surface until nightfall, where his daunting task of training started all over again. They traveled for several days stopping each night in some secluded area where they could all rest. For Tannis and Jadeance, the evenings were filled with grueling training exercises. Each morning drew crisp and cold informing all that winter was fast approaching.

CHAPTER 4

THE GREAT RED WOOD

Atrius, did you have to buy the thin walled tents?" Samous complained, as everyone was getting up.

"A tent is a tent." Atrius replied. "Did you get wet? Any bird droppings land on you during your slumber?" Atrius asked with a mocking smirk.

Samous looked back and drew his cloak tightly around him. "I guess all wines are the same to you then. I'll remember that when we arrive at Astrothen."

"Now, you can't be serious." Barvik laughed. "Men drink ale. Wines were invented for the weak."

"What would a giant, blundering oaf know of refinement?" Samous glared.

"Want proof?" Barvik laughed again. "You are complaining about being cold."

"Not all of us are half beast," Samous mocked.

Barvik's face took on a hurt expression. "I'm not that hairy," Barvik complained, looking down at his arms.

"Not at all," Cyres replied with a large smirk. "You're no more hairy than a night hound."

"A dog, is it!" Barvik shouted. "Perhaps you need your memory adjusted," Barvik warned, grabbing his huge battle axe.

"Enough," Kainan replied. "We must be on our way."

"Will we reach the Great Red Wood today?" Atrius asked.

Kainan looked at the sun, and then he turned to Samous.

"I doubt it." Samous replied. "We'll get close, maybe within ten miles or so."

Atrius smiled, "One more day of sunlight, then."

"What does that mean?" Tannis asked.

"When we cross into the Great Red Wood, you won't see the sun again for weeks. Many get hopelessly lost in the Great Wood. There are few ways to navigate, also is it near impossible to tell distances. It is easy to forget where you are and how far you have come," Kainan replied.

"Isn't that dangerous?" Brie asked.

"To most, yes," Kainan replied. "Not to worry, we have certain advantages."

"You mean Master Wurwick?" Jadeance asked.

Kainan looked over to Jadeance. "Traveling with Wurwick always grants you an advantage. However, the advantage of which I speak of lies with Vel. Ulmich eyes don't work like our own. When it is dark to us, he still sees light. He can navigate the wood with ease. Samous also can see quite well in the dark. I think it has something to do with similar Elvin ties."

Jadeance looked over at Vel. The dark man had become important in his life. In the few weeks he had been around, he had saved their lives and kept them safe time and time again. His thoughts drifted as his eyes fell upon Samous. He was a strange little fellow, sure enough, yet he was incredibly intelligent and always seemed to know where he was heading, as if he could read the world as a man reads a map.

"Is there anything you can't do Vel?" Tannis asked with a smile.

"No, there isn't," Atrius replied, smiling also.

"There are a great many things I am unable to do," Vel replied. "In truth, I have a great many failings."

"Being human is not a failing, my friend," Kainan replied.

Vel looked to the road. "We must be on our way."

Kainan smiled. "Yes, the day is slipping by."

They rode on through the day, and as evening started to set they came across a large group moving back towards Astole. Samous rode out to great them.

"How fares the North Road, friend?" Samous asked politely.

A man in the front looked at him suspiciously. "Who said we're friends?" The man replied, looking at the others menacingly.

"Just being courteous," Samous replied. "If you say not friends, that's fine with me. Still, have you any news on the road?"

The man looked at Samous with contempt. "There is no road. Only death lies in that cursed wood."

"The Great Red Wood can be dangerous," Samous agreed.

"No, you don't understand." The man replied. "Everything is dying in there. Even the trees wither and fall." Then he looked back at his group. "We lost many to the evil that now owns the wood. We were forced to turn back or face death. We have turned back. Take care and do the same now, before you also dig needless graves."

Samous looked back at to Kainan. "Forgive the intrusion, my not friend," Samous replied cautiously.

The man shook his head. "Only death awaits you in there, mark my words, stranger."

Samous watched as the group rode past. "What

did you make of that?"

"Superstitious fool," Barvik said with a grunt. "That forest has always been feared."

"I don't think so," Atrius replied with a worried face. "Something about him seemed wrong."

"What do you mean, old friend?" Kainan asked.

"I'm not positive, but I think he was hiding something."

"What could he be hiding that can hurt us in any way?" Cyres asked looking back towards the group.

Atrius looked up sharply as if remembering something. He rode up to Brie. "Child, give me your hands." Brie looked at him with her eyebrows raised. She obediently gave him her hands. "Good," Atrius said. "Now close your eyes and think about the man we just met."

"What is he getting at?" Barvik asked puzzled.

"Hush now," Wurwick said sharply.

Brie looked at Wurwick, and then she looked over at Jadeance, almost as if she were trying to draw strength and courage from him. Closing her eyes she bowed her head slightly.

"Yes, now remember you have nothing to fear, nothing matters except that man. Find him." Her chin tightened as she frowned slightly.

"Concentrate on him, and nothing but him," Atrius urged. Her hands began to tremble slightly she turned her head away from Atrius. He held her hands tightly, "Tell me child, what do you see?" Atrius asked.

She screamed, and tried to pull her hands away, but Atrius held on tightly.

"That's enough, come back now," Wurwick barked. Brie screamed and pulled her hands back. She looked like she was lost and her eyes stayed distant.

Wurwick struck her leg with the tip of his staff, and a bright green aura surrounded her for a moment. Then her eyes focused and tears began to stream down her cheeks. Atrius pulled her in tight and pulled her off her horse.

Jadeance slid off his horse and knelt next to her. She flew into his arms and wept hard. He held her tight, rocking her slightly.

"Tell us what you have seen, dear child," Atrius said with a sad face. "It will help."

"The first few visions can be incredibly painful," Wurwick said as he kneeled down next to them.

"What do you know of the visions of the Dream Keepers?" Atrius asked curiously.

"I have many secrets, Master of Astrothen," Wurwick replied firmly.

It took several minutes for Brie to calm down. When she was finally able to open her eyes, she looked over at Atrius. "We can't," she said. "We can't go in that awful place."

"What did you see child?" Atrius urged.

"I could feel his pain," she replied. "That, and so much more. There is a deep hatred and an unspeakable evil in those woods. There is a great wave of death, and it is spreading quickly, looming over every living thing, nothing has been spared. I also saw great beasts roaming in the dark, somewhat like a wolf but..." she hesitated.

"They are called Volkru," Cyres replied with a shudder. "Fearsome beasts."

"Please continue," Atrius said softly.

Brie shook her head, "The beasts are enraged and something is driving them through the wood, to what end I can't tell, but death is on their minds."

"Thank you, my child. I know that was not an easy task. We must be on our way. I feel a hard road ahead," Atrius replied standing.

"But you don't mean to go in there, do you?" Brie pleaded. "We will all perish."

"It will be ok, child," Atrius replied trying to comfort her. "There are few dangers that forest offers that Samous and Vel can't guide us around."

Kainan looked at the sun, "Let's be on our way."

They moved steadily onward until they crested a slight hill and came within eyes view of the great north red woods. It was like a vast wall stretching on as far as the eye could see. It was limitless and immoveable. To Jadeance it seemed as if the very sight of this great entrance was warning any and all who came within view to turn and leave. Jadeance normally enjoyed forests. He had spent many years hunting and playing in the forest lands surrounding Windhold. This forest however, seemed different, it felt different. It was old, far older than any wooded area that Jadeance had ever been to and there was an unmistakable feeling of fear hovering underneath its thick canopy. Even the giant Barvik seemed to ride with his hand on his hip axe as they entered the vast emptiness. Jadeance was only able see a few paces in any direction. He could feel a strange fear creeping up his back. He looked over to Tannis, who also seemed a bit uneasy about entering the woods. Vel took point as they crossed the distinct line that proved to be the entrance to a strange new place. It was dark and Jadeance couldn't see very far. He was able to make out the shapes of closer friends, yet try as he might he couldn't see up to where Vel was riding, nor back to where the pack horses were. Jadeance felt himself begin to panic when he heard Wurwick's voice.

"Don't worry, your eyes will adjust in time and it won't seem so dark."

"It's kind of unnerving that you are able to enter my thoughts at whim," Jadeance complained. "Can you hear all my thoughts?"

Wurwick chuckled, "Maybe I can and maybe I can't."

"That's not funny," Jadeance fired back. "I can't help what I think."

"We'll see about that. You will have to discipline your mind someday; fortunately for you that day has not yet arrived. Now it's time to get down to business, you must keep your head in here. Many enemies can feel your fear, don't feed them. They hunger for fear and will be drawn to it. You must be calm, yet fierce. Do you know why the serpent is so feared?"

"No, I guess I have never really thought much about it," Jadeance confessed.

"They are unpredictable, you don't know if or when they are going to strike. They do not show fear or aggression like other animals, generally speaking of course. It is this unknown factor that adds to the fear and respect they demand. Don't show your hand, keep your mind calm and firm, and you will demand respect from nature around you."

"Enemies?" Jadeance asked, looking into the trees. "What enemies are you talking about?"

However Wurwick was gone. Jadeance looked around as they rode on. It was silent. Every other forest Jadeance had ever been in was full of life, with birds and deer. This forest had no sounds. In fact, there was no evidence of animal life at all. Jadeance moved up and fell in with Tannis.

"Is it just me, or is it too quiet in here?" Jadeance asked.

"What do you mean?" Tannis asked.

"Well, have you heard a single bird, or seen a single chipmunk?" Jadeance asked.

"That is a bit strange," Tannis replied looking around. "Maybe they avoid the road."

"I wouldn't count on that." Cyres said from right behind them. "Something is wrong here. I can feel it in the air. Keep your weapons handy. There are many dangers in these woods. I get the feeling that there is something unnatural going on here."

They rode on for hours, and with every passing mile Jadeance got the feeling that something was watching him. He looked around constantly, searching for whatever it could be that was definitely following them. Brie rode close, her cloak pulled tightly around her. She looked at him.

"There is something out there," Brie whispered.

"You can feel it too?" Jadeance asked.

"It's more than that." Brie said. "I can almost sense something, like a hatred, or anger. It's hard to explain."

"Do you think the others know?" Jadeance asked.

"I don't think there is much that gets past Kainan. I get the feeling that he knows more than he lets on. It's almost like he is hiding something," Brie said.

"Hiding what?" Jadeance asked.

"I don't know," Brie replied.

Jadeance looked up as the column stopped. Vel led them off the road and into the trees. As they were dismounting, Kainan made his way to them.

"Don't any of you wander off," Kainan said seriously. "Stay together, and stay with Wurwick, Cyres, Barvik, Vel or myself."

"What of Atrius and Samous?" Tannis asked.

"They will also be staying close. There are many dangers in these woods," Kainan said looking into the trees.

"Yes, we have heard that," Jadeance complained. "When are you going to tell us what is out there? I don't like surprises, and if we are expected to keep our heads if something happens, it will be easier to do if we aren't in shock."

"Jade," Tannis scolded. "That is no way to speak."

"No, it is alright," Kainan replied. "He makes a good point. To put it lightly, there are many dangers. Most of them you wouldn't really have a hard time with. There are a few that can be a bit unnerving. The first are the Volkru. They are simple enough to understand. Legends tell that they were once wolfs.

Sometime a Millennia ago, they were transformed slightly. You see they can walk like you and me, but only for a short time. They are taller than most men, and they are extremely intelligent. They don't like pain, and can be frightened easily enough. They have sharp claws on their front paws that are venomous, and that is typically their major weapon. You can use that against them, by cutting off the threatening appendage as they swipe at you with it. They are by far the most deadly creatures in these woods. Next in line of things you don't want to see while you're traveling through these woods are Crain Spiders, or Argos Spiders as they are more commonly known. They are your basic venomous spider. What seems to drive people to the brink of insanity is the size of the beasts. They are every bit as large as a standard wagon. An unnerving sight, I promise you. They aren't very intelligent and can be easily confused. The last one rarely bothers humans. However, if they do you, won't have time to do anything about it. They are hardly seen, and they are as silent as the clouds drifting in the sky. To my knowledge they are the largest snakes in the world. They hunt at night, so if one comes for you, you will be asleep. But I wouldn't worry about them; they don't bother humans, unless you bother them first, that is."

Jadeance shook his head. "You're telling me

that there are giant spiders running around here! You have got to be outside of your mind, thinking I'm going to go through a dark, spider infested death trap!"

"Come now," Barvik laughed. "You're not afraid of a spider are you?"

"That's easy for you to say," Jadeance shot back. "A giant spider will only come up to your knees. The same spider will swallow me whole."

Tannis began to laugh. "Jade doesn't like spiders. He used to bribe me to get the last ale barrels from the pantry. The ones in the back were always covered in spiders."

Jadeance started to reply to Tannis when Kainan interrupted him.

"You will be kept safe. Just keep close, like I said." Then Kainan stood up. "We need to get camp up, we need rest. It's a long road, and there is something unnatural going on here. We will want to get through as fast as we can."

"Yes," Samous said. "Something is giving me a bad sort of feeling. We will have to get to the West River tomorrow. We are almost out of water."

"Great," Jadeance complained, "more good news."

Cyres laughed. "Your fear is hopelessly misplaced my young friend. Argos fear fire, and are only a threat in large numbers. The Volkru on the other hand, they can be troublesome."

Jadeance fixed Cyres with a hard look. "Oh good, now I feel much better."

"Will you fools stop discussing the weather and get to helping," Wurwick said irritably.

Cyres looked at Jadeance. "I fear for you, my young friend."

"Why?" Jadeance asked, confused.

"Well, I fear you have no hope. Wizards, you see, seem to live for a very long time, and the longer a man lives, the looser his head gets," Cyres said with a smile.

Barvik and Samous began to laugh. Wurwick's face hardened. "Cyres, your mouth is going to get you into trouble one day."

"My apologies, ancient one," Cyres replied with a bow. Then he quickly left to help Atrius.

"Will you two stop that!" Wurwick complained bitterly to Barvik and Samous, who were laughing.

It took them several hours to get camp set up and supper cooked. They all set around a large fire talking.

"Do you get the feeling that something is tracking us?" Samous asked.

"Most of the day..." Kainan replied looking into the darkness.

"Any ideas?" Atrius asked.

Jadeance could tell that he was also nervous and that made him feel a bit better. He was beginning to think that he was the only one who was afraid.

"No, not yet," Kainan replied. Something in Kainan's eyes told Jadeance that that wasn't true.

"Can you see anything Vel?" Samous asked the dark man.

Vel looked around. "Nothing, not even brush critters."

"What is happening here?" Brie asked. "What could make all animal life leave the woods?"

Kainan looked into the fire. "I don't think they all left. I think most died, and the rest have fled."

"There is something else," Wurwick said. "The very trees are dying, all of them."

"What could do this?" Atrius asked shocked.

"I don't know," Wurwick replied.

"We're going to want to change things up tonight," Kainan said, looking into the night.

"What have you got in mind?" Cyres asked.

"Just a little something to keep...," there was a sudden crack off into the dark that cut Kainan off short.

"Right," Barvik replied. "But to keep us from what?"

"What is going on?" Jadeance asked nervously.

Atrius smiled, "It's an old trick. It comes from an

Astrothenian legend."

"That's just great," Samous replied sarcastically. "Now, I was wondering when you might get around to telling us what this great legend is?"

Atrius shook his head. "Samous, have you ever heard of patience?"

"It's something old people say when they need everyone around them to slow down to their level," Samous complained bitterly.

Atrius fixed Samous with a hard look.

"We will set up one large tent," Kainan replied. "Attach all our canvas together."

"We have a similar tradition in Ver-Ulmich," Vel replied.

"Then let's get set up." Kainan replied.

"What does that mean? Wur, I mean, Master." Jadeance asked.

"Very good," Wurwick replied with a grin. "It will take some getting used to, however it is absolutely critical in many circles. Best to get used to it now, and save an embarrassment later," Wurwick replied.

"You didn't answer my question," Jadeance replied bitterly.

Wurwick smiled. "Call it a gut feeling. You will have to learn to listen to your gut, my boy."

Jadeance could feel his temper rising. "But what does this all mean?" he asked, as nicely as he could muster.

"It means we're going to have visitors tonight," Tannis replied, looking around into the darkness nervously.

It took nearly an hour to rig a tent that would house them all. They got everyone inside and closed it up.

Cyres came over and put his hand on Tannis' shoulder. "Keep Brie in-between you and Jade tonight. And sleep in your gear."

"All right," Tannis replied.

Cyres nodded, and then he looked to Brie. "I know you have an exceptional bow arm, however it will be dark in this forest, and until we get back out into the open you should rely on his arm for protection. You may end up making a costly mistake otherwise. Keep your sword close and stay in the group."

Brie looked to her bow then nodded her head. "Ok, I'll put it away for now."

"Let's get some rest," Atrius said.

As Jadeance lay down, he felt uncomfortable and jumpy. Exhausted, he slowly drifted off into slumber.

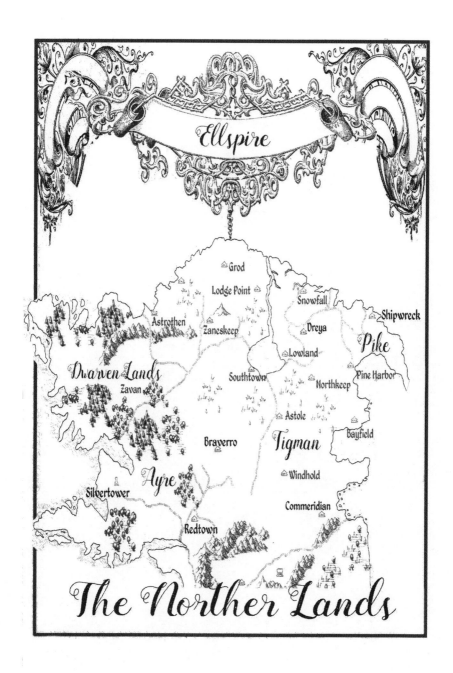

CHAPTER 5

HARROWMON

Jadeance awoke early the next morning. He sat up slightly and looked around. It was dark. Jadeance loved the early morning sun, and he felt as if someone had robbed him of that slight joy. Then, as his eyes fell upon Brie he realized that nothing had happened. Everyone had thought that there was going to be some sort of an attack. Looking around, everyone was sleeping, in fact several of them were snoring loudly. Jadeance got out of his blankets and belted his sword on. It was by far the finest thing he had ever owned. Actually, it was the finest thing he had ever handled. Walking outside, he drew the fine blade and looked it up and down. There were intricate markings on the blade that ran up and down on both sides. Some were a beautiful design, and some were Elvish lettering. In many parts of the world the greatest of sword makers gave their weapons names, because they believed that the sword itself had a life force all of its own. This sword was no exception. Jadeance couldn't read the Elvish writing, however he knew that somewhere its name appeared. Tyuru was unlike any blade Jadeance had ever held. For one thing, it had little to no weight, and Jadeance could swing it easily. His sword training had been going much better with this weapon in hand.

"That is a fine blade," Vel said from behind him.

Jadeance turned around. "I have a lot to learn, don't I?"

Vel smiled, "We all have much to learn."

"Not you," Jadeance protested.

"We never stop learning," Vel replied. "It is when we think we have learned all that we become a danger to ourselves."

Jadeance sheathed his sword. "We weren't attacked last night like Kainan thought we might."

"They are out there," Vel replied looking into the trees.

"What is out there?" Jadeance asked.

The dark man looked at Jadeance. "Argos. It is curious to me that they are acting different than usual."

"Spiders act like spiders," Samous complained as he came out of the tent. "Put a fire by one, he'll move. Simple as that."

"Not so simple," Kainan replied, also emerging from the tent. "What is driving them? I have never seen spiders act with a pack mentality before. These ones are hunting." He hesitated, looking around. "Hunting or tracking us, whatever the case may be, it is not their normal behavior."

"It must be the same thing that is killing the trees and the birds," Jadeance replied.

Kainan smiled. Samous however, shook his head. "All right, Master Jadeance, why don't you shake your staff and show us all what that is?"

Jadeance fixed Samous with a hard look.

"Oh wait," Samous said theatrically. "Don't do it, you might accidently turn me into a toad!"

"That is absolute garbage!" Wurwick roared, emerging from the tent. "How many times do I have to tell you that wizards don't turn people into toads! It's bad form. The very thought of it implies an utter lack of taste and dignity. Now, if you are all done, we need to be on our way. With any luck we'll make the river by noon."

They broke down the tent, and after a quick breakfast they were on their way. Jadeance rode next to Brie and Tannis as usual, yet the feeling that something was following them had them all in a somber mood. Jadeance found himself scanning the trees, looking for any signs of movement. Then,

Jadeance started to see light up ahead. At first he thought it was a trick, but as they rode closer the light grew stronger. The party started moving faster, and it didn't take long to break free of the tree line. The party stopped and Jadeance looked at the wide, sweeping river. It was large enough that the sky was clearly visible. One by one they all stopped dead in their tracks at the sight of it. Hundreds of dead animals lay on the banks of that river. The dead lined both sides and stretched out as far as the eye could see.

"By Thamis, what could have caused this?" Atrius asked in a shocked voice.

"This is what we have been looking for," Kainan said in a sad voice. "Driven by thirst, they have come here to die."

"What could have poisoned the whole river?" Barvik asked.

Wurwick looked to Jadeance. "All right boy, you're up."

"What do you mean?" Jadeance asked puzzled.

"Water is your Element, so now this task falls to you. You must locate the source," Wurwick replied firmly.

"Can he do that?" Tannis asked.

"He is your brother, what do you think?" Wurwick replied his old eyes emotionless.

Jadeance got down off his horse. Walking to the river bed, he closed his eyes and held his staff tight. "Show me," he whispered into the air. Opening his eyes, the elements came to life and he once again saw the world through a slight blue tinge. The river flowed red as blood. Looking to the east end of the river, there was a slight blue glow. He knew that was what he had to follow. Running up the river, he followed the lights with his friends following close behind. Slowly, the light turned to a bright red, and Jadeance could finally see what was causing the problem.

Everyone had dismounted and joined Jadeance on the river bed.

"Well, boy?" Wurwick asked.

"It's a necklace," Jadeance replied, pointing to the river. "There is a low spot. It's very deep, and the current is at its strongest here."

Wurwick began to swear. "It must be a Harrowmon, a horrible curse placed on an object. Few can even attempt it. The last successful attempt that I know of was nearly eight hundred years ago."

"Can you destroy it?" Kainan asked.

"No one knows enough about them to even attempt it." Wurwick replied scowling into the water.

"How can we move it?" Atrius asked.

"You don't want to touch it," Wurwick replied.

"Well need to grab it with something."

"That solves one problem," Barvik grumbled. "Last I checked no one here can breathe under water."

"I can get it," Tannis replied confidently.

"It's too dangerous boy," Wurwick replied. "It could be sixty feet down for all we know."

"No," Jadeance replied. "Tannis is half fish, he can get it. I can help with the current."

Kainan looked at the two boys, "Half fish is he?"

"Care to make a bet?" Jadeance asked hopefully.

"Aren't you a bit young for gambling?" Samous replied, his eyes narrowing.

"Am I?" Jadeance replied. "Or are you scared to take me up?"

"You bet on your brother's life?" Kainan asked, his face darkening.

"No," Jadeance replied. "I bet on how long he can hold his breath. We have been doing it for years."

"Ever lost?" Samous asked with an evil grin.

"Nope," Jadeance replied confidently.

"Enough," Kainan said firmly. "Can you can really get it?"

"Yes," Tannis replied confidently. "That is, if Wurwick can find me something to grab it with."

"I don't like it," Wurwick replied bitterly. And with that, he held out his hand and produced a pair of blacksmith tongs and a necklace with a large box at its center. "These are enchanted," Wurwick said as he handed them over. "They will protect you." Then he grabbed Tannis by the wrist. "This is no game boy! If you drink any of that water…"

"I'll be ok," Tannis interrupted. Then, to cut off further conversation he began to undress. Tannis was very strong, and when he removed his shirt, his chest rippled with muscles as he moved.

"I'll be watching you," Jadeance said. "Just wave at me if you need any help. I'll also take care of the current, but I don't know how long I will be able to hold it, so don't take your time."

Tannis nodded his head, and then dove head first into the river.

"That has to be cold," Cyres shuddered, watching Tannis disappear underneath the ripples.

Jadeance pointed his staff at the river. It only took a moment to stop the flow of water running past. What shocked him was how easy it was to stop the great waters. Stopping up a massive river is no small task, and yet he seemed to do it with little effort. The moments dragged on as Tannis continued to descend to the river's floor. What at first appeared to be a simple task of holding back the fierce current soon became far more challenging. Jadeance couldn't stop the new water from coming down the river, so he had to hold more and more back, forcing the standing water line to rise.

"Are you sure you know what you're doing?" Samous asked nervously.

"Don't break the boy's concentration," Wurwick barked sharply.

The pressure became intense, and Jadeance began to wonder if he could hold it all back.

"Keep your balance," Wurwick said sharply in the back of Jadeance's head.

Jadeance watched Tannis swim deeper and deeper. "Come on Tannis, hurry! I can't hold this up too much longer," Jadeance said, struggling under the intense pressure of the great river.

"You can do it, Jade," Brie said reassuringly.

It was Cyres who called the alarm, and Jadeance turned his head to see the hillside above them covered with giant Argos spiders. Each was a strange grey color, and they had thick fur covering their bodies and legs. What took Jadeance's breath were the huge fangs they had.

"What now?" Atrius asked alarmed.

"Ever had spider soup?" Barvik asked with a huge grin as he pulled out his monstrous axe.

"Have you ever considered that a fight could be a bad thing?" Cyres complained as he drew his two massive swords out.

"I doubt it," Kainan replied with a shrug, also drawing a sword.

"There are too many," Atrius said, drawing a sword.

"Put that away," Wurwick barked at Atrius. "You and Brie get your bows out. Aim for their heads or their sides."

As the spiders started down the hill, Barvik, Cyres, Kainan and Vel charged up to meet them. Wurwick held out his hand and a ball of fire emerged and floated just of his palm. He waved his staff over it and the single ball of fire split into two. He tossed them up the hill. They hit the side of the hill and a wave of energy flew up the hill sending dozens of the monster Argos flying.

"Wurwick!" Atrius shouted. "Do something! We're going to run out of arrows long before we run out of spiders."

Wurwick grunted, and sent another group of Argos flying. "We need to find whatever is driving them, and stop it," Wurwick shouted back.

Almost in answer to Wurwick, another spider crested the top of the hill. Argos spiders were large but this one however dwarfed them all. He was easily twice as large as the rest, and it grunted and hissed in a manner that left no question. This was the driving force, a spider king. Everyone stopped momentarily as the giant came into view.

"There are too many of them!" Vel shouted to Kainan. "We cannot hold this much longer."

"We can hold a bit longer," Kainan shouted back

Jadeance was sweating, straining to hold back the still climbing river. Then Tannis emerged from the river and made his way to shore.

"Glad to see you didn't take your time," Jadeance grated; sweat now dripping down his face.

"What is going on here?" Tannis asked, shocked.

"Be careful with that, boy!" Wurwick shouted.

Tannis looked down at the amulet he had retrieved. It was a dull silver, and overall very plain. However, you could feel death heavy in the air surrounding it. Tannis tossed the amulet to the ground, and as it landed it sent sparks flying and the very earth it landed on blackened and dried up. That blackness slowly began to spread.

"Noo," hissed the giant Argos. "He hass it." The giant spider began down the hill, completely surrounded by an army of Argos.

Just then Jadeance had a good idea. "Kainan," Jadeance shouted. "Fall back."

"Fall back!" Wurwick shouted his reply, and sent another blast, giving Kainan and the others room to fall back.

"This is stupid," Barvik swore. "Now we're pinned

up against the river."

"It will be ok," Kainan replied. "Jade has a plan."

The spiders were now nearing the shore line. "Now would be a good time!" Cyres yelled.

"We have iiitt." The giant Argos hissed with delight.

With a smile, Jadeance simply turned loose the strength of the massive river he had been holding back. Instead of sending it back down the river, he redirected it, going around his friends. Jadeance lifted his staff, and the river waters climbed in response. Then he pushed the mass to the ground. There was a great rushing noise, and the earth shook under the pressure as the wave hit the charging spiders full on. There was a mass of furry grey legs mixed in with the churning waters as the spiders were all carried downstream. Jadeance struggled under the pressure, his legs buckling under the strain. Concentrating with all his might, he finally managed to revert all the water back down the river bed.

"Brilliant!" Wurwick shouted, and he began to dance with glee. "Ha! Did you see that? Taught him all he knows, I did," Wurwick laughed, dancing in circles.

Barvik however, wasn't laughing. "Could you have waited a little longer?" he shouted. "They didn't quite reach us."

"Easy Barvik," Cyres said sheathing his swords. "He had to get them all."

"Well, he didn't have to wait so long." Barvik grumbled, dropping his great axe.

Brie ran up and hugged Jadeance tightly. "You were wonderful!"

"Brie," Jadeance wheezed. "You don't have to let go, but can you loosen up a bit? I can't breathe." She released him, and he nearly fell to the ground.

"Are you ok?" Brie asked.

"I'm ok," Jadeance replied. "I'm just a little tired."

"We have a problem," Kainan said as he approached the amulet Tannis had retrieved.

"More than one," Atrius replied.

"Wurwick, can you do something about this?" Kainan asked.

"I can't destroy it," Wurwick replied. "But I can trap its evil." Wurwick produced a small wooden box from under his robe.

"Where did you get that?" Samous asked curiously.

"None of your business, you little sneak," Wurwick replied.

Wurwick opened the box, then he held the tip of his staff over the amulet, obediently it began to rise.

He lifted it gently into the box, being careful not to touch it at all. As he closed the lid, the box flashed a bright green.

"Is it safe now?" Atrius asked.

"It's evil is contained," Wurwick replied. "I have sealed the box. But its evil can still be used. We need to make haste to Braverro."

"What is going on?" Tannis asked shivering.

Brie brought him a blanket from one of the pack horses.

"No time for that," Wurwick replied. "We need to be on our way." He held his staff over Tannis' head. A bright light erupted from the tip of staff and surrounded Tannis. After a moment the light flickered and vanished. When it was gone, Tannis stood dressed in his clothes, and he was completely dry.

"Right," Kainan said looking around. "We had better get a move on before they come back."

"We can't leave yet," Brie said, folding her arms.

"What are you talking about?" Samous replied, dropping his bow. "Do you think that we should just sit here and wait for them to come back? Maybe instead of fighting this time, we can..."

"That's enough of that, Samous you little thief." Wurwick interrupted.

"What's this about child?" Atrius asked Brie.

Brie pointed to the river. "Just removing that thing isn't enough. Life can't return here until there is water to drink."

"What can we do?" Atrius asked her.

"Jade can fix it," She replied confidently.

Atrius looked to Wurwick. "Can he?"

"How should I know?" Wurwick replied. "I wasn't the one creating the giant wall of water." Then he looked to Jadeance. "Well boy, will you bring life back to this wood?"

Jadeance looked at Wurwick helplessly. He felt so tired.

"You can do it, Jade," Brie said smiling.

"Yea, Jade, you can do it," Tannis said reassuring him.

Jadeance looked at the river. How could he cure an entire river of a poison that had overtaken everything?

"Well, boy? Will you?" Wurwick pressed.

Jadeance looked down at his staff. "Will you give me strength?" he whispered. His staff sent a strange tingle through his hands. It seemed to breathe new life into him. He waded into the river until he was waist deep. He looked to Brie and Tannis one last time, and then he closed his eyes and took a deep breath. He opened his eyes and held his staff up over his head. Drawing in his strength, his staff fed him sending a slight throbbing sensation up his arms. A bright blue smoke began to encircle Jadeance. As his strength grew, he could feel a chorus of voices ringing in his mind, calling to him from a place he couldn't even begin to understand. Then, when he felt like he couldn't possibly hold it any longer, he dropped the tip of the staff into the water, screaming "now!" As the staff hit the water, it began to react almost violently. The sound was near deafening, the water began boiling and churning as far as the eye could see. The smoke that had been surrounding Jadeance began to rise from the river in a mesmerizing way that left the group speechless. All the dead that lined the river banks vanished and thinned into the mist. Slowly, the river started to settle and return to normal. The water was crystal clear, and a calm peace set over the banks of the once dead river. Jadeance numbly started to make his way to shore. He felt completely drained, and as he reached the shore he nearly collapsed. The giant Barvik picked him up with apparent ease, and carried him back to the horses.

"We have truly seen a wonder here today," Samous said with great excitement. "Have you ever seen anything like that?"

"Hush now, Samous," Wurwick replied quickly. "We must keep our heads and move on."

"Is he going to be ok?" Atrius asked, a little worried.

"He will recover," Wurwick replied confidently. "He is far stronger than he looks."

"Have you ever seen the Argos combine like that?" Kainan asked Vel.

"Never," Vel replied. "Always before, there have been a dozen or less."

"They were clearly after the amulet," Kainan replied. "But what could possibly have united them?"

"The water," Wurwick mused. "There were hundreds of dead lining the banks of this river. Did you see a single Argos? Something very powerful is at work here, and whatever it is, has to be supplying them with fresh water."

"That's crazy," Atrius replied shocked. "Who could be so powerful?"

"I don't like it," Samous said. "Something doesn't sound right."

"No, it makes perfect sense," Kainan replied with a smile. "It's genius really. You create something with great power, you hide it in a place that no one will be able to find, and then you use it to manipulate your own force of bodyguards to protect it. It's worry free. Whoever put it there won't have to think twice about it, if it's there or not, because who could possibly get past all the Argos, and retrieve it from the depths of a poisoned river?"

"Two young brothers from Tigman," Atrius replied with a smile. Then his smile faded. "This seems like a very special kind of evil. It might be a good idea to get on our way."

"Yes," Kainan replied. Then he turned to Wurwick. "Is the river safe now?"

"Yes," Wurwick replied. "In fact it is probably cleaner than any river flowing in any part of the world."

"Good," Kainan replied. "Let's fill our stores then be on our way."

"Can young Jadeance ride?" Atrius asked.

"I'll ride with him." Brie replied. "We'll be all right."

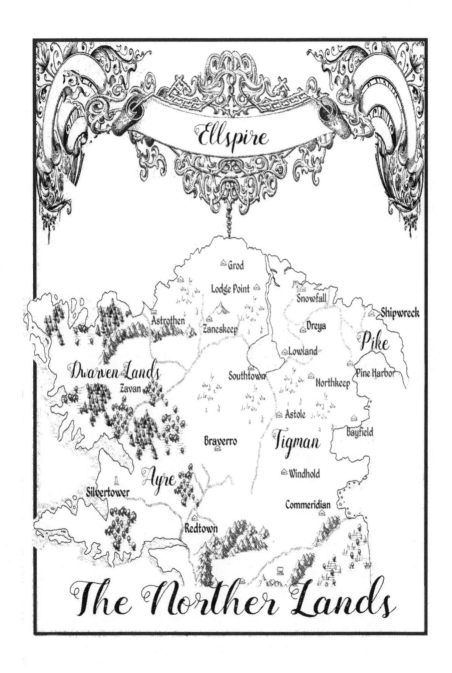

CHAPTER 6

MORE VISITORS

They moved back onto the road, and rode hard into the night. The woods still steamed with an overwhelming sense of evil. Fears fueled by knowledge that there was an army of Argos trailing them kept the party riding hard. The days and nights began to merge in the darkness. Jadeance struggled to keep himself alert as they made their way through the great woods of the north. It took nearly two days for Jadeance to start to feel like himself again. Despite his returning health, he still rode with Brie. She was a comfortable riding companion, and they were both fairly lightweight. The horse didn't seem too bogged down by having two passengers.

"We'll stop here for the night," Kainan said aloud after a hard day of riding.

Jadeance fell gratefully off the horse he had been sharing with Brie. "I don't like riding all day,"

Jadeance complained, rubbing his backside.

"You will get used to it," Cyres replied with a grunt as he also slid off his saddle. "Sooner or later you will lose feeling altogether, and then you will be ready to be a proper soldier."

"That's not very encouraging," Tannis complained, also rubbing his backside.

"Let's keep with a single tent again tonight," Kainan said as he surveyed the area.

"Right," Atrius replied.

"Great," Samous laughed. "Another night sleeping next to a giant, snoring bear."

"I hardly snore at all," Barvik complained. "You wouldn't even notice it, if you fell asleep first."

"Just like you wouldn't notice the changing of the seasons, if you were as old as Wurwick is." Samous laughed.

"Samous, have you ever considered the possibility of waking up at the top of a mountain range? Or possibly at the mouth of a dragon's den?" Wurwick asked, his old eyebrows narrowing.

"Do you know where to find a dragon's den?" Kainan asked with a smile. "I thought they were extinct."

"Dragons are most certainly not gone forever," Wurwick replied firmly. "They have been persuaded to stay indoors, you might say. And if we are going to talk of dragons, pray they stay where they are. I fear this world would most certainly burn if they were to return to the skies."

"Why, Master?" Jadeance asked curiously, his mind aflame with the thought of seeing a real dragon. "I thought they lived peacefully in our lands."

Wurwick grunted, "There isn't a lot of peace in a dragon. They are easily the most fearsome animal created by the Divines. Suffice it to know that in the elder days there was a power that could control them, a power that has long since vanished. That is one of the saddest tales of this world's history, and a story for another day."

It didn't take them very long to get camp set up and a supper on the fire. Jadeance sat next to Tannis, watching Barvik and Cyres sharpening their weapons, and thinking about dragons.

"How long until we reach Braverro?" Brie asked Atrius.

Atrius looked upwards, trying to locate the sun through the mass of trees. Then he turned to Samous.

"At least another week," Samous replied quickly.

Brie sighed and looked into the fire. "I miss the sun," she said quietly.

"Take care, child," Atrius said comfortingly. "This darkness will not last forever."

"It would be nice if we knew more about what is out there," Samous grumbled.

"There may be a way," Atrius replied looking at Brie.

"Planning to offer her up as a sacrifice?" Samous laughed. "You are starting to sound like that black Magi, Balseer."

"Don't be ridiculous," Atrius scoffed, looking highly offended.

"No, Atrius is right," Wurwick mused. "Brie, would you do me a favor? Close your eyes and relax."

"Why?" Brie asked, looking at Atrius curiously.

"You will be safe," Wurwick replied, as he filled his pipe and lit it.

Brie closed her eyes and took a deep breath. After a moment she opened her eyes and looked at Wurwick questionably. "Was something supposed to happen?"

"You need to relax. Try again. This time do as I say and relax," Wurwick grumbled. As Brie closed her eyes, Wurwick's pipe began to produce more and more smoke. It moved out in waves towards Brie. Jadeance could feel the old man's magic flowing in a calming wave, as if the smoke numbed all emotion and a calm peace swept over them. "What's in the darkness?" Wurwick asked quietly.

"It's not just darkness," Brie said, looking off into the darkness through the smoke. Then she closed her eyes and fell silent for a time. "There is an evil in this wood and it soon bears down on us, though we see it not. It will find us divided and confused. But fear not, for hope is not lost at the cross road. Be diligent, for there is a hidden strength in the deep, and in its finding you will hold the key to awakening a great lost power."

"What are you talking about Brie?" Samous asked confused, his long pointy ears twitching slightly.

"Hush now," Wurwick barked looking intently at Brie. "What lost power?"

Brie shook her head as if waking up from a long nap. "What?" She asked looking around confused.

Atrius sat in front of her and grabbed her hands. "Don't worry, child. You have the ability to see into another plane of existence. I believe you already knew that. You have seen something just now, and I desperately need you to remember what you have seen."

"I don't know if I can," she replied softly, looking slightly embarrassed.

"You can do it Brie," Jadeance said, sitting next to her. "I'll be right here to help you."

She smiled at him then closed her eyes. "Ok, I will try to remember what I can."

"What lost power?" Wurwick asked carefully.

"It's hidden," she replied. "It has been sealed and

kept away for a long time." Then she frowned, "I can't see anything now, just darkness."

"Hidden from what?" Wurwick asked.

"I...," she stuttered. "I just don't know," Brie replied.

"What evil sets itself against us here?" Kainan asked.

Brie began to frown. "I see thousands of eyes..., there is a great hunger, and a shadow."

"That's not obscure at all," Samous complained bitterly. "Standard gibberish, all who claim to see beyond our world speak in riddles."

Atrius shrugged. "Well, if you think you can do any better, go ahead."

"He has you there," Cyres smirked.

"Hush now, all of you," Kainan commanded. "She spoke of a division amongst us. Let's not make it any easier."

"Is the lost power a dragon?" Jadeance asked hopefully.

"No, I don't think so." Brie replied with a smile.

Vel came into the fire light and began to speak to Kainan in a language Jadeance couldn't understand. There was one word unfortunately that he could make out, 'Volkru'.

Kainan looked around and said, "It's time to retire for the night." Barvik grunted and began to feed the fire.

"I thought we were going to bed?" Brie asked.

Barvik looked into the forest. "We are," he said simply. "This is just a precaution."

"For what?" Tannis asked.

"Not now," Cyres said as Kainan began herding them all into the tent.

"Keep Brie in between you and Tannis again tonight," Wurwick said to Jadeance as they started laying down bed rolls.

"Stay armed again tonight," Cyres said to Tannis as he passed.

Jadeance laid his head down, and despite his excitement, he fell fast asleep.

Jadeance awoke suddenly to a creak outside the tent. He looked around, and everyone was asleep, in fact everyone was snoring loudly. Brie reached out and pulled him in tightly. "I'm scared", she whispered into his ear.

"It will be ok, Brie," Jadeance said to comfort her.

"Something is out there," Brie whispered.

"We need to wake Vel," Jadeance replied.

"They're all awake," Brie whispered as she turned her head to face Cyres. "Have you ever heard Cyres snore before?"

"But why would they all pretend to be asleep?" Jadeance asked puzzled.

Then, as if it were an answer to Jadeance's question, several large beasts burst right through the tent wall. The Volkru expected to find their prey asleep. Much to their surprise, they were met with shouts of alarm, and drawn weapons. The Volkru looked like huge wolves that had learned to walk upright. Their eyes were large and frightening, and they had a slight yellow tint that was utterly un-nerving. The hunger in their eyes paled to the sight of their horrible teeth. Jadeance grabbed Brie's hand and followed the giant Barvik out of the tent and right into the fire light. The beasts were everywhere. Jadeance couldn't quite decide what to do, until he saw Tannis fighting next to Cyres. He didn't seem to fear them at all.

"Teach them to fear you!" Wurwick's voice sounded off in his head. He turned to see one lunging towards Brie.

"Not today!" Jadeance shouted as he leveled his staff at the beast. "Fire!" he commanded. A bright light burst from his staff as the Volkru was thrown into the forest, completely engulfed in flame. He began sending the beasts flying. One of the beasts came out of the tent, carrying the box that contained the amulet with an agility that surprised Jadeance. Vel cut him off. His spinning staff made short work of the beast.

"This is getting old," Samous shouted as he spun around one of the fearsome beasts, sticking his short sword into the creature's back.

"Ha!" Barvik laughed. He was able to spin his monstrous axe in a peculiar way, almost as if it were dancing around his massive arms. He moved his way right through the beasts, cleaving many of the beasts nearly in two. "I'm just getting warmed up," the giant cheered as he beheaded a Volkru.

Cyres fought next to Tannis and Kainan. Kainan's movements were strong and precise. One by one the Volkru fell, as Kainan kept methodically chopping at the creatures as they attacked.

Cyres style was similar to Vels, more of a continuous motion. Despite his stature, his movements flowed with speed and agility. His sword danced and spun around him, it was simply mesmerizing. The ground around him was littered with dead Volkru.

Jadeance watched Wurwick send a Volkru spinning through the air. Then the remaining Volkru broke and ran back into the forest howling.

"Where did they go?" Samous asked his eyes searching.

"They did not have the numbers required to achieve their objective," Vel replied, picking the box that contained the amulet off the ground.

"There seemed to be plenty of them to me," Atrius complained looking around.

"Anyone get the feeling things are only going to get worse?" Samous asked.

"We need to keep moving," Kainan replied as he cleaned his sword.

"Right," Barvik replied. "I'll start on the tent."

"What's left of it," Samous remarked, looking back at the torn canvas.

They broke camp quickly and were off, the events of the morning completely filling Jadance's mind. The shrieks and howls of the beasts echoed over and over, as if the battle was still raging. A fear began to creep into the very depths of his soul the thought that he would never again see daylight. This dark, horror filled wood would certainly claim them all. Still, they had faced such insurmountable odds and were as yet unscathed. Jadeance began to look at his new friends differently.

"That's what you have been waiting for isn't it," Tannis shouted to Kainan as they rode through the expanse that is the Great Red Wood.

"What?" Kainan replied.

"That attack," Tannis pressed. "That's why we have been crammed into one tent."

Kainan laughed slightly. "Yes, I have felt it coming for a time now. It's an old trick. You see, the attackers think that they are taking you by surprise. When in reality you are not asleep, and it is they who are caught by surprise."

"Do you think we are out of the danger now?" Brie asked. "We have defeated two of the major threats this wood offers."

"It's hard to say," Kainan replied. "There are a great many dangers you haven't even considered. Let's just travel hard, and make our way out as fast as possible."

They rode on through the day, and made their camp that evening near a great ruin. Very little of what once was, now remained. A few standing walls was just about it.

"What is this place?" Tannis asked.

"They say it was once a Dwarvin village," Samous replied. "We have so little information about them it's hard to say for sure. The southern elves have far more records than we do. My people didn't venture very far into the mountains. Of course, it would have been generations ago, back before they sealed themselves in their mountains. Now they are more secret and mythical than anything else. Few men who have ever lived have been allowed inside their great mountains.

"Why did they disappear?" Brie asked.

"They were betrayed," Wurwick replied quietly.

"You see, there are chapters in human history that we would erase if we could. One man with an evil heart found his way to power. He sought domination of the Dwarves. There was a great betrayal. To his great astonishment the Dwarves proved to be too resilient to be enslaved. They retreated to their mountains and locked the door behind them."

"Never to return?" Brie asked.

"Well, you see the Dwarves are not like the elves. The elves turn more towards philosophy. They are a race full of compassion and most of all forgiveness. They are for the most part immortal, and they tend to look on the brighter side of things. The Dwarves, on the other hand, are a very emotional, very courageous race, and they have strong values. But they don't easily forget, and are notorious at holding a grudge. And when it comes right down to it, we need them far more than they need us," Wurwick said, sitting down.

"Why do we need them?" Tannis asked.

"Well you see, there are no finer stone workers, or metal smiths in the world. We have very little to offer them, except our ales and wines. Then Wurwick sighed. "Enough talk for tonight. We all need to get some rest."

Jadeance retired, wishing he was back at Wagstaff and out of these woods. "Tannis, what do you think

Uncle Keldon and Aunt Suena are doing"?

Tannis stretched in his blankets. "Closing up for the night probably," Tannis replied.

"Do you wish we could go back to just Jade and Tannis? Lowly innkeepers, listening to stories brought to us by the trading caravan," Jadeance asked.

"Yes," Tannis replied with a slight smile.

"No you don't," Brie popped up. Then she half rolled over Jadeance. "There was no one in all of Windhold for you."

"What are you talking about?" Tannis replied with a slight blush.

Brie smiled. "Don't you try to hide from me, Tannis," Brie replied firmly. "I have always known that true happiness for you meant leaving Windhold."

"Now you're being ridiculous," Tannis replied, blushing harder.

"No, I'm not," Brie replied with a slight smile.

"It looks like she hit something there," Jadeance laughed.

Tannis turned his back on them both. "I'm not going to listen to this anymore," Tannis declared.

Jadeance and Brie laughed for a time, before Jadeance took a deep breath trying to calm himself. "Good night, Tannis," Jadeance said with a huge smile on his face.

"Shut up you," Tannis barked.

Brie looked down at Jadeance. "Where is my good night?" she asked.

Jadeance shrugged, "Good night, Brie."

"I think you can do better than that." Brie replied with a slight grin.

Jadeance looked confused. "Um... have pleasant dreams, too," he replied, not really sure what she wanted.

Brie rolled her eyes. "You are an impossible boy," she declared. Then, without saying anything else, she bent over and kissed him soundly. Brie was warm and comfortable. Jadeance found himself blushing furiously as he realized that he truly enjoyed it when she kissed him. Brie backed off slightly and said, "That is how you wish a girl good night." Then she started back to her blankets. Suddenly, her face took on a look of near horror and she grabbed Jadeance's still blushing face. "Not any other girls," she replied firmly, "Ever!" Then she bit her lip slightly and also began to blush.

"Just you. I think I understand." Jadeance laughed, and then he pulled her in tight and hugged her. "Go to sleep, Brie," he whispered. Brie smiled, still blushing and quickly disappeared underneath her blankets.

CHAPTER 7

DARKNESS FALLS

Morning dawned cold as Jadeance stirred up the fire. Slowly, his friends started to make their way out. Wurwick emerged last, and he didn't look very happy.

"Feeling your years this morning?" Samous asked with a smile.

Wurwick gave him a hard look. "Didn't sleep well", he grunted. "Kept having…," then he shook his head. "No matter. I think I have been too close to the amulet. I'm not going to carry it under my robe today. It seems to be affecting me."

"We can take turns with it," Kainan replied. "We should have thought of it sooner," Kainan apologized.

Wurwick shrugged, "It is pure evil, and I should have known better than to keep it so close for so long."

"I'll carry it for a time, Master," Jadeance replied.

Wurwick grunted, "Thank you. I have placed it over on the large stone, near the fire pit."

Jadeance nodded and looked to the stone Wurwick had spoken of. The stone had become a table of sorts. Jadeance made his way to pick it up, and then he looked at Wurwick. "If it can affect him so bad, maybe I'll wait to carry it until were leaving," he thought. Jadeance stretched and noticed Brie sitting near the fire. She smiled and motioned to him.

"How did you sleep?" Brie asked as Jadeance sat down next to her.

"Fine," he replied blushing slightly. "Aren't you going to ask me how I slept?" Brie asked with a slight smile.

Jadeance couldn't look into her eyes without blushing. He looked to the ground, angry with himself. "How did you sleep?" he muttered out.

"I slept wonderfully," Brie replied. Then she turned his head towards her. "Why won't you look at me Jade?"

"No reason," Jadeance replied.

"I think you need to wish me good night more often," Brie said, her smile broadening.

Jadeance began to blush again and quickly looked away.

Brie laughed. "I'm sorry, Jade. I'll be nice." And with that she hugged him tightly and fell silent.

"We'll be nearing the great basin soon," Samous said. "Braverro lies at the far end. We'll arrive by end of the week if we're lucky."

"Our luck hasn't been the good kind lately," Cyres complained.

"Then we're due," Atrius replied with an encouraging smile.

Cyres let out a deep sigh. "Due for what is the question."

"Cyres!" Atrius said sharply. "If you don't cheer up I'll..."

Atrius was cut off by a deep drum note. Everyone fell silent for a moment. There was another drum note, and then another. They were everywhere. Kainan turned to Barvik and motioned to the horses.

"What's going on?" Tannis asked.

"They are talking to each other," Cyres replied as he rushed to pack up the essentials from camp.

"Who?" Jadeance asked. However, before anyone had a chance to answer him, dozens of Trolls burst through trees. There were shouts of alarm, and Jadeance found himself split up from his friends. One of the Trolls grabbed the box containing the amulet and broke into the woods shrieking with delight.

"No!" Kainan yelled. "They cannot have it back." Jadeance didn't take time to think, he burst into the trees at full speed after the Troll. Excitement filled

Jadeance as he ran. He could tell other Trolls were chasing him, but he paid them little thought for he was far faster and was easily pulling away from them. It didn't take him long to close the gap on the running Troll who carried the box containing the amulet. The Troll shrieked and tried to lose him. Jadeance was light on his feet, and he overtook the Troll. With a burst of light, Jadeance sent the Troll flying with his staff. He stooped and picked up the box without missing a step. A spinning spear nearly got him as he bent over. Swearing, Jadeance flew off into the trees again hoping to lose them. He came out into a small clearing and stopped dead in his tracks. The clearing was full of armed Trolls. He turned around to see more Trolls come out of the trees behind him. Looking around gave no hope. He was completely surrounded. Jadeance's stomach lurched slightly with terror. Fearing the end had come for him, Jadeance was not going to die without a fight. He drew his sword and stood sword in one hand, staff in the other. The Trolls that had trailed him charged, and Jadeance began felling them as fast as he could, sending many flying into the woods with his staff, slicing others with his sword. Jadeance was not a warrior and he was badly outnumbered and it didn't take too long for one of the Trolls to pin him up against a tree. He was stripped of his sword and staff and held tightly against the tree. The Troll that held him was one of the Trolls he had nicked with his blade. The Troll groaned slightly and looked at its now bleeding arm.

"You are a feisty little one. I'm going to enjoy this," the Troll laughed as he bent over and picked up Jadeance's sword. "I'm going to kill you with your own sword!" the Troll laughed. He placed the blade on the gash that Jadeance had cut in his arm and applied a light film of blood to the spotless blade. With a terrifying grin, the troll held the blade to Jadeance's cheek, and the sharp blade easily dug deep into his flesh. Jadeance screamed as the Troll cut, mixing Troll blood with his own. The pain was intense and the wound burned. The Troll brought the blade to his lips and licked the fresh blood off the blade. Jadeance could feel blood running down his cheek, and the burning in his cheek intensified as time went on. Holding back tears, he watched the Troll as he raised the sword high above his head. Suddenly there was a shout of alarm, and the Troll dropped the sword, and Jadeance was set free and fell hard to the ground. When Jadeance looked up to see what was going on, he felt a rush of excitement. Cyres was there, his twin blades spinning violently. Jadeance grabbed his staff, and looked for his sword. The sight of it made him sick and he had to concentrate to hold his stomach. The Troll had not dropped the sword, his arms had been cut off, and one hand still gripped the hilt as it laid there lifeless.

"Get on your feet Jade!" Cyres shouted, as he continued to fell any Troll who dared come within sword's reach.

Jadeance used his staff to flip the dead arm off his sword, and then he ran to Cyres. Standing back to back, the trolls completely surrounded the two cutting off any hopes of an escape.

"What happens now?" Jadeance asked.

"I'm working on it," Cyres replied, looking around.

The Trolls parted, and a single Troll made his way to the front. He had an elaborate headdress made of bones. His body was covered with horrible scars. His right hand carried a terrible looking staff, made of two huge bones belted together and covered with feathers and totems. The head of the terrible staff was made of two human skulls facing away from each other.

"That doesn't look good," Cyres said, as the Troll approached.

"You have something that belongs to me," the Troll hissed.

"As you can see, we have nothing," Cyres replied slowly.

The Troll growled. "I see right through your pathetic lies." He shrieked as he raised his staff, sending a small ball of intense darkness straight at them. Jadeance jumped in front of Cyres, dispersing the darkness with the tip of his staff. Unfortunately the blast was more than Jadeance could hold, and he was sent flying.

"You pathetic fool. You will never be strong enough to overpower me," the Troll laughed.

Jadeance pulled himself to his feet and looked at the Troll with hate. "I'm not afraid of you!" Jadeance yelled defiantly, sending a blast of energy at the Troll with all the power he could muster. The Troll stepped forward and thrust his staff into the burst Jadeance had sent. As soon as the skulled staff hit the energy, it was mirrored and intensified throwing Jadeance and Cyres to the ground. Jadeance made his way back to his feet, when suddenly he was lifted high in the air, and the box containing the amulet slipped out of his pocket and flew toward the Troll. Jadeance tried with all his might to stop the box. The more powerful Troll flicked his finger towards Jadeance and he was thrown back several feet into a tree. Jadeance felt as if he had been crushed. The wound on his face was numb now, his bleeding was getting worse and the blood had started to make its way down the front of his chest. The front of his robe clung to his chest as he struggled to stand. Cyres pulled him to his feet.

"Rest now, my brave friend," Cyres said holding Jadeance up.

"You cannot escape," the Troll laughed. "Throw down your weapons! Your lives belong to me now."

"No," Jadeance grunted. However Cyres shook his head. "They have won this battle, little one," Cyres said. "The only way to fight now is to submit." Cyres dropped his swords. "We will submit," Cyres said to the Troll.

CHAPTER 8

PRISONERS

Cyres and Jadeance were placed in shackles, and force marched deep into the forest. To Jadeance it all seemed far too much to bear, and his pain and exhaustion began to get the better of him. Tears lightly streaming down his cheeks, he began to stumble and finally he collapsed. Cyres picked him up and placed him on his shoulders.

"We'll be all right Jade. They are keeping us alive for a reason. We'll have a chance to get out. Just trust me, and do exactly as I say. And if nothing else, you must look to keeping yourself alive, even if it means leaving me behind. Also, I don't know what they want. So no matter what they ask, you don't give them any information," Cyres said seriously.

"But what if..." Jadeance started.

"No," Cyres cut him off. "No matter what they do, or what they promise. Whatever it is they want, we can't give it to them."

"All right," Jadeance replied. He was struggling to remain conscious. Weakened by his wounds, he soon succumbed and fell unconscious. Jadeance awoke later that night as Cyres sat him down, and sank gratefully to the ground himself. There were well over fifty Trolls guarding them. The Trolls didn't speak to them; instead they only spoke to themselves in a Trollish language.

Even though Jadeance couldn't understand the Trolls, it wasn't hard to see that they hated him and Cyres. Whatever contact they did have was brief, and usually bore some kind of violence. They walked for several days with little to no food. Jadeance felt weak and scared. He often drew strength from Cyres. The large man seemed to be immoveable, despite the conditions. He took most of the abuse, and at times found them edible roots and berries as they walked. It didn't take Jadeance long to realize that without Cyres, survival would be impossible. His cheek was getting worse. The bleeding had long stopped, now it was swelling and oozing a horrible puss. Despite Cyres best attempts to treat it, it continued to worsen. The pain was now overwhelming. Despite his best efforts to think about something else, his pain completely filled his mind.

"We're going to be all right," Cyres said as he

applied a mixture he had made to Jadeance's cheek.

Jadeance had stopped talking. The pain surged every time he even attempted to move his mouth. One of the Trollish guards walked up, and made a kick at Jadeance with a glare of hate. Cyres intercepted it with his own leg. "Move out," the Troll grumbled.

Cyres stood up, and then picked Jadeance up off the ground and carried him along. The column moved steadily though the day until they broke out of the trees, and into a large clearing.

The clearing was completely filled with Trolls surrounding a large stone structure. It was two spherical towers perched on either side of a large gate way. For the first time in a long time, Jadeance was in the sun. It was a wonderful feeling that didn't last long.

In fact he was so sick he could barely notice it.

The Trolls lead them deep into the passage way. It descended downward into a well-lit expanse of caves and tunnels. The Trolls pushed on for several miles, until they were brought into a large cavern that was filled with dozens of horribly deformed and mutilated corpses, many of which appeared too small to be full grown men. The Troll shaman who had captured them sat upon a gruesome looking throne that was built of human bones and skulls.

"As you can see you are very lucky to still draw breath," the Troll said calmly.

"You have been spared for a reason. If you give me what I seek, I shall spare your lives. If you resist...," he waved one of his hands at the mutilated corpses that surrounded the room.

"You will become another one of my amusements. As a token of my good will, I will give you something special."

The shaman set his staff down as he got out of his throne. He walked over to an altar, and picked up a small vial filled with a slight yellowish liquid. He walked up to Jadeance and began to pour that liquid out on Jadeance's cheek. The pain was excruciating, and Jadeance fell to his knees holding his cheek and groaning in pain. Slowly the pain subsided, and Jadeance looked up astonished. His wound was completely healed.

"Take one night to think over your possibilities," the Troll said. He waved his hand again and Jadeance and Cyres were escorted out of the throne room and much farther down into the expanse of caverns. Jadeance was hopelessly lost. The caverns and passageways zigzagged back and forth. Finally they found themselves in a holding area. It was a large cavern that was separated into several different cells by large iron bars that ran the length of the cavern. The guards chained Cyres and Jadeance to the wall and left. Without the guard's torches it was absolutely dark. Jadeance couldn't see anything at all.

"What do we do now?" Jadeance asked quietly.

"We wait," Cyres said. "We need to see how often the guards come by."

There was something in Cyres voice that told Jadeance that there wasn't much hope. "You can't get us both out of here can you?" Jadeance asked.

Cyres sat quietly for a time. "We'll get out," he replied finally. "Together. Now get some sleep and we'll talk more in the morning."

Jadeance had a hard time getting comfortable on the hard stone ground. The hours drifted by and he soon fell asleep. His sleep was troubled and Jadeance was awakened by the creaking of iron, and the torches of the guards. The shaman stood in front of their cell.

"Ready to talk?" he asked in a hoarse voice.

"You won't get anything you want out of us," Cyres replied firmly.

The shaman smiled. "I was hoping you would say that. It's more fun for me that way. You see, they all say that at first and yet I always get what I want. Take these pathetic fools," the shaman lit up the opposite side of the cavern. There, suspended on the wall were three Dwarfs. They had been beaten, and were completely unresponsive. "This fool has watched his own people die slow and painful deaths, in vain," the Troll said, pointing to the one in the middle. "He will soon tell me what I want to know."

The Dwarf opened his eyes and looked at the shaman with hate. "Never," he said. "Kill me if it be your way. But I will never tell you."

"You are powerless," the shaman laughed. Then he lifted his staff, and the Dwarf went rigid.

The shaman lowered his staff and the Dwarf was able to relax. "You can't hang there forever," the shaman barked.

"You are slowly dying of hunger."

Then he turned to face Jadeance. "You are not a warrior like him," the shaman said, pointing to Cyres.

"Are you ready to hang from a wall and watch as I slowly kill your friend? I will kill him slowly and then the only thing you will be offered will be his scarred flesh. If you do not eat him, you will starve to death. You don't want that, do you? Think, as you watch these stupid Dwarves die. I'll be back tomorrow. If you're ready to help me, your friend will live. If not, you will be responsible for his death. You see, your blood is special and I need it. You will help me invoke the powers of this realm to bend to my will and deliver to me the blade that will set my place atop this world."

"You will get nothing from him," Cyres replied with heat.

"From you, yes I can see that. But you will see that in the end I always get what I want."

Then the shaman turned to leave. "Leave them torches," he commanded.

"I want the boy to see what suffering looks like."

The shaman left and several of his guards took steel spikes and wedged them in between the wall and the suspended Dwarves, forcing their backs to bend outward.

The guards laughed as they left. The Dwarves cringed with pain. Despite the pain, they all stayed mute.

Cyres kicked at his chains. "If we're going to make a run for it, now is going to be the time."

Jadeance looked around for a moment, then he felt a sudden burst of energy, and he could feel the shaman leaving.

"He left," Jadeance said, shocked.

"What are you talking about?" Cyres asked puzzled.

"That stupid Troll with the staff, he left. I felt him leave. I didn't know you could travel with Magic," Jadeance replied almost in wonder.

"Can we talk about your Magical education later?"

Cyres demanded.

"I don't think you understand," Jadeance replied with a grin. He held his hand out and said, "Come back to me." He almost whispered. His staff appeared in his hand with a light pop.

Cyres looked at him with surprise.

"You see, with him gone, he can't hear me," Jadeance said as he loosened his shackles, and then Cyres'.

Cyres smiled. "Get the gate." Jadeance knew if he opened the gate the hinges would squeak, and the guards might hear, so instead he simply melted away the center of the gate, and stepped right through it. "Get ready to catch them," Jadeance said, and Cyres ran to the first Dwarf. However the Dwarf objected.

"Not me, free him first," and he jerked his head towards the Dwarf in the center of the three.

Jadeance looked to Cyres with a confused look on his face, then shrugged slightly and undid the bolts that held the Dwarf hostage, and he fell in Cyres's awaiting arms. The Dwarf let out a groan of relief as his feet touched the ground. He dropped to one knee, and held his back. Then he looked up.

"Free my men, for I have not the strength," the Dwarf nearly begged.

Jadeance freed the other two Dwarves. They were all in bad shape.

"I wonder if the potion that healed my cheek can help them?" Jadeance asked.

Cyres looked at the doorway. "Jade, I'll go get our weapons, and see what I can do about that potion. You have to stay here and protect them."

"You can't go out there alone," Jadeance protested. "You're unarmed! You won't stand a chance."

"Remember this now," Cyres said grabbing Jadeance by the shoulders. "Your mind is your greatest weapon, and as long as you keep your head you are never unarmed." Then Cyres looked over to the three Dwarves. "Do not abandon them even if you think I am dead." Then he grabbed a torch and disappeared into the passageway.

Jadeance looked at the three Dwarves. The one that the shaman had attacked was obviously important. The other two seemed to be protecting him. He seemed to be young and yet Jadeance could tell that he was considerably older than himself. He had long black hair, and a medium length black beard.

The other two were an odd mixture.

One of them was older. He bore a long, gray-black beard and his long hair was nearly all white.

The third was young, maybe even as young as Jadeance. He had blond hair and he also bore a medium length beard. The older Dwarf began to cough and he sounded terrible.

"Can I get you anything?" Jadeance asked them.

"Not unless you smuggled any food or water in with you," the youngest Dwarf replied.

"Water," Jadeance replied, smacking his forehead. "I think I can help with that." He closed his eyes and concentrated as hard as he could. At first he tried to make water skins. Struggling, he simply couldn't get his head around it. In the end, he was able to create five small steel canteens, complete with cork stoppers. He then pulled water elements from all over into the canteens. One by one they flashed a slight blue tint, and then returned to normal.

"Here," Jadeance replied, handing the three startled Dwarves a canteen. "Keep these. You will find the water to be as pure as it gets. Also, no matter how long you drink from them, they will never run dry."

All three Dwarves drank deeply, for nearly half an hour they drank, and rested.

"The great Divines have smiled upon us this day," said the Dwarf with black hair.

"My name is Orin, son of Dimlun, King over all Dwarves. This is my young friend, Borun, son of Gilbick," Orin said as he looked at the young Dwarf. "The newest addition to my now decimated guard."

Then he looked to the older Dwarf.

"And this is Grik, son of Irban. We now find ourselves in your debt, a debt I fear we won't live to repay."

Grik started to rise, until Borun stopped him. "You must rest. Tell me what must be done and I shall."

"There is no time for this," Grik interrupted. "We can't sit here and wait for them to come back. We must move."

"No!" Jadeance shouted, "I won't leave Cyres. He will come back."

"We can wait a little longer," Orin replied looking at Jadeance.

"My prince, we cannot take the risk involved in..." Grik started.

"It will be safe for a moment longer." Orin interrupted. Then he glanced around the room, "Besides, we will need the tall warrior and this brave Magi before the end."

Jadeance looked at Orin with gratitude. "Cyres will come back. He doesn't know how to fail."

"Won't do him any good if he is dead," Grik grumbled.

Orin shook his head disapprovingly and Grik looked away. Then Borun looked to the doorway. "Someone is coming," he warned.

"Fan out and take their weapon arm first," Grik

instructed.

Jadeance and the Dwarves spread to either side of the doorway. Jadeance strained his ears, trying desperately to hear anything at all. The bleak silence of the tunnels was unbroken, and Jadeance wondered how the Dwarf could have heard anything at all.

Without warning, Cyres burst back into the room. He was carrying a large weed sack and breathing hard.

"This was everything they had in their holding room," Cyres explained. "There were several other Dwarvin weapons, however I couldn't carry everything." Cyres apologized.

"This will do," Orin replied, pulling a chain mail shirt on.

Cyres looked at the three Dwarves. "I only found one of these. I hope it is enough to help you all." He handed a small vial to Borun.

"Let me see it," Jadeance said reaching for the vial.

Reluctantly, he handed it over.

Jadeance looked at it for a time trying to piece together what he wanted. "Drink it, but not all the way," Jadeance finally said as he handed the vial back.

"You take it first," Borun said as he handed the vial to Orin.

Orin took the vial and drank gratefully.

He began to cough and fell to one knee as he handed it back to Jadeance.

"Not the best swill to cross the lips, whatever it was, it works."

Jadeance whispered to his staff, "Refill it," and slowly the vial reacted and filled. Smiling, Jadeance passed it to Grik, who looked down at it.

"My prince," Grik began to refuse as he was cut short.

"Drink your share," Orin ordered. Grik sighed, then took a drink and passed the vial back to Jadeance, who once again filled it. Borun drank gratefully.

"How do you feel?" Jadeance asked.

"Good," Grik replied, grabbing an axe from the sack.

"I see you found your swords," Jadeance said, looking at Cyres.

"Yes," Cyres replied. "The only thing I didn't find was that amulet. He must have it with him." Then he looked at the Dwarves. "You're a prince, do they know?"

"Yes," Orin replied. "We will save the introductions for later. For now, we must get out of here."

"Can you lead us out?" Cyres asked.

Grik stepped forward. "There is no cave in this world nor the next, that a Dwarf can't navigate blindfolded."

"Good," Cyres replied. "Lead on."

CHAPTER 9

INTO THE DEEP

They wound their way further into the caves for hours. Jadeance was lost beyond hope, and the caves seemed to have a strange pressure. The deeper into the mountain they went, the harder Jadeance found it to breathe. "Not to doubt your logic," Jadeance said, holding his staff high for light, "but doesn't it seem as if we are going the wrong way?"

"What do you mean?" Grik growled.

"Well," Jadeance replied looking around. "Don't we want to get out of this place? It seems to me as if we are headed deeper."

Grik grunted. "We can't go out the way we came in. There is an entire Troll army there. And if we can't make it out that way, we must travel through the passageways to the other side of the mountain."

"Is there such a way?" Jadeance asked.

"Several," Grik grunted. "We must simply find

one that hasn't caved in yet."

"Caved in!" Jadeance shouted, his heart beginning to race.

"This mountain was carved out by goblins, and they don't reinforce anything. Their doorways have a tendency to give lose and cave."

"Won't the Trolls use that to their advantage?" Cyres asked, looking back the way they had come.

"Trolls won't venture much deeper," Grik replied.

Cyres looked at the old Dwarf. "Why won't they follow us?"

"There are far too many things to fear in the deep, and Trolls are poor cavers. They will soon abandon this chase," Grik said, looking into the dark.

"Will there still be Goblins wandering the deep caverns?" Cyres asked.

"We must be swift," Grik replied, looking Cyres in the eyes.

"Do not fear," Orin said. "There are no greater cavers than Dwarves. Let's keep moving."

As the hours dragged on Jadeance began to stumble, his feet numb with exhaustion. Everything looked the same, and the passageways were beginning to blur together. The only light available was the light that Jadeance could produce from the tip of his staff. The passageway they were following opened into a huge cavern.

"We can rest here for a while," Grik said, looking around.

Jadeance sank gratefully to the ground. Cyres sat down next to Jadeance. "How are you holding up?"

Jadeance set his staff into a crevice, holding it upright. Then he closed his eyes. "I don't think I have ever been so tired in my life," Jadeance admitted.

"Get some rest, you will need it," Cyres said with a smile.

Jadeance slept for hours. Despite lying on the hard, rock covered ground, he slept surprisingly well.

"It's time to move on," Cyres said, as he gently shook Jadeance.

Jadeance opened his eyes and looked around. The cavern was huge, and it went on endlessly in all directions. His staff gave off a clear blue light, warding off the impending darkness. Unfortunately his staff was only able to light up a small portion of the cavern, and the great wall of darkness that completely surrounded them played on Jadeance's imagination in a terrifying manner. The Dwarves were sitting together talking, as Jadeance and Cyres approached. "I don't suppose you managed to steal some food when you were getting our weapons back?" Orin asked hopefully.

Cyres smiled, "None at all."

"Great," Jadeance grumbled. He stood up slowly,

looking into the darkness. Despite his hunger, he felt more awake than he had in a long time. Orin looked up at him. "Is there much food to be found in these caves?" Jadeance asked.

"There can be," Orin replied. However, he didn't sound very convincing.

Then Jadeance had a sudden thought. Cyres was gone when they had made all their introductions. Jadeance threw a quick guilty look to Cyres, then to the Dwarves. "Umm Cyres, I, I mean we didn't have time to..., well what I mean to say is you missed our introductions earlier."

Cyres laughed. "You have been more than slightly out of it. Did you honestly think I have been following these three Dwarves without so much as finding out who they are?"

Jadeance blushed, "Well, I have been slightly out of it, haven't I?"

Orin stood up. "We need to keep moving, as our young friend has been hinting at, food will be scarce. If we stop, we die. Time to test yourselves, we have to keep pushing."

Cyres nodded, "We'll be right behind you."

"I'll try to give you as much light as I can," Jadeance offered.

"Don't," Grik grumbled. "There are many dangers in the deep. We must tread lightly. See that you keep your light to a minimum. It will betray us from far off."

Jadeance looked around. "I hadn't thought of that," he confessed.

Jadeance followed on blindly. As the hours passed, he could feel his heart beating in his throat. He had never truly known fear in his life until he had been captured by the Trolls. He had been in tight spots, sure enough. The Neering Janston had killed was dangerous. Being chased by the Trolls the day they had meet Vel was not one of his better days. But in all of his past experiences, there had been two constants. Tannis had always been there, a pillar in his life. And always before, he had been able to draw upon courage, as if it were a well deep within him. A well, that for some reason he could no longer find, no matter how hard he tried. The depths all around him seemed to press upon him. He could feel an unseen danger looming, a danger none of them could see. It sat in the darkness, watching and waiting.

Sensing Jadeance's fear, Orin beckoned. "Come here and walk with me, my young Magi. The deep holds nearly as many mysteries and wonders as it does dangers. We tread lightly to avoid the dangers, true enough. Perhaps it's time to consider the wonders. It has been said that if you look for death, surely you will find him. And yet if a man would spend his time looking for the greatness this world holds, surely he will find it. Search your thoughts for your friends, and use that as your axe. Use your thoughts to battle your fears. This is our way, as passed to me by my father and his before that. No doubt, the same will hold true for a young magi as it has the Dwarves of old."

Jadeance smiled and nodded, then followed Orin, with Cyres close behind. Despite being in the midst of his friends, the unknown that was the dark all around him brought a fear so strong he could nearly taste it. Tannis was not with him, and he wondered if would ever see Tannis again. Then his mind wandered to Brie. Fighting tears, he wished he was back at Wagstaff, serving beer and eavesdropping on old Cradalo. As the day went on, his hunger began feeding his fear. Time seemed to slip into the very darkness that haunted him so. Finally Grik grunted and halted.

"Let's stop for some rest. Age seems to be getting to me," Grik said as he sank to the stone floor.

"I don't think its age," Cyres replied, also sinking lightly to the ground. "We have been walking for hours."

Grik grunted. "When we get out of this we'll have drink to that, Master Cyres."

"I can't wait," Cyres said, as he closed his eyes.

"The old stories tell that Dwarves make excellent drinking companions."

"There are none better," Grik replied with a smile. "We Dwarves pride ourselves on our ability to drink to our friends misfortunes."

"Ha," Orin laughed. "We also drink to anything else we can find a reason for."

Jadeance looked at his companions, as they sat in the darkness that seemed to be slowly destroying him. The smiles slowly faded from their faces. And they fell silent, the dark seeming to stifle even their slightest joy. Jadeance was now begging to be consumed by his fear. It dominated his every thought. Then, from somewhere deep inside of him there was a voice. It was warm, like a summer's day. Jadeance focused all his thought on it, trying to hear the words spoken from afar. Then all of a sudden, it came to him like the loosing of a great dam. Brie's voice was undeniable. Though he knew she was far away, she sounded as if she were there next to him.

"Jade, why are you so sad?" Brie's voice sounded in his head.

"Brie, is that you?" Jadeance asked, his voice echoing in the halls of his mind.

"You know it's me," She replied softly. "Are you hurt?"

"No, not anymore," Jadeance replied. "Cyres

saved me. You wouldn't believe how brave he is."

"Kainan says he's the best," Brie replied.

"He is," Jadeance replied sadly.

"No, I think he will come in second best," Brie replied happily.

"What do you mean?" Jadeance asked.

"You do not yet know your abilities," Brie replied warmly.

"I am not his equal," Jadeance replied slowly. "I am a coward."

"I have known you most of my life, and you are anything but a coward. Now you listen to me, Jadeance. You will find whatever it is that you have lost. Pull yourself together, and do it now. You must come back to me."

"Wait a minute," Jadeance shot back a little hurt, "I..."

"No time," Brie interrupted. "Promise me, Jadeance, promise you will do whatever it takes to find me. Promise."

"I promise," Jadeance fumbled.

"Promise me, Jadeance." Brie insisted again.

"I promise, I promise." Jadeance replied shyly.

"Don't forget that you promised me, Jadeance. You do what you have to do. Find a way back to me. Oh and Jade, I love you."

"Jade!" Cyres shouted.

Jadeance shook his head, "Yes?"

"We will be leaving soon, and you seemed to be sleeping," Cyres replied grabbing his gear.

"Ok," Jadeance grunted. "Couldn't you have waited another minute?" Jadeance asked himself. "Brie, are you still there? Brie?" Jadeance sat silently, straining, however Brie was gone. Focusing all his thought and straining as he was, he did notice something. It took him several moments to recognize what he was feeling.

"Jade, are you coming?" Cyres asked confused.

"Wait," Jadeance replied, still trying to pinpoint what was now calling out to him.

"What is it lad?" Grik asked.

"Water," Jadeance replied. "Lots of it."

"Water?" Cyres replied. "Jade we don't need water remember?" He shook the canteen that he had made them all. "Now, if you feel a large deer or something, then we can talk."

"How much water are we talking about here?" Grik asked.

"A lot," Jadeance replied. "It seems to be a well or something, a lot of standing water."

Borun smiled, "that might be our path."

"I don't like it," Orin replied.

"Water will mean food," Borun replied.

"Yes it will," Grik replied. "We won't be the only

ones to know that."

"I don't like it," Orin repeated.

"There's nothing for it, we need food. It could be days to the end of this nightmare. How long can you walk with no food before your mind shuts off completely?" Grik asked.

Orin looked to Jadeance, "Where is this water?"

"That way," Jadeance pointed. "I don't think I can get you there."

"We are the cavers," Borun replied. "We'll find it. You just keep it firmly in your mind." Then he slapped his hands together. "I see dinner tonight."

They moved on for hours.

The strong sense of water grew with every passing mile. The cavern finally opened up and grew into immensity. "Here it is," Jadeance exclaimed, as he rushed forward. With a smile, Jadeance threw the light that was resting atop his staff into the darkness. It flew obediently over a large mass of water. It stretched for miles, easily the biggest lake Jadeance had ever seen. The water just kept going and going.

"I never would have imagined that I might find a huge underground lake," Cyres replied in wonder. "What feeds it?"

"Surface rivers meet underground wells," Grik replied. "They are not uncommon. I have never seen one so large myself."

"Are there fish in there?" Cyres asked.

"Most certainly," Grik replied. "However, they will not be like the fish you are used to."

"What do you mean?" Jadeance asked.

"There is no sun here, nothing to give them nutrients. The only food they get is the spring that flows from the surface. The fish here will have adapted to that. Usually they are smaller, and will taste different," Grik replied.

"I don't care if they can talk, they will be just fine for me," Cyres said.

"Yes, well, getting one will be difficult," Orin replied.

"I don't think so," Jadeance replied with a grin. He held his hand out as if he were reaching for something. A pillar of water began to form. It matched Jadeance's outstretched hand perfectly. He opened and closed his fingers slowly, and the giant water hand matched him. Closing his eyes, he sent the huge hand deep into the water, cupping as it went. When it reemerged, he threw dozens of flipping fish onto the bank.

"We are truly blessed to have such a worthy companion!" Borun yelled, snatching up a fish and banging it on a rock.

"Yes," Orin yelled out. "Gather them up!"

Jadeance made several balls of pure light and

began setting them about the beach, so that they could find the fish more easily. Then he ran up the beach, gathering up fish. As he reached down and picked one up, he looked it over slowly. It was strange. Its flesh had almost no color at all. Just pasty white, it looked similar to the catfish he used to catch out of the canal back home. What struck Jadeance the most was that they didn't seem to have eyes. Jadeance made his way back to where the others had gathered.

"Funny looking things," Cyres said as he turned one over. "Hope they taste better than they look."

"I wouldn't get your hopes up," Borun replied, looking down at the pile.

"Well, maybe under different circumstances," Orin replied. "I bet Goff could make them up."

"Oh, I miss old Goff," Borun replied sourly, looking down at the fish.

"Right now, I miss firewood," Grik replied looking around.

Jadeance began to laugh. "I'll make you a deal. I'll find fire, you clean the fish."

Grik looked at Jadeance thoughtfully. "My lad, you find us some fire and I'll honor you in the house of my fathers."

Orin and Borun looked shocked. Jadeance smiled, and looked around. The lights he had strewn along the beach began to flicker and move, each one finding a sizeable stone and bringing it obediently back to Jadeance. He gathered up the stones and arranged them into a fire pit. Then he started spinning the balls together. They spun faster and faster, merging and glowing, until they appeared a slightly deeper color. Jadeance lowered them into the pit. As they landed, there was a shimmer and suddenly there were no longer several balls of light, but a great warm fire.

"By the Divines!" Borun exclaimed. "How did you do that?"

"It's complicated," Jadeance replied, sweating. "It is also very tiring."

"Well, rest now my friend. You have earned your supper," Borun replied.

Jadeance sat back and watched as the others cleaned out the odd looking fish. "Why don't they have eyes"? Jadeance asked.

"For the same reason they have no real skin color," Grik replied. "There is no sun here, nothing but darkness. They undoubtedly have other senses to replace their eyes."

"I don't think we should think about it so much," Borun said, eyeing the odd looking fish. "Let's just call them fish and leave it at that."

Cyres pulled one off the flames and set it on a rock

he had placed on his lap. "Blind or not, I'm hungry."

Jadeance shuddered as he watched Cyres take his first few bites. However after noticing that he didn't fall over dead, his hunger got the best of him and he too pulled one from the flames. Using his knife, he removed a small bite and slowly lifted it to his mouth. It didn't smell funny.

He blew on it, delaying the inevitable.

Jadeance closed his eyes and bit down. It had a strange texture, but all in all it wasn't too bad. In fact, he felt foolish for his cowardice.

They all ate for the better part of an hour. It felt good to rest and to get a hot meal. Jadeance sat, comfortable for the first time in days. Suddenly there was something tugging at him, deep inside of his mind - pulling, urging him to take notice. Jadeance shook this feeling off. It came again, this time stronger. Something seemed wrong, as if a strange presence was looming over him. Jadeance turned slowly, completely unprepared for the monstrosity standing over him.

The creature was easily eight feet tall. Its thick skin formed knots to armor the creature. Its features were strangely human, two huge eyes staring right at Jadeance. Its mouth had large jagged teeth. It bore little to no hair. Jadeance stumbled back, trying to retreat from the beast. Bending down, it simply grabbed and hefted him high into the air. Jadeance dropped his staff. He tried desperately to reach his sword.

"Damn that fire!" Orin yelled. "It gave us away."

Cyres stuck both his swords into the monster's back. It screamed an animal-like sound. Spinning more quickly than Jadeance could have ever imagined the creature smashed its fist in Cyres, sending him flying through the air. Jadeance could hardly breathe; the creature was squeezing him so tightly. He felt himself slipping into unconsciousness as Borun and Orin lunged themselves at the creature's legs, chopping deep into its flesh with their Dwarvin battle axes. The creature groaned in pain and tossed Jadeance in its furious attempt to get at the Dwarves who were circling him. Jadeance looked up, coughing.

One by one, the creature was knocking the Dwarves around.

It grabbed Grik as he tried to jump onto the creatures back.

Holding him tightly in one hand, it grabbed a large stone with the other and swung it at the helpless Dwarf.

Howling in pain, it dropped the stone as one of Cyres blades lobbed of half of its hand. Cyres spun and stuck his other sword into the creature's belly. It howled again, and with another show of agility, it kicked Cyres square in the chest sending him sailing into the lake. Looking down at its mangled hand it howled again and threw Grik out of sight. Orin jumped and stuck his axe deep into the creature's side. Spinning, the creature smashed Orin into the side of the Cavern.

Borun rushed the beast to pull its attention from Orin. Screeching in anger, the creature jumped slightly and pinned Borun to the ground with its foot.

Then it pulled Orin's axe out of its side with its good hand and hefted it high above Borun. The Dwarf struggled desperately to free himself. Jadeance had gotten to his feet and grabbed his staff. Surging with anger, Jadeance formed a claw with his hand again. A huge watery hand hefted the creature high into the air.

Borun scrambled to his feet and stood in awe as the creature helplessly attacked the hand that held him captive.

Orin's axe merely slid harmlessly right through the watery hand with each clumsy swing. Jadeance shook the creature slightly until it dropped the axe.

"Don't let him down," Grik barked as he slowly made his way to Jadeance.

"No," Jadeance replied. "I was just wondering if it can breathe under water." He then sent the creature spinning deep into the center of the lake. After several minutes, the bubbles stopped rising to the surface. Cyres slowly dragged himself to the shore.

"Nice touch with the giant hand there," Cyres wheezed. "Good thing you didn't think of it a bit earlier."

Jadeance ran up to Cyres and helped him up the shore. "You mean before he kicked you into the lake?" Jadeance asked with a slight smile.

"Yes, before that," Cyres replied shaking his head.

"Get some rest," Jadeance replied. "I'll be right back."

Borun was helping Grik over next to Cyres as Jadeance ran to Orin.

"Are you hurt?" Jadeance asked.

Orin grunted. "I live, how do the others fair?"

"Everyone is fairly banged up. I think we will want to take a few days to rest."

"Help me," Orin said as he extended his arm. Jadeance grabbed it and hefted the Dwarf to his feet.

"We'll sleep here tonight," Orin said as they reached the others.

"Not likely to find many other living things in here with that Troll."

"That was a Troll?" Jadeance asked, shocked.

"A Cave Troll, not related to the Iurkan Trolls that captured us earlier," Grik replied wincing.

"Are there many of them here?" Jadeance asked,

looking around.

"Dozens," Grik replied.

"Don't worry," Orin said lying back. "They don't stay together, they prefer solitude."

CHAPTER 10

DISCOVERY

adeance grunted as he got to his feet. Though he felt tired and stiff he wasn't really hurt, unlike the others who all had an injury of some kind. He made his way around the shoreline, collecting the weapons that had been flung in the fight with the Troll. After gathering them up, he decided to look around. As he walked he realized that he no longer feared the deep. Though he couldn't see past the light of his staff, it didn't seem to matter. Something deep inside of Jadeance told him that there was something else to be seen here. He walked along the water's edge for a time, his eyes searching the ground for anything that might seem out of the ordinary. His eyes stopped suddenly as they fell upon a set of huge green eyes. They were reptilian, and they seemed strange, as if they were searching him for something. Jadeance stopped dead in his tracks. He could clearly make out the huge lizard's body as it slowly stepped out of the water. It was much longer than a pair of horses standing end to end. Its mouth bore row upon row of razor sharp teeth. Jadeance knew he should fear this lizard, however he remained calm. A strange voice sounded in his head.

"What are you looking for?" The giant Crocodile asked.

"I don't know," Jadeance replied carefully.

"But you are searching for something, yes?" the giant Crocodile pressed.

"I hadn't really thought about it," Jadeance replied.

"Why walk along this sandy grave if not to find something?" The giant Crocodile asked, its eyes searching.

"Grave? What grave?" Jadeance asked.

The creature turned its head. "Everywhere you look, this place is nothing but a tomb."

"Who has died?" Jadeance asked.

"Many have died here, some looking for gold, some looking for prestige and honor, others seeking knowledge and power. All were willing to risk death in exchange for their dreams. The question becomes, what are your dreams? What are you willing to trade?"

"I'm not willing to die for anything." Jadeance

said defiantly.

The giant lizard's eyes fell on Jadeance again. "This is not so. Can you think of nothing you could trade? Even if it were to save her?"

"Is Brie in danger?" Jadeance asked.

"Are not all in danger?" The giant Crocodile replied calmly.

"What are you?" Jadeance asked with some heat.

"Matters not what I am, only what you think I am." The giant Crocodile replied.

"What do you want?" Jadeance pressed.

"I am here to do as I have always done." With that the giant turned back towards the water. "Will you follow?" it asked.

Jadeance stood still, his heart pounding. His mind was torn. On one hand he should fear this giant, especially in the water. Jadeance could tell he was made for the water. On the other hand, as strange as it was, he didn't feel that the Crocodile had come here to kill him. And how did it know so much about him?

"What will I find?" Jadeance asked.

The lizard didn't answer, it only slid slowly into the water's edge and turned to face him.

"Well, I am also at home with water", Jadeance said to himself. "He has physical strength. I have a power all my own." Jadeance drew his sword and stuck it deep into the beach. Then he looked at his staff. "Remember that, it will keep us from getting lost." Jadeance took a deep breath and followed the giant into the lake. As his head dipped below the surface, the elements became visible yet again. As he swam, the water began to illuminate with light blue sparkles that moved and flowed. He could see them concentrate by his mouth. On impulse he took a breath, expecting water to flood his lungs. In amazement, he found he could breathe normally. Looking to the giant, it appeared different than any other life form he had ever seen before. Instead of glowing a single color, he showed a full spectrum, as if all the elements resided within him. Deeper and deeper they swam. Jadeance held his staff in front of him by both hands and used its power to propel him. The giant swam with a grace that was mesmerizing. It swayed from one side to the other, almost as if it were dancing. Its movements were graceful and elegant, a stark contrast to its fierce and demanding appearance. After a time, Jadeance could make something out. It seemed like a large structure, an old sunken ship perhaps? As he approached it he discovered something far more frightening. It was a graveyard. Rows upon rows of bones littered the ground.

"What is this place?" Jadeance asked in his mind.

"The final resting place of the last Great One."
The giant replied. "But that is not the question."

"What do you mean?" Jadeance asked.

"What will you find? What final secret does the great one have to give? Look, young one and know that you have my blessing and have passed the test placed before you. May you continue to follow that heart that has hither to lead you to greatness. You will yet have many tests placed before you and there will be great sorrow and heart ache before the end. Heed it not, for all fate rests with you. Should you fail, all fail with you. Then the giant started to fade, yet the lights inside him began to brighten. Jadeance watched as it changed into the form of a man. He looked old, and powerful.

"Thank you,' Jadeance muttered. "May I ask your name, great one?"

"I am the father of all. Go now, for time is short."

Jadeance was left with the great voice ringing in his mind as the figure disappeared. He turned to look at the graveyard of bones. What great one? There seems to be hundreds of bones here. He swam around it for a time wondering what he was supposed to find, then he noticed something so frightening he stopped dead in his thoughts. He had made his way to the front of the mass, and there on the ground was the largest skull he had ever seen. It looked for lack of better words like a giant lizard skull. Jadeance struggled to comprehend its massive size. It was easily the size of a full wagon plus a large team of horses. He swam easily into one of the vacant eye sockets, and with a slight turn, out the other side. Then the gravity of the great one struck him. It was one skeleton, not many. Jadeance stopped and marveled at the sheer size of it. It stretched for hundreds of feet, resting there hidden from the world. Jadeance couldn't imagine anything to massive. There was no mistake; Jadeance had found the remains of a great dragon. Swimming down the throat of the beast, Jadeance was lost in thought wondering what it must have been like to merely be in the presence of such a massive beast. There ahead of him in the dust was something shiny. He made his way to it, and there was a skeleton lying there, gazing upward. It was clearly a man's skeleton. He was wearing an elaborate chest piece, and near his left hand was an elaborately decorated sword. He looked up at the huge skeleton and realized he was where the stomach would have been. Whoever this man was, he had clearly attempted to fight the dragon and failed. Jadeance couldn't even imagine facing something so terrifying. Clearly the warrior hadn't won. Jadeance carefully retrieved the sword and chest piece. There was deep set writing on them. Jadeance couldn't make any of it out. As far as he could tell, there were at least three different languages written upon them. He could barely lift them both and swim at the same time. He finally placed them on his staff, and used it to propel them once again. Jadeance looked back wondering what had caused the giant to die, or even to become lost so deep beneath the earth. Jadeance shook his head and started back towards the surface.

"Can you still find my sword?" Jadeance whispered to his staff. His staff tugged him slightly off to the right. Jadeance smiled and continued towards the surface. As he emerged from the water he could see he was in a bit of trouble. Cyres and the Dwarves were waiting for him. Cyres had his swords drawn and was standing directly in front of his sword that was still stuck half deep into the sand.

"Where the hell have you been?" Cyres raged as Jadeance slowly began to surface.

Jadeance was taken aback. Cyres had never been anything but calm, and even under the worst of situations he usually made jokes. "I...," Jadeance stuttered. "Well I just went to...."

"Went to what!" Cyres shouted. "Throw away everything we have all been working for? Do you have any idea how many lives have been lost just to keep you safe? Then you plan on repaying them by leaving the ones who have been set to protect you and going into the deep by yourself?"

"Cyres, I had to." Jadeance protested.

"Had to what!" Cyres interrupted again. "Go for a swim?"

"No," Jadeance shouted. "Something was calling me, I didn't realize it at the time, but there was something I needed to do, and I had to do it alone. He said it was a test."

"Who said what? What was a test?" Cyres shouted looking around.

"Slow down," Jadeance said sinking to the ground. "I can only tell you what I have seen. I just felt like walking and looking around. Everyone here was hurt and I went to scout around. When I got here, I met him."

"Met who?" Cyres asked again.

"I don't know his name. I came upon a giant crocodile and..."

"How big, lad?" Grik interrupted.

"I don't know, maybe thirty feet long or so." Jadeance replied.

"Giant crock," Grik exclaimed. "They are rare this deep, but they can survive on just about anything. Dangerous beasts, totally at home in the water. One thing is for sure, you will only see one if it wants you to and that will most likely be the last thing you ever see. Master of the ambush, incredibly quick and powerful, they feed on Trolls mostly. What was it doing?"

"It just walked out of the lake." Jadeance replied.

"It did what?" Grik asked shocked. "It would have looked at you as a good meal, lad."

"He wasn't here to eat me." Jadeance interrupted. "Well I didn't know that right at first, but then it started talking too."

"It was talking to you?" Cyres interrupted.

Jadeance was starting to lose his temper. "Do you want to hear the story? Or perhaps you want to tell it for me?"

Cyres didn't look pleased, however he cleared his throat. "Ok, no more interruptions. Go on."

"It asked me what I was looking for. I didn't understand that. I really wasn't looking for anything. I just, well, I don't know. I felt like something was calling out to me. So I guess I was looking for something and just didn't know it."

"Lad you're rambling." Grik grunted. "Get on with it."

"Well I told him that I wasn't looking for anything. He asked me why I was wandering a graveyard if I wasn't looking for anything. I didn't understand that, either. Then he asked me if I would follow him, and he went back into the lake.

I knew that he was trying to show me something, so I followed him. The lake is very deep, we came upon what I thought was a massive bone yard. Huge bones, taller than most of the caverns we had been traveling through. We moved through them for a long time until he turned on me. He spoke to my mind as he transformed from the crock into a human. He must have been one of the Divines. He was huge, and perfect. I asked him for his name, and he told me he was the father of all."

Cyres dropped to one knee. "Did he have golden robes of light, perfect grey hair and a look of power upon his face?"

Jadeance looked at Cyres. "Yes, but he was more see through than anything, almost as if he wasn't really there at all. Who was he?"

"His name is Thamis." Cyres replied softly. "I have seen him once before. What did he tell you?"

"He told me that I had his blessing, and that I had passed the test that he had placed before me. I was supposed to search the great one."

"What great one?" Cyres asked.

"Well I didn't know it, but as I swam a bit further I discovered that I had been swimming through one giant skeleton, not many. The skull was big enough that it wouldn't have fit in the barn back at Wagstaff."

"A skeleton of what, exactly?" Orin asked.

"I don't know for certain, but I think it was a dragon." Jadeance replied. "It looked like the crock, long neck and tail and a massive set of wings.

The Dwarves looked at each other in silence. Finally Grik spoke.

"Did this great one have a large horn atop its head?" Grik asked.

"Well," Jadeance thought about it. "I was looking at the teeth." Jadeance confessed. "Let me think, I swam though the eyes and..."

"Hold it," Cyres interrupted. "You swam though the eyes? Don't you mean you put your arm though the eye?"

"Oh no," Jadeance replied firmly. "I swam right though. No problem."

"Yes, he was massive," Grik replied quietly.

"What are you talking about?" Cyres asked. "Do you know what he is talking about?"

"It is a Dwarvin legend," Grik replied. "There was a great flying beast. Drakk A Thudul. Translated into common it means dragon of doom. He was the great destroyer; whole villages were lost to his furry. Death was his mission and he hunted us Dwarves to near total destruction. The Dwarves were not the only race to fall in great numbers to the dragon. This was, of course, after the loss of the great dragon masters.

The elves had amongst them a mighty champion. It was said that he had a great vision. In his vision he was told how the great beast could be destroyed. He came to our elders, who presented him to the king, High King Uirbus. Desperate to save our people, he took the champion and two Elvin Magi deep within our halls of Zavan, past the great mining halls to the halls of Grungnaz. There our finest weapon smiths and armorers crafted for him a great suit of armor. Also he was crafted a sword and shield. It was said that Grungni himself blessed the champion and all of his new armor. We have no history of where he went, or what he did after that. As legend tells, the champion was never seen again, and that he failed to kill the beast. Failed or not, the dragon also disappeared. It is said in the halls of Zavan that the champion failed and was killed. In sorrow, the great Divine Grungni found the beast and sealed it deep within the earth, in a hole so deep that only Grungni could have made. He was sealed there to die, punishment for the death that was set upon his people and retribution for the bravery of the champion who died so worthy a death."

"The dragon is certainly dead." Jadeance replied. "Also I was sent to search the great one. At first I thought the great one was the dragon. However, now I believe it was the man who I found in what would have been the belly of the beast."

"You have seen him?" Orin shouted excitedly. "You actually saw him?"

"Well, what was left of him." Jadeance replied softly. "I found these," Jadeance hefted the beautifully decorated breastplate and sword. The Dwarves all fell to their knees. Orin stood and with shaking hands, took the sword and hefted it.

"We have been blessed beyond all Dwarves. All will come to know this to be hallowed ground. The great cave created by our lord Grungni to cage the great Drakk A Thudul, the mighty destroyer. You have truly proven to be a worthy friend, Jadeance of Tigman. You have earned the loyalty of Orin, Warrior Prince of Dimlun, High King and Overlord, ruler of the great hall of Zavan." Orin then bowed deeply to Jadeance. Jadeance looked to Cyres for guidance. Cyres bowed slightly and waved his arm. Jadeance looked back to Orin and returned a gracious bow. Orin was looking at the sword with wonder. Jadeance made his way to Grik and extended the Breastplate.

Grik shook his head and took a quick step backwards. "That is holy, meant only for the hands of royalty. I must not defile it with my unworthy hands."

"Well, I'm not royalty," Jadeance replied a little concerned. "Have I defiled it?"

"You are wrong," Orin said standing. "You have been blessed by the Divines, guided by the very hand of Thamis. Your name will be sounded in the halls of Zavan for years to come."

"An honor set upon no man in my lifetime," Grik replied, with a look of wonder.

"Well, not to upset the mood, but this is just a little heavy for me," Jadeance said, hefting the mighty Breastplate.

"Yes," Orin replied. "I think I know just what to do with that." Smiling, Orin looked at Cyres's Breastplate, which had been badly damaged by the Troll. "Master Cyres, will you bow your knee before a Dwarf?"

"I will gladly bend a knee before you," Cyres said as he fell to one knee. "But I don't think that I am the right one to carry..."

"Hush now, my new friend," Orin interrupted. "You have not only saved our lives, and retrieved our weapons. You have proved to be a man of honor and respect. If not for you, Grik would have been cleaved in two by that foolish Troll. That action exposed yourself to the attack that so damaged your armor. Also, the best way to hide something is to make it inconspicuous. If we were to carry it, it would stick out. If it lies upon you, it will be better protected. By my command, remove your Breastplate."

Cyres looked shy, and moved slowly removing his breastplate. Borun grabbed Cyres's Breastplate and gently rested it upon the sand in the same spot Jadeance had come out of the water. Orin then turned his head to Jadeance and nodded. "Take this mighty piece and may it protect you from all harm," Orin continued. Jadeance handed the Breastplate to Cyres and helped him latch it on. "When we arrive at the city of my father's, even Zavan itself, I will see to it that a new Breastplate be crafted in your name, and set to fit you. Until then, I charge you to protect this most holy relic and carry it to the great hall of my father. Will you accept my charge?"

"I will," Cyres replied looking down at his chest.

Orin nodded, and then he belted the great sword across his back and placed his axe next to Cyres's old Breastplate. Then he turned and said, "You must excuse us for a time", then he began to talk to the other two Dwarves in their native tongue. They all fell to their knees and began to sing. It was a slow song. Their voices were deep and the song seemed to catch Jadeance somewhere deep within the bounds of his mind. It was almost as if their voices carried to the walls and back again endlessly.

"It's magnificent isn't it?" Cyres near whispered.

"Can you understand what they are saying?" Jadeance asked.

"No. Let's move back a bit so we won't interrupt them," Cyres replied.

Jadeance nodded and followed Cyres back away from the kneeling Dwarves. Jadeance felt as if his body were soaring.

"There is a great Magic in Dwarvin song," Cyres explained. "They are praying."

"I didn't think, well it just... everyone talks about the elves and their Magic. You don't hear about Dwarvin Magic much," Jadeance said as he looked back to Cyres.

"The Dwarves keep many secrets, far more than any other race. They are close knit, and rarely like outsiders. Do not be surprised if some people hate us when we reach Zavan," Cyres replied firmly.

"Cyres, Thamis said something else I don't understand. He said that I have many more tests ahead of me, and there will be heart ache. If I fail, all fail with me. What was he talking about?"

Cyres looked up, and then sighed, "I'm not the right one to tell you. If I know Kainan, he will find us when we get out of here. Ask him, he may have a better answer."

"You know something!" Jadeance complained bitterly. "You said that."

"I know what I said," Cyres interrupted. "I was angry. Forget I said anything."

"I can't just forget," Jadeance complained.

"I know," Cyres apologized. "Just stay close and let's get out safely."

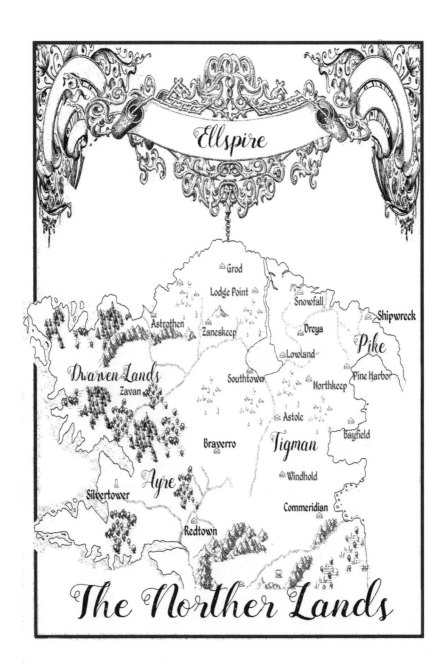

CHAPTER 11

BATTLE ON THE CLIFF

Tannis was running behind Brie. They had been running for days and were exhausted. So far they had been unable to lose the Trolls that trailed them so diligently. During the chaos everyone had been split up, and all Tannis could do was run, and do everything he could think of to keep Brie safe. The morning was cold and they had not been running long when by sheer luck they ran right into Vel.

"Vel!" Brie shouted and jumped into the silent warrior's arms. "I am so glad to see you!"

"It is good to see you both as well," Vel replied looking around.

"Where is everyone else?" Tannis asked.

"I do not know. I have been feeling the urge to run west all day now," Vel replied solemnly. "I believe I am being guided to our friends, a hope that has been intensified by finding the two of you. Hopefully, we will find the rest of our friends soon."

"What happened back there? It all happened so fast I didn't have time enough to think. Before I knew it, we had been separated, and have been chased ever since."

"I do not know how they came upon us so quickly, but I do know that we are in danger standing around here." Suddenly Vel's head shot around violently. "They will soon be upon us, run!"

They ran on and on, a tremendous fear hovered in the air all around them as they could now hear the sounds of Troll feet behind them. Tannis heard lighting behind them and a few hollowed shouts. "What was that?" Tannis shouted to Vel.

"I do not know," Vel yelled back. "Keep going."

Something had been troubling Tannis for some time now. Jade was never so far from Brie. Where had he gone? Deep inside he could tell his brother was still alive, but the Troll attack had been too much for even Kainan to foresee and he feared the worst. Just then, Tannis heard another lightning bolt somewhere off behind him. Confusion filled his mind. He could hear them coming from behind, but for some reason they were unable to overtake them. It was dark now and the trees seemed to grabbing and slicing them as they ran hopelessly through the wood.

"They are gaining on us!" Tannis yelled to Vel.

"Keep going!" Vel shouted back.

As they ran, the trees started closing in, almost as if they were moving closer together. Tannis could feel himself starting to panic. Brie tripped and fell. Tannis bent and hefted her onto his shoulder. "We can't fight Trolls and forest!"

"We do not have to fight the trees," Vel shouted. "The trees will shelter us but we must keep moving!"

"What is going on?" Tannis yelled as he looked back. Right behind them the trees were closing completely. He could hear the Trolls shrieking and hacking away at them.

"Wurwick is giving us a chance," Vel shouted.

Tannis continued running, and as he ran he noticed the trees had begun to thin. Soon he could see sun light shining through the tree tops. Running was easier now that he could see. They had also met up with Samous and Atrius. The trees were now becoming sparse.

"What is this?" Tannis asked. "Are we leaving the wood?"

"I don't know," Samous shouted back. "I have never been this way before. I don't like it though; this feels as if we're being herded."

"Herded to where?" Brie asked.

"Where do you lead stampeding cattle?" Samous asked.

"I'm closer to a barmaid than rancher," Brie shrieked back.

"You lead them to a place you can control them," Atrius replied looking back.

"What are you talking about?" Tannis asked. However he skidded to a stop dumfounded at what he was looking at. They had come across a cliff face. With a quick glance up the mountain he could clearly see a dried up river bed. This had at one time been a colossal waterfall. It had cut deep into the gouges into the Valley below. The Valley below them was completely filled with Trolls, the sound of their war drums, and the whole Valley boomed and shrieked and moved. The sound was defining. Tannis could feel the earth shake as they pounded the ground with their feet.

"What now?" Brie cried.

"Up here!" Kainan shouted.

Tannis looked up and saw Kainan, Barvik and the others were scrambling up the cliff face.

"Go," Vel barked, and he ran and started up the face.

"We won't be able to outrun them like this," Samous grunted as they reached the others.

"There is an outcrop just ahead," Kainan said. "Look up another fifty feet or so. We will hold them from there."

"Right," Barvik said.

Tannis didn't feel as comfortable with the plan as Barvik did. Then it hit him, Jade wasn't there.

"Where is Jade?" Tannis shouted.

Wurwick's face looked sad. "We must keep moving! We can't help him now."

"I'm not going anywhere without Jade," Tannis shouted with heat.

"The Trolls have broken though my tree line," Wurwick shouted. "We have no time, now move!"

It didn't take long to reach the outcrop. Kainan helped Tannis up; his face also bore a deep sadness. "We can't help them now. We must stay alive to find them."

"Them? Who else is missing?" He looked around quickly. Then it hit him and he turned back to Kainan.

"Cyres will keep young Jadeance safe, do not worry," Kainan said confidently.

"That was ill timed," Samous said, looking down. "I think it's a great time to worry."

"We don't have to worry about the ones in the Valley," Wurwick said pointing down. "The cliff is too great. It's not graduated like this one. I have also set a barrier of sorts along the ridge top. It will take them several hours to break it."

"Great," Samous grated. "Now all we have to do is

fight off the several hundred who are tailing us."

"We have bigger problems," Atrius replied breathing hard. "They now have the amulet."

"No, I put a tracer on it," Wurwick replied.

"Can we discuss this later?" Samous asked, pointing down the cliff.

Tannis looked down, and the Trolls had reached the cliff basin.

"Right," Wurwick replied. He extended his staff and several loose rocks began to fly upward and come together forming a platform. It flew higher and higher as Wurwick raised his staff until it collided with the cliff face twenty feet above them or so.

"Tannis you take Atrius, Brie, and Samous up there," Kainan shouted. "We'll hold them from here."

"You expect me to just sit back and watch?" Tannis shouted.

"No, I expect you to give them hell with rocks and arrows, anything you can. Your heart is in the right place but you don't have the experience to stay here." Kainan's voice left no room for argument.

"Come on boy!" Wurwick shouted as he began to climb to the upper ledge.

Tannis helped Brie up, and then he looked down. The Trolls had already started climbing. Barvik, Vel, and Kainan drew their weapons and spread themselves along the ledge. Brie, Samous, and Atrius drew their bows and started loosing arrows. Tannis had given his bow to Samous and felt useless. "I should be down there with them," he told himself. He watched several Trolls fall as the arrow storm hit. Wurwick also began blowing large numbers of Trolls off the cliff as they climbed. Despite their efforts, the Trolls started reaching the ledge. Tannis started lobbing rocks down, grunting with satisfaction as he watched a Troll fall, knocking several others down with it. It didn't take long to see that Kainan, Vel and Barvik were getting outnumbered in a hurry.

"This isn't working!" Atrius shouted to Wurwick. "Can't you help them?"

"There are too many for me," Wurwick grunted as he cast a shield preventing the Trolls from entering the ledge from one side.

Tannis watched in frustration as one of the Trolls sneaked behind Vel as he was defending against three others and threw his spear at his exposed back with deadly accuracy.

"No!" Tannis shouted. "I've got to get down there," he thought. Then Tannis was frozen in shock as the spear stopped in midair, turned and flew with surprising speed back into the surprised Troll. Tannis looked to Wurwick. The completely shocked look on his face told Tannis that he was not the one who had saved Vel's life.

"Done be a worryin' now, young master, we be here ta save da day!"

Tannis looked above up to see old Meshire and Janston sliding down the rock face to join them.

"Meshire!" Brie exclaimed.

"Ha," Wurwick yelled. "How good of you to come."

"Wouldn't miss it fer da world," Meshire said as he landed next to Wurwick.

Janston continued right past them and slid down to fight next to Vel.

"We be a needin ta help da boy!" Meshire shouted.

"I thought we needed him to help us!" Samous shouted as he loosed another arrow.

"What has happened?" Wurwick asked.

"Da Troll's done grabbed em," Meshire replied. "Der be a powerful dark Magi, I dare not confront em alone. It be he who brought da darkness upon dis wood."

"Figured that," Wurwick grunted as he sent a blast of green light from his staff.

"Is Cyres still with him?" Atrius asked.

"Till death," Meshire replied.

"What can we do to help him?" Samous asked. "We have our hands full here. That fool Cyres will have to get them out himself."

"Wit dat dark Magi holden em, der be no hope fer em ta escape," Meshire replied firmly.

"You want to bring a dark Magi against us?" Samous asked in shock. "I thought you said he was too strong for you?"

"Dat be true," Meshire agreed. "But good master Wurwick be his equal."

"So how are you planning to draw this Magi out?" Atrius asked. "Will he just come if you call?"

"No," Wurwick said with a smile. "This is all about that amulet. I put a tracer on it just in case the worst should happen." Wurwick smiled, and then he drew a large symbol on the ground with his staff. Wurwick extended his hand and it began to glow slightly. Snapping his fingers, a bright flash of light burst from the symbol and the amulet appeared in its center. "Now we wait," the old man laughed.

With the added aid of Meshire and Janston, they were easily holding the Trolls off. Things appeared to slow for just a moment, and then suddenly there was a commotion on the ground. The massed Trolls spread and made way for a single Troll. He was a horrible looking Troll with a huge headdress and a staff that seemed to radiate pure evil.

"How dare you!" The dark Magi roared. "I shall feed on your corpses before this night ends." He lifted his staff and a black mist began to surround him. He began spinning his staff slightly, and the mist also began to spin, then like a giant wave it flew towards the ledge Kainan was fighting on. Just before it struck, it stalled and then began to fall in upon itself and imploded. The sound was earth shaking. Tannis was nearly sent to his knees.

"You're going to have to do better than that," Wurwick shouted down.

The Magi shrieked and sent another blast Wurwick's way. Wurwick shielded himself and there was another thunderous shock as Wurwick blocked the blast. His face set firmly, Wurwick sent a blast of green down towards the Magi. The battle intensified quickly and raged on all around Tannis. Wurwick and the evil Troll were locked in a death match, and despite the help of Meshire, the Trolls were starting to overwhelm Vel and Janston.

"There are too many on Vel's half of the ledge," Tannis shouted to Meshire.

"No, der be too many o em. I can't keep up!" Meshire sounded back hurling flames at the Trolls as fast as he could.

Tannis looked down again, and he knew what he had to do. He drew his sword and closed his eyes. "Run, Jade," he whispered to the wind. And then he jumped off the platform Wurwick had made. Even though it was steep, it wasn't a straight fall, so he was able to slide down to the lower ledge. He landed not far from Janston.

"What are you doing boy?" Janston yelled.

"What I must!" Tannis yelled back, as he charged. The closest Troll turned to face him and swung a heavy axe directly for his head. Tannis easily ducked under the blow and lunged at the Troll. His sword slid surprisingly easy into the surprised Troll's ribcage. A dark red blood began to spurt from the wound as the sword slid deep inside the now mortally wounded Troll. The Troll made a deep grunt as he backed off the blade that had just killed him. Tannis didn't have time to notice. All his mind was focused on was the blood that had splattered upon his arm. It was a deep red color, and he felt as if it had stained him, a stain that he knew he would never truly wash clean. As he backed away slowly staring at his arm, a voice began to call from deep within his mind.

"Not yet, you can't stop yet. You must push through this." Tannis snapped back to reality. There was a spear floating towards him, which he easily knocked aside. Tannis wondered how anyone could have possibly thrown a spear so slowly without having it fall right out of the air. There was little time to think on that, as suddenly there were more Trolls. They were everywhere. Tannis began moving through them with an ease that he simply couldn't believe. Their movements were so slow! He had a rhythm worked out. He would let the Troll attack first, and he would simply block that attack and then strike himself. His sword slipped in and out of the attacking Trolls. One by one they fell, and for a time it seemed as if they could defeat this terrible Troll army. Meshire's efforts had caught the attention of the evil Troll Magi. He twisted his staff, and there was a defining sound. Wurwick was consumed by fire. He then sent a blast at Meshire. Meshire tried to block the blow but it was too strong for him, and he was sent reeling into the mountain. As Meshire fell, so did his protections. Trolls were now coming from everywhere.

"Now what?" Janston yelled.

"We fight to the last!" Kainan roared. "We will teach them to fear us!"

Suddenly there was a blast that surprised them all. A large group of Trolls were blasted off the ledge. Then the entire side of the ledge caught fire. All the Trolls that were climbing on it caught fire and fell. Tannis looked up and could not believe his eyes. There, standing next to Wurwick, was Balseer. Together Wurwick and Balseer started to bombard the evil Magi. It didn't take long for Kainan, Barvik, Vel and Janston to clear the ledge. Tannis watched as Wurwick and Balseer continued to overwhelm

the infuriated Troll. In desperation, the Troll tried
to flee. Wurwick grunted and forced his staff to the
ground. The Troll was flung to the ground. Laying
there, the Shaman screamed, and reached for his
staff. Just as his hand reached it, Balseer's hand flew
skyward palm up. The Magi's staff flew effortlessly
into the air.

"No," cried the Troll in desperation.

Balseer got a wicked grin on his face. His palm
burst into bright flames, and the Troll shrieked as if
he were in great pain. Tannis looked up to the staff
hanging effortlessly above the howling Magi. The
staff had burst into flame and bright sparks flew
from its head.

Meshire, who was slowly getting to his feet
grunted, "Be done wit it already."

Balseer gave a short chuckle and closed his palm.
The explosion was deafening. The Magi's staff burst
into hundreds of pieces. The Troll began to flail
uncontrollably. A trickle of blood began to flow
from his nose. The Trolls on the ground looked at
their leader being held captive and lost their resolve.
Tannis had never experienced a feeling quiet like it.
The sight of so many running from so few, it was
a moment lost in time and it filled Tannis with a
resounding resolve.

"The boy?" Wurwick asked firmly.

The Troll grunted, a slight smile crossed his pain stricken face. "He thought himself my equal, and was punished for that treachery."

"I want answers!" Wurwick Barked. "Speak."

"Or what?" the Troll chuckled. "What more can you do? You have not the power to destroy me."

"You have secrets?" Balseer asked. Then a light smile crossed his face. "I too have secrets. Wouldn't it be strange if we happened to share one? For example you have a backup plan, something to give you courage in the face of your betters."

"You know nothing of betters," the Troll screamed. "I have summoned powers you could never have imagined. I have torn the Vail, I have walked where none could follow."

"Lot of good it did you," Balseer smirked.

"Enough," Wurwick raged. "The boy!"

The Troll grunted and crossed his arms.

Balseer lifted his right hand, his fingers flexed as if squeezing something. The Troll shrieked and grabbed helplessly at his chest. He began to cough blood and spasm.

"Stop it." Brie screamed.

Balseer relented his grasp, and the Troll began to breath. His breath came in short gasps. Still clutching at his chest, he fixed Balseer with a look of pure hatred.

"If you can't be killed this is going to be a long night," Balseer shouted.

Barvik began to laugh, "I for one hope you don't talk. I prefer to watch you cringe there on the ground. Reminds me of a fish I caught once."

"The boy will be dead long before you can reach him," the Troll said with a smile. "I left orders to kill them both in the morning. If it makes you feel any better, he will watch as his friend is slowly disemboweled, all the while knowing that is how he himself will die. My only regret is not being there to enjoy it myself."

Wurwick began to laugh. "Your arrogance is your undoing, just as you came here to destroy whatever was in your path without giving thought to what you might find. Tell me, did you leave them under guard?"

The Trolls eyes narrowed slightly.

"I thought not," Wurwick began to laugh. "Cyres and Jadeance are already on the move."

The Troll closed his eyes for a moment then began to shriek horribly.

Balseer began to laugh again. "Your failure is now complete, but not to worry, I will help you. Time for me to reveal my secret, I know you empowered the Harrowmon with your own soul. I will now set you free."

"No!" the Troll shrieked.

Balseer snapped his fingers, and the amulet appeared at the tip of his staff. Balseer then began to chant in a language Tannis had never heard. The amulet began to emit a thick black liquid. Finally Balseer tipped his staff towards the withering Troll. The amulet soared down. As the two collided a great burst of energy flew in all directions, and the Troll's skin began to melt and boil, oozing off in all directions. It didn't take long until the Troll was definitely dead. All remained of the once powerful Shaman was a scarred skeleton.

Tannis was shocked to his core. There was a strong breeze, and Tannis felt cold. He looked down and noticed that his cloths were sticking to him from the dark Troll blood that had been splattered everywhere. He looked at his sword; it had a light covering from hilt to tip. Several small chunks of flesh had gotten caught on the edge of the blade. Tannis looked around and all he could see was charred and bleeding Troll corpses. For the first time, the smell caught him and he couldn't hold his stomach any longer. Dropping his sword, Tannis fell to his knees and began to retch violently. Tears seemed to flow from his eyes no matter how hard he tried to hold them back. He felt someone kneel next to him.

"It was never your skill that I doubted," Kainan said softly. "Battle is a horrible thing. I have seen the bravest of men with years of training turn and flee when the battle starts. There is one thing that no teacher, no matter his skill can teach, or prepare you for. Taking life makes you look into the beyond. I often wonder what I will see when my times comes. I had hoped to spare you from the nightmares you will now undoubtedly face."

Tannis looked at Kainan. It was easy to see how he could command the respect of even the greatest of men. It only took one look into Kainan's eyes and Tannis could clearly see how much Kainan cared for his men. Tannis coughed and looked down at his clothes. "I didn't expect the blood to spray at me like that," he admitted shyly.

Kainan nodded. "A wise man told me once that the Divines made war so gruesome for a reason. It's not supposed to be easy. You can take it to be a good sign that it bothers you so much."

"I thought you would think of me as a coward," Tannis confessed.

"No coward would run into a hopeless fight just to save a friend," Kainan replied seriously.

Tannis laughed slightly. "Jade would. I doubt it would even have to be a friend. He would go merely because someone was in trouble."

"There is greatness inherent in you both." Kainan replied. "A trait given to you by your father, who was a great man, amongst the bravest I have ever had the pleasure to meet."

Tannis smiled, and then looked around and his smile faded. "How do I get past all this?"

Kainan sighed, "You will have to find your own path. Every man copes in his own way."

"Does it ever get any easier?" Tannis asked.

Kainan stood, "That depends greatly on you."

"We can't coddle the boy all day," Balseer complained bitterly. "We need to get a move on and fast. There are still several thousand Trolls around. They will get back to chasing us soon."

"Why don't you shut your mouth, if you plan on being an ass," Barvik shot back, jumping to Tannis' defense.

"All of this coming from a giant blundering oaf. I am quite amazed you have made it this far, what with all the running and all."

Barvik spun his giant axe in his hands. "Why don't you come down here? I'll send your soulless body to join your precious night father."

"Enough!" Kainan shouted. "Balseer, you watch your mouth or I'll have you muzzled."

"Can none of you spot your betters?" Balseer retorted. "Or perhaps you…"

"I said enough!" Kainan roared. "I fear neither the demons of hell nor the Lords of the Silver Tower. I have stared into the eyes of death and have been blessed by the very hand of Thamis, himself. You will obey my will or be banished. There is too much at stake."

Balseer held his resolve for a moment; however Tannis could clearly see that no one could stand against the large man indefinitely. Balseer lowered his eyes and grunted. "We do need to move."

"He is right," Atrius said solemnly. "But I fear the path."

Samous looked up, "Atrius is right. We have to go up and we'll hit snow tomorrow or the next day. This mountain is treacherous in good conditions. The road will not be easy."

"No one said the road was going to be easy," Kainan replied.

"We must be cautious," Vel replied. "The Trolls still hold the advantage. Their numbers are too great, and we could easily be cornered and ambushed in the high mountains. Trolls are excellent mountaineers."

"What about Jade?" Brie asked. "We aren't just going to leave them?"

"Cyres and Jadeance will be on their own," Kainan replied sadly. "We cannot help them now. The entire Troll army lies between them and us. Cyres will lead them out another way."

"You put entirely too much faith in that curly haired buffoon," Balseer said sourly. However after a quick look from Kainan, Balseer looked the other direction.

"Vel is right," Barvik grumbled. "We can't have them on our backs like this. They're too close."

"I will take care of that," Balseer said confidently.

"Playing the hero?" Wurwick asked curiously.

"No," Balseer sneered. "I'm doing what I do best."

"And what is that?" Atrius asked.

"Causing distractions," Balseer replied with deep laughter. "I'll buy you time, but don't dawdle. They will move and I'm not going to stick around to do this again."

"Are you in a hurry?" Barvik asked.

Balseer fixed Barvik with a hard look. "No simpleton, I'm on orders and I need to report back."

"I don't mean to doubt you," Atrius said. "How do you plan on shaking an entire army?"

Balseer began to laugh, "You will see. Just know when it starts, you need to keep moving. There are several people working at this, and you will have a certain amount of protection."

Wurwick began to shake his head. "That is too dangerous. What could they possibly be thinking?"

"Don't be such a baby," Balseer sneered. Zunshi is convinced that it will happen naturally soon, anyway. We will just be pushing it."

"To what end?" Wurwick growled.

"Will you cross the council?" Balseer asked with a mocking smile.

"We needs ta be trustin' da council," Meshire said.

"Let's move," Kainan said. "It's going to be a rough road."

As Tannis reached for his sword, the sleeve of his shirt stuck to his arm and he cringed from it. Janston reached down and retrieved his sword.

"In time you will learn how to keep most of it off," Janston said softly. He then bent and began to clean the blade. "Haven't we been here before?" Janston asked with a slight smile.

"It seems like such a long time ago," Tannis replied. "Last time was easier, for lots of reasons."

"Yes," Janston replied. "I bet it was. Well, we might as well make our way up towards the others."

Tannis nodded, and followed Barvik up to the ledge Wurwick had created to keep Brie and Atrius safe. When they reached it, Meshire approached.

"Dat was a brave ting ta do," Meshire said.

"No," Tannis replied. "It was foolish. I should have listened to Kainan."

"Hum," Meshire replied. "It be a good ting ta

listen rightly enough. Kainan knows what ta do an what not ta do. Den again, ye must listen to yer gut. Tinkin' on da moment cun save yer life an da live's o yer friends."

"I think I have heard you say something like that before," Tannis replied.

"Well, I don talk ta hear da sound o me voice. Der always be a reason," Meshire said smiling. "Don forget yer gut just cause someone said not ta." Then Meshire laughed, spoke a word Tannis didn't understand, and a bright flash erupted from Meshire's staff. Tannis closed his eyes for a moment. When he opened them, his clothes were dry and clean. No sign of the fight that he had been involved in remained.

"Come on, Tannis," Brie said, and she gave him a tight hug. Tannis held her for a moment and he could almost feel a deep sorrow coming from deep within her.

"Jade is going to be alright," Tannis said. She pulled away, and a tear slid down her cheek.

She wiped her cheek. "I keep telling myself that," she replied, her lip trembling. "But I don't know where he is and what they have done to him. He said he punished him."

"Jade is too strong to worry about," Tannis said. "He is probably worrying about our safety." Brie looked grateful, however another tear slid down her cheek. "Do you think he misses me?"

Tannis smiled. "I'm sure he does."

"Keep up," Samous yelled back. Tannis looked and they had started to climb higher.

"Are we going to scale this whole blasted mountain?" Barvik grumbled. His great bearded face was covered with sweat.

"There is a path half a mile or so higher," Janston replied. "It takes us up towards the high passes. From there it will be a straight shot to Astrothen."

"Don't tease me," Barvik grumbled.

"Oh, come now Barvik, it hasn't been that long since you were drunk," Samous laughed.

"I think we're all going to wish we were drunk come morning," Atrius groaned, looking at the snow covered passes.

Tannis looked back as he turned onto the path. The vast sea of trees was never ending, and it went on as far as he could see. "Good luck, Jade," he thought.

"Don't worry too much," Barvik said between breaths. "Cyres is with him. Say what you will about him. He may be a joker, but he is the best of men and he will keep your brother safe."

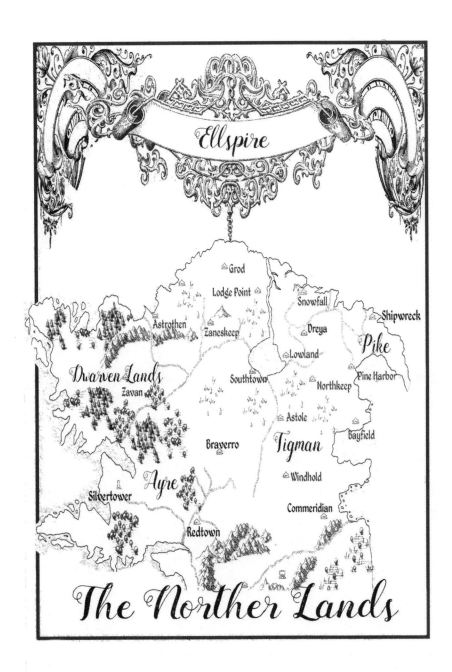

CHAPTER 12

THE HIGH MOUNTAINS

Tannis smiled and then followed Janston along the long road to Astrothen, a city he had never seen, yet couldn't wait to get to. As nearly as he could tell, it was the ancestral home of his father. They had no sooner reached the top of the cliff than half of the mountain broke free and crumbled down towards the still fleeing Troll Army. The sound was deafening and the earth shook violently. The group moved on quickly and Tannis followed, leaving that terrible place behind him, his thoughts weighing heavily on the battle. He had never killed anything that wasn't an animal. He could never have imagined how that would have felt. He could clearly see the faces of the Trolls he had killed, watching as they realized they were wounded. Each one had its own defining moment that he feared would stick with him forever. Then there was Jadeance. He knew that he was bound to be separated at some point, but he had hoped that it would be under better circumstances. As he walked, he looked back at Brie who had kept close behind him in silence all afternoon. They continued to walk for hours, and as they walked he watched her intently. She didn't so much as make one peep. Finally, as dusk was setting in, Kainan found a small outcrop on the trail to make camp.

"We'll rest here for tonight. Unfortunately without the packs, it will be cold."

"Don't worry about that," Wurwick replied, groaning as he sat down. "Ah," he sighed in relief, "I'm getting too old for this."

"Um, Wurwick, aren't you forgetting something?" Atrius asked gently.

"His mind has finally slipped," Samous laughed.

Wurwick gave Samous an icy stare, which only made him laugh harder. "Are you done?" Wurwick demanded irritably.

"That all depends," Samous laughed. "Are you going to turn me into a fat toad if I'm not?"

Wurwick took a deep sigh and closed his eyes. Shaking his head, he lifted his staff. "You're going to be the death of me Samous," he said, as he waved his staff and the packs all appeared. "Couldn't do anything about the horses," Wurwick replied as he got out his pipe. "Trolls like the taste of horse. They are all long dead."

Kainan twisted his head and seemed to convulse slightly. "Trolls are disgusting", he mumbled. "Well, they wouldn't have been much help up here anyway."

It took the better part of an hour to get a makeshift camp set up. Wurwick made several rocks light on fire. All in all, it was nice to sit and relax. The whole camp was quiet, the absence of Jadeance and Cyres weighed on everyone's mind.

Barvik nudged at Tannis, "Grab your sword."

Tannis was confused, but with a shrug he drew his sword and handed it over to Barvik. Looking it over, he grunted. "When you fight, your sword takes a beating," Barvik explained, handing the sword back. "If the sword is poorly made, the cuts will sink deeper. Yours is in good shape, but you still have to clean up the edge." He reached into a pack and pulled out several large stones. "You use long even strokes. Count as you go," Barvik explained. "You don't want to grind more on one side than another."

Tannis rested his sword on his lap and began to rub it with the stone Barvik had given him. While his hands were busy, his mind was allowed to wander. He found himself looking upon the face of the first Troll he had killed. There was a deep hate in his eyes. Tannis struggled to keep his thoughts on other things than the dead of the day. The night lagged on until finally Tannis retired to his bed roll.

Brie watched Tannis as he slept. She could
tell he was troubled. She took a deep sigh. There
was so much to worry about. Everyone seemed to
have something troubling them. As for her, it was
easy. Jadeance was gone, and in trouble. She closed
her eyes and pulled her blanket tightly around her
shoulders. She felt light, as if she were falling. With
a flash of light she found herself lying in a meadow.
The sun was warm, sitting up she looked around.
There were hundreds of beautiful flowers covering
the meadow like a blanket. It seemed so homey and
comfortable, all her cares and worries melted away.
Then she spotted the cabin. A light smoke rose from
the chimney. Brie got to her feet. She had been here
before, the day they had meet Vel. As she approached
the cabin she smelled fresh bread, and with a smile
she reached for the door.

"Come in hun," A woman's voice came
from inside.

Brie opened the door. There was the same saintly
woman sitting at her table once again. She was
beautiful, with long silver hair. Her face was smooth
and pristine.

"Come in and sit down," the woman invited,
waving her arm at the chair opposite her.

Brie sat down and looked around. The cabin looked

the same as it had last time.

"Nothing has changed, hun," the woman said with a smile.

"Please?" Brie asked trying not to be impolite. "Who are you?"

"That is still complicated," the woman replied with a smile. "You wish to classify me with a name. I have many, and I fear you are not yet ready for that yet."

"Where are we?" Brie pressed.

"This is a special place, a sanctuary you might say." Then the woman smiled. "Why don't we talk about why I have brought you here?"

Brie nodded.

With a smile the woman leaned forward. "Do you remember what we talked about last time you came to visit?"

"Yes," Brie replied.

"Good, it is time for you to start fulfilling your destiny. Your path is difficult, yet you will find it to be a rewarding one. What a man dreams is personal, and important. Dreams can utterly consume your mind or free it. There is a deep Magic in dreams. An old Magic most have long forgotten. For some spare few moments, you are free or enslaved. You will come to find that you have power over dreams and in time, power over the mind and therefore power over most men. Many will fear you, many will love you. Some will attempt to bribe you. Kings will plead for your love and attention."

"What are you saying?" Brie asked. "What am I to become?"

The woman's eyes grew distant. "Your future is uncertain and clouded. We do not yet know how you will handle the Burden. You see, you will be able to see into a man's future, and his past. See the true nature of his feelings. Feel his sorrows and pains, and if it be your will, take them on yourself. This is where it gets complicated. You do have the power to clear these feelings from your mind, but it is a difficult thing and most who have your great power never learn to handle the Burden. You are able to purge sadness and sorrow but it is a difficult discipline to learn."

"How do I clear these feelings? How do I rid myself of the sadness you spoke of?"

"For you, a key has been provided. You must find this key and use it to unlock your true and full potential. Only when you truly have it to be your own will its power be able to merge with your own. Only together will you find peace and do what must be done."

"But what does all that mean? Please give me a hint where will I find this key?"

DAVID MUNSON

Then a smile hit her perfect lips and in a flash
Brie caught a glimpse of Jadeance sitting in a dark
cave. "Time is short," the woman continued on. "You
won't be able to read everyone. There will be some
that hold to their sorrows too deeply. For others you
will be blocked for different reasons. Your friends
will need your talents if they are to survive. Go now,
unlock your true power and take my love and my
blessings with you."

"What if I fail?" Brie asked.

"You are much like the boy you so love. Many
people think that you are incapable of failure."

"Am I?" Brie pressed.

"I do not yet know what you are capable of." Then
she stood up. "You will do what you set your mind
too. Now go and fulfill your destiny."

Brie awoke, it was late and the stars were bright.
The air was cold, and she found herself shivering.

"A storm is coming on," Tannis said softly.

Brie jumped. "Tannis, what are you doing awake?"

"Can't sleep," he shrugged. "Keep thinking
about Jade."

"Tannis, do you think I'm special?" Brie asked.

"I thought you were in love with Jade," Tannis
said with a slight smile. "Don't you know that flirting
with his older brother is bad form?"

"Tannis, did you know that you're a far larger

dunce than Jade could ever be?" Brie shot back with an irritated look.

Tannis began to laugh. "No one is a bigger dunce than Jade."

"Well then, don't be silly," Brie said firmly.

"Why do you ask?" Tannis asked.

She looked at the stars. "I had a dream."

"What kind of dream?" Tannis asked.

"I met a woman. She seems to be important. I have met her before, she is the one who told me Jade was in danger the day we met Vel. Do you remember?"

"How could I forget?" Tannis asked. "That was the day our lives all changed."

"Sometimes I think it started the day we met Meshire," Brie said.

Tannis began to laugh. "Here we are, sitting around in the middle of the night, freezing and trying to figure out who is responsible for ruining our lives."

Brie also began to laugh. Then she pulled her blanket tighter. "Tannis I miss him."

"Don't worry about Jade," Tannis said. "He can take care of himself."

"That doesn't make it any easier," Brie complained.

"No probably not," Tannis agreed. "But what

can we do?"

"Sleep?" Brie suggested.

"You can," Tannis said looking around. "I have given up on it."

Brie knew what she had to do. "Tannis come here."

"Brie, it's cold. I don't want to get out of my blankets," Tannis complained.

Brie sighed. "Ok I'll come to you," and she started to get up, but Tannis moaned.

"No, I'm not going to make you get up." He rolled out of his blankets and leaned over her. "Ok, now that I'm freezing what do you want?"

"She also told me how to take your pain away," Brie said softly. She reached up and held his head in her hands. His mind opened up to her. She was able to see him running as a child. His mother's face appeared, a beautiful woman. Then she felt his pain. It wasn't the loss of his brother that had been so troubling him, it was the Battle. He felt the dead calling to him. "Be at peace, dear brother," she whispered into his ear, and then she gently kissed his cheek. At first the pain was sharp and near unbearable. It took her a few moments to shake it off. Tannis pulled away from her, shaking his head. He looked confused. "Go lie down now Tannis," she commanded. He numbly made his way back to his blankets. As she sat trying to deal with what felt like a presence in her mind, she closed her eyes. "Oh Jade, I need you," she whispered. "Jade...", then her mind faded and she could see him. She could feel his sadness.

"Jade why are you so sad?" Brie's voice sounded in his head.

"Brie, is that you?" Jadeance asked.

"You know it's me," she replied softly. "Are you hurt?"

"No, not anymore," Jadeance replied. "Cyres saved me. You wouldn't believe how brave he is."

"Kainan says he's the best," Brie replied.

"He is," Jadeance replied sadly.

"No, I think he will come in second best," Brie replied, a slight smile forming on her face, a smile that slowly began to ease the pressure in her mind.

"What do you mean?" Jadeance asked.

"You do not yet know your abilities," Brie replied warmly.

"I am not his equal," Jadeance replied slowly. "I am a coward."

"I have known you most of my life, and you are anything but a coward. Now you listen to me, Jadeance. You will find whatever it is that you have lost. Pull yourself together, and do it now. You must come back to me."

"Wait a minute," Jadeance shot back a little hurt, "I..."

"No time," Brie interrupted. "Promise me Jade, promise you will do whatever it takes to find me, promise."

"I promise." Jadeance fumbled.

"Promise me, Jadeance," Brie insisted.

"I promise, I promise!" Jadeance replied.

"Don't forget that you promised me, Jadeance. Do what you have to do, find a way back to me. Oh and Jade, I love you." She felt their connection fade and she wasn't even certain he had heard her. Knowing he was alright made her feel better and she looked at Tannis, who was now sound asleep. With a smile she closed her eyes and drifted off.

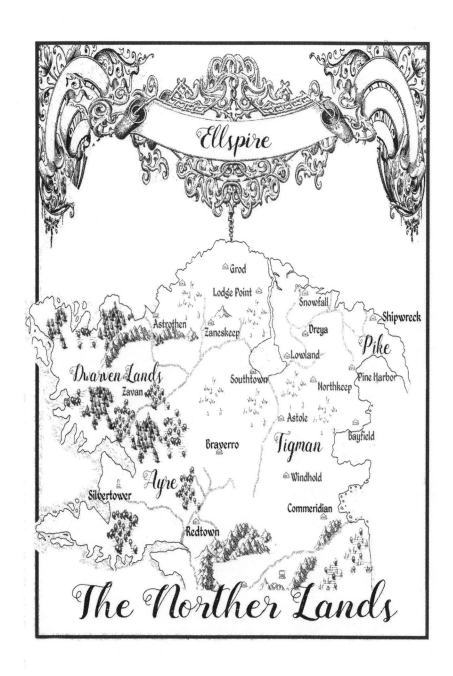

CHAPTER 13

WINTER WOES

Tannis was awakened by Vel. "Come on, it is going to be a long day." Tannis looked out the door to the enclosure they had taken shelter in. Snow was falling and it looked cold. Brie tossed a large pack into his lap.

"Barvik said he made all this, but I have never seen this pack before. I strongly suspect Wurwick had something to do with it," Brie said with a laugh.

Tannis smiled and opened the pack. Inside there were several large fur bundles wrapped together. "Barvik made these?" Tannis asked with a smile.

"What?" Barvik grumbled. "Don't think I could?"

"This one has my name tagged on it," Tannis laughed. "You did that too?"

"There is no faith in today's youth," Barvik complained.

"It's funny you should mention faith," Samous

laughed. "Because that's just what it would take to even think you could make anything like this at all."

Barvik smiled, then without warning he grabbed Samous with his massive hands, hefted him easily into the air and threw him out into the snow. As Samous rolled down the hill, Barvik yelled back, "Strange that you think so, because I just made you really cold." Wurwick and Atrius began laughing uncontrollably. Samous was swearing outrageously as he stammered back into the tent.

"Looks like your mouth finally got the best of you," Wurwick laughed. "Next time you intend on insulting something twice your size, why don't you make sure you're not within arm's reach."

Barvik looked at Wurwick. "Don't think I don't know you're digging at me when you say that."

"Don't even think about it. If you attempt to toss me out the door you will find yourself beardless."

"You wouldn't!" Barvik shouted, his hands going protectively to his beard. "You can't just go around threatening a man's beard like that, it's unholy."

"There is nothing holy about your beard," Atrius barked. "You're going to curse us all with talk like that."

Tannis continued laughing as he watched Samous put on his fur clothing.

Tannis had been out in the snow plenty of times.

This was the first time he felt completely warm and comfortable.

"It's Pikeman," Wurwick said, pointing to the new fur clothing. "They like the cold, yet they don't actually like to be cold. There is no finer winter clothing in the world."

Tannis looked at Barvik.

"Yes, he is a Pike," Wurwick laughed. "So yes, he might have wanted to make the clothes. However Samous was right. That man was made to destroy, not to create."

"Still," Tannis wondered. "How did you know my size? And Brie, she looks smaller than she really is. She hides her...well she," Tannis stammered and began to blush.

Wurwick grunted. "I am a wizard my boy. I have my ways."

"That was an interesting conversation," Brie said coming up from behind them.

"Brie," Tannis stuttered. "I thought you were up there with Vel. That is I..."

"Nope," she replied with a smile. "I was right behind you the whole time. So what is it that I am so good at hiding?"

Tannis began to blush furiously. "Um, never mind. I think I'm going to go talk with Barvik." Brie began to laugh as Tannis ran to join Barvik.

"Hasty retreat," Barvik laughed. "I like that."

"How did you?" Tannis started to ask.

"My ears are good boy. If you're going to be a man of action you need to learn that your surroundings are everything. Your ears can save you from many dangers."

"Like what?" Tannis asked. "Few things will be out in a snowstorm like this."

Barvik began to laugh. "Well if you had been using them you might have noticed Brie sneak up on you to listen."

Tannis groaned inwardly. "Set myself up for that didn't I?"

"Yes you did!" Brie shouted. "And I don't sneak, nor do I eavesdrop."

Barvik laughed harder. "You could have fooled me."

"If you don't stop laughing you're going to wake up with your beard braided." Brie warned.

Barvik looked shocked. "Now listen here girl, a man's beard is private property. You don't see me threatening your belongings."

"What, are you afraid of little me?" Brie asked.

"I don't see this going your way, old boy." Atrius laughed.

Barvik scowled. "See what you have done," Barvik said, pointing at Tannis.

Tannis shrugged, and walked on listening to Brie laugh softly. As the day dragged on, the snow began to get deep. The trees started to thin out as the terrain began to get rocky.

"If this gets much deeper, we're going to have some real problems," Barvik grumbled as they all sat around a small fire that night.

"There is a path," Wurwick replied. "It is passable for at least another month or better."

"Unless the Trolls are there waiting for us," Samous said, looking into the fire.

"He might be right," Atrius said. "We can't think in conventional terms here. It appears as if the Trolls have taken this mountain for their own. They will most certainly have all known paths under watch."

Wurwick took several large puffs, and then removed his pipe. "Well I can't blast right through the mountain. What do you suggest?"

"The snow is going to be too deep to make our own way," Samous mused. "There are several canyons that will be passable, however. If I was going to plan an ambush, that's where it would be."

"I don't see why we don't just take the most direct route," Barvik growled. "If we stay high where the snow is deep and the road is narrow, they will have to come at us one on one. We make some Troll soup, and be on our way."

"No good," Samous replied shaking his head. "They will merely send some scouts to the peaks. One good avalanche in the right place and we won't stand a chance."

Kainan looked around. "They won't be watching all known passes towards Astrothen."

"What are you talking about, old boy?" Atrius asked.

"Zane's Keep," Kainan replied.

"That's not a good idea," Atrius replied firmly.

"There will be an entire garrison there," Kainan replied.

"They don't like visitors," Atrius replied firmly as he folded his arms.

"We'll be fine. Before I..," then Kainan hesitated. "Well, I put one of my best there."

"And you think he is going to forgive you for that?" Samous asked. "If you had exiled me up here I'd have your head."

"No," Kainan shook his head. "He requested it. His wish you might say."

"Um, excuse me," Tannis asked. "What is Zane's Keep, and why don't they like visitors?"

"It is a fortress," Kainan replied. "It was originally built to protect the southern borders, or so they say. It isn't anywhere near the Ayre border."

"There are more stories about Zane's Keep than

facts," Atrius said darkly. "Even among the chamber brothers, there are few who truly know what its real purpose is."

"So, what do we do?" Janston asked. "Between Atrius and Kainan they will more than likely let us through, but what if they don't?"

"I fail to see what choice we have," Samous replied. "I'd rather talk with some zealot crazed Aryens than face the stinking Trolls."

Barvik was looking around. "I don't really know the way anymore."

"I know where it is supposed to be," Samous replied with a mischievous grin.

"That's not very comforting," Brie said looking around hopelessly.

"I know where it is," Kainan said as he looked into the night.

"There is an entrance into the lower catacombs not two days from here," Wurwick replied.

"What catacombs?" Barvik asked.

Wurwick smiled as he removed his pipe, "It's a secret, you see. I couldn't possibly tell you more. What with old promises and what not, you will just have to trust me."

"I have heard tell of such a thing," Atrius replied. "But if we are worried about getting into the castle, how are we to gain access to some secret passage?"

"Trust me," Wurwick replied, putting his pipe back in his mouth.

"Not likely." Samous grumbled.

"It's going to be a cold couple of days," Atrius interrupted. "We need to get some rest."

Tannis set his bedroll down and sank gratefully into his blankets. He sighed and closed his eyes. The air was cold on his face. He pulled his blanket tighter around his shoulders.

"What do you think Jade is doing?" Brie asked quietly.

"Sleeping," Tannis replied. "Jade is a morning person, not too good at staying up late."

"I wish he was here with us," Brie said sadly.

"I do too," Tannis replied. "Don't worry about Jade. He will find a way back to us."

Brie sighed. "Yes, I know. Good night Tannis," Brie said as she rolled over.

"Good night Brie," Tannis said with his eyes closed.

Tannis slept little during the night. He didn't enjoy being cold. In fact, the only one who slept was Barvik. The giant seemed to be indifferent to the cold.

"Do you ever get cold?" Tannis asked Barvik as they were getting ready to leave.

"I have once," Barvik replied with a great laugh. "When I was a small boy, and to be fair that was a particularly cold winter."

"You were never a small boy," Samous laughed. "You clawed your way out of a bear, or don't you remember your early days as a cub?"

Barvik looked at Samous, who had backed up to the stone wall. "You think that's funny do you? That's ok, I have a sense of humor too." Without warning he threw his axe at the stone ledge just above Samous. A great wall of snow broke free and slid down the rock face completely covering Samous.

Tannis watched as Atrius and Janston dug the little man out of the snow bank.

"You don't seem to learn very well, do you?" Atrius asked as he pulled the little man out.

"That lumbering fool tried to kill me," Samous complained as he tried to get the snow out of his long pointy ears.

Barvik was laughing so hard he began to cough.

"Enough of this nonsense, you two fools are going on like we are not running for our lives," Kainan said as he retrieved Barvik's axe. "I'll have no more of this. There are great dangers on this mountain, and your fooling around could risk it all. You nearly brought down the mountain!" Barvik looked ashamed as he took his axe back from Kainan.

"And you," Kainan said to the shivering man. "If you don't curb your tongue, I'll help Barvik toss you off this rock myself. We need to be swift and silent, not slow and dangerous."

The mood was somber as they made their way back to the road and it was quiet for most of the day as they traveled on. The snow was getting deeper, and Barvik took the lead. Using his giant axe as a walking stick, he plowed a path for everyone else to follow. By the time they stopped for rest that night everyone was exhausted and cold. The skies had opened up and fresh snow blotted out the sky. Meshire used the rock face and the snow all around to make a shelter.

"If we go inside that, it will bury us in the night," Samous complained. "I'm freezing as it is."

"It be warm an safe," Meshire replied. "Sides I gave it me own little encouragement ta stay up."

Tannis was doubtful as he climbed into Meshire's shelter. Much to Tannis's surprise it was rather warm and he slept better than he had in while. In fact, he had been sleeping much better sense the night Brie had kissed his head. "I wonder if that's why Jade fancies her so much," Tannis wondered to himself. She did have a power Tannis could never explain. Whatever the reason, he awoke refreshed and looked around.

"Gather yer strength, young master," Meshire said. "Der be a storm brewin'. A cold an windy day be waitin' fer us."

As they emerged from the shelter Meshire had made, Tannis was nearly swept off his feet. The wind was intense, a blizzard that Tannis had only imagined from the stories that old Cradalo used to tell.

"What now?" Barvik yelled pulling his heavy cloak tighter.

"We can't stop here or well be buried alive," Atrius yelled back.

Brie grabbed onto Tannis. "I can't see!" She yelled.

"Everyone hold onto the person in front of you!" Wurwick yelled.

"Wait," Meshire Yelled back. Then he began to chant lowly, and a bright red rope appeared around Tannis. It looped around his waist and over to Atrius. Even though the rope was bright red he could hardly see up to Wurwick and Barvik.

"Now we be linked," Meshire yelled.

"Right," Wurwick shouted. "Follow me, I'll get us through."

Tannis struggled on for hours. With each passing mile the wind seemed to pick up. He could no longer see Brie behind him or Atrius in front, just the rope sliding into the sheer blanket of snow. Then the road turned, and the full force of the wind struck them.

Tannis had to turn his head to breathe. He felt numb, each step was a new struggle. Finally he stumbled into Atrius.

"Why have we stopped?" Tannis shouted to Atrius.

"We are here," Atrius shouted back. "Get back towards the wall."

They all huddled together as Meshire stepped forward. With his staff held in front of him he created a barrier against the wind. Wurwick began to sing in a language Tannis had never heard before. The song was slow but strangely inviting, as if he heard it somewhere before. The rock face opened into two large doors. They made a slight grinding noise as they opened.

"Everyone inside," Kainan shouted.

The doors shut behind them. There was nothing in the darkness. No sound from the wind and snow slamming against the wall they had just come through. Meshire and Wurwick lit the tips of their staffs. They began sending balls of light around to light up the cavern. It was large, and covered in spider webs. It didn't look as if anyone had been there in years.

"What now?" Brie asked.

"Now we wait," Wurwick replied. "It won't take them long to find us. And when they arrive, don't expect a warm welcome. They don't per say like it when anyone enters without knocking first."

"How will they know we are here?" Samous asked.

"The spell I used to open the passage is an old secret," Wurwick said as he pulled out his pipe. "It does have one drawback. Anyone who was listening would have heard it."

"And you think someone was listening?" Atrius asked.

"Most definitely," Kainan replied.

Tannis sat down next to Brie and Janston. "How long do you think it will take them to find us?"

"Hopefully long enough to calm down," Atrius replied as he lit his pipe.

They waited into the night. Tannis was just starting to close his eyes when he heard the rush of footsteps. He looked up to see several dozen men charging with weapons drawn.

"Calm down," Kainan shouted. "We surrender. We need to talk."

"Shut it!" A man in the back shouted. "Set your weapons on the ground."

"Take it easy," Kainan replied. "Hear us out."

"I do not know how you found this place, but you will sorely regret the discovery," the man said raising a bow.

'I wouldn't do that," Wurwick warned. "It was no accident that brought us here. We need to get..."

"Silence you old fool!" the man shouted. "I will do the talking."

"I am a friend," Kainan replied. "I must see Hesih, your commander."

"How do you..," then the man hesitated. "No matter, you are under arrest. You will see no one."

"You are making a mistake," Wurwick said. "You will hear us. Now why don't we..."

"Enough!" The man shouted, aiming his bow directly at Kainan. "Your weapons or your life."

"I'm afraid you leave me no choice," Wurwick replied. With a flash, all their weapons disappeared. They all looked around astonished.

"Will you hear us now?" Kainan asked.

The man nearly fell when his bow disappeared. He nodded slowly. "My name is Kainan. We travel to Astrothen. We have been running from the vast Troll army and we must see the king."

"You truly know Hesih?" The man asked.

"I do," Kainan replied. "He bears a serpent crest upon his bracers. Gold trimmed."

"How do you know this?" the man asked.

"Simple," Kainan replied. "I gave them to him."

"You gave them to him?" Then the man swallowed hard. "I will take you to him, and pray for us both that you don't lie. Death will be welcome to our punishment if you do." He started up the passage way then paused. "May we have our things back?"

Kainan looked to Wurwick.

Smiling, the wizard lifted his staff. A bright green light filled the chamber for a moment. When Tannis opened his eyes, all the guards had their weapons.

The man looked around then shook his head. "Say nothing. No introductions. The least I know the better. I will let Lord Hesih sort all this out."

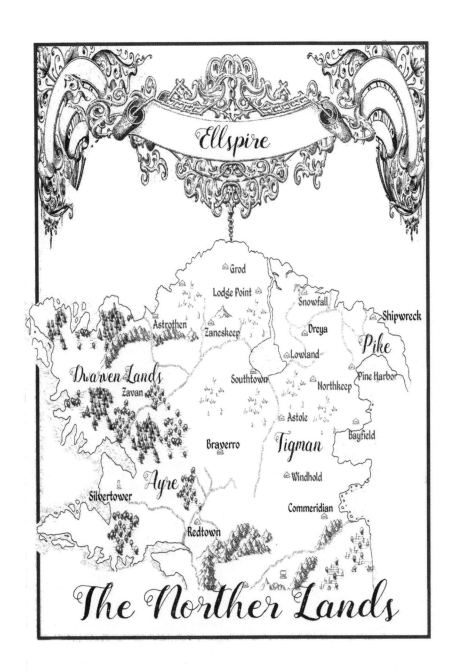

CHAPTER 14

ZANE'S KEEP

It took several days to reach the upper levels of Zane's Keep. Tannis had never seen so many soldiers, most looked forbidding. It was clear that they were not welcome. It was a strange place, with was no sign of laughter, music, or comradery. This was alien to Tannis. Music and laughter was such a part of life in Tigman. His whole life he had believed men worldwide enjoyed music and singing. There seemed little joy in these narrow, dimly lit corridors. The thing that caught Tannis the most was the stone work. Every few feet on both sides of every corridor they went through were lifelike stone statues of a man in armor. Thousands of these solid, mute soldiers stood guarding the dark corridors leading to Zane's Keep. The castle of Zane's Keep was neat, and almost perfectly built. The walls were straight and smooth, as if they had been sanded and smoothed by the gifted hands of Master Gideon. They looked much like the perfect table tops turned out of his shop. Looking around, Tannis missed Wagstaff very much and wanted to be back home again, waiting tables and watching Jadeance snoop over every conversation he possibly could. Despite the seeming perfection of the walls, they were bare, almost desolate. The only decorations Tannis could see were the soldier statues that continued to line the hallways. The statues here in the castle had a different style armor carved onto them. Despite the almost depressing state of the castle, the soldiers that lived here seemed to be solid, almost the mirror image of the stone ones that filled the castle's walkways. Tannis thought after a year of walking through this depressing looking castle, all signs of joy would leave him. And yet every soldier he passed looked him straight in the eyes without a trace of depression. There was something deep in those eyes, something Tannis couldn't quite understand. A pride that was barely recognizable and deeply hidden. There was something here, a secret that could only be seen deep in the solid men that stood as a great wall, a protection against the world, keeping whatever was here safe and unknown.

They were taken into a large room that had a dozen large stone pillars stretching from floor to ceiling. Large fire pits dotted the room, giving ample light. Tables stretched from one side of the large room to the other. Charts and books seemed to be neatly organized upon them. Armored men stopped whatever they had been doing and got to their feet as Tannis and the others were brought up to a large cascading fountain that stood dead center in the room. A man approached the lead guard. He was normal sized man, older than the rest of the troops in the room, however not so old that you would think of him as past his time.

"What is the meaning of this?" the man demanded. "You desecrate the great..."

"Hold it Pathues," a man interrupted, as he approached. He was smaller than Cyres and Vel, but slightly taller than Atrius with light brown hair and a well-trimmed beard. He wore elaborate armor that bore a resemblance to Kainan's.

"My Lord Hesih, we cannot allow this rabble to be admitted to..."

"This is no mere rabble, Pathues," Hesih replied, bowing before Kainan.

"You honor me with your presence," Hesih said with deep respect.

"Get up, my friend," Kainan replied, helping Hesih to his feet. "Forgive this intrusion. We require aid. I must deliver this boy to Astrothen. We have been set upon by the vast Troll army that dominates the wood and lower range to the south."

Hesih looked at Tannis for a moment, his eyes searching. "Is that?"

"One of them, yes," Atrius replied.

"One of them? Where is the other? Noble Magistrate, tell me that all I not lost."

"He is ok," Kainan replied. "Cyres is with him."

"Cyres? Where are they?" Hesih asked. "What is going on here?"

"We'll explain everything," Atrius replied. "May we sit?"

"Yes, over here," Hesih said, leading them to a long table. It only took a few moments to have it cleared. "I'll have food and drink prepared. We can talk while we wait."

They sat down at the long table with Tannis and Brie up near Kainan, Atrius, Barvik and Hesih.

"Magistrate Atrius, would you do me the pleasure of making the introductions?" Hesih said, looking down the table.

"Former Magistrate," Atrius replied with a grin. "I, like many of our friends here, have come out of retirement. Of course you know Kainan, Barvik, and Vel-Imein. This little fellow is Samous, a very clever Meerman," Atrius said, pointing at the little man. "He is a thief and a liar, among other things. However he is also son of Prince Tifnar, of Meurl in the Meer Forest and is a valuable asset."

Tannis exchanged a shocked glance with Brie. He didn't know that Samous was the son of a prince. "Wait until I can tell Jade," he thought.

Hesih nodded his head. "I have fallen into royal company."

Samous smiled, "Don't worry about it. My title is proof that the Divines do have a sense of humor."

"That is enough of that!" Atrius barked. "I'll not have you blaspheme!" Samous laughed as Atrius continued. "This is Warwick, First Seat on the High Council at the Silver Tower, our guide, and protector of a promising young Magi."

"Former seat holder," Warwick replied. "I, too have reason to come out of retirement."

"And that explains how you found our tunnels," Hesih laughed.

"This old friend is Meshire, also a Wizard from the Silver Tower."

"An honor ta make yur acquaintance," Meshire said with a smile.

Hesih nodded and looked to Janston, "One of our own, if I'm not mistaken."

"Janston, of Grad, Mirrorman Seeker of the Third Order, assigned to the Silver Tower, and by extension to Meshire here."

Hesih pulled a silver amulet from his breast.

It was the same amulet that Tannis has seen the night Janston had killed the Neering. "I too was once a Mirrorman Seeker. I served under the Fifth, Ninth, and finally the First Order. You are welcome here, brother."

"I know of you," Janston replied. "The work of the First Order is legendary. I am honored to meet another of that great company."

Hesih smiled, "There are few of us left."

"Last, but not least, we have the children," Atrius continued. "This young man is Tannis, eldest son of Taggard."

"Is he really?" Hesih replied shocked. He looked at Tannis for a moment, and then he looked to Kainan. "Does he...?"

"No, not yet," Kainan replied firmly.

"Do I what?" Tannis asked. The table fell silent. "You must tell me," Tannis pleaded.

"I'm afraid we can't," Kainan said slowly. "You will know more in time, when it is safe."

Tannis sat frustrated, wondering what they were holding from him.

"And this great beauty is Brie," Atrius continued, "the greatest lute player in all of Tigman, and a valued friend."

Brie blushed slightly.

"Beautiful indeed," Hesih replied with a smile.

"Now, what is this about Cyres?"

"We traveled through the great wood. An unspeakable evil has run rampant. Most of the creatures are dead or dying," Atrius said.

"That has been my report as well," Hesih replied. "The Troll army has taken the wood. They will push into Tigman soon."

"We found the source of the killing in the wood," Atrius continued. "An amulet was cursed and placed into the river, killing any who drank from it. We managed to retrieve it, and sometime later destroy it."

"Good," Hesih replied with a smile.

"It came with a price," Atrius replied. "Before we could destroy it, the Trolls attacked. There were too many to hold and we became separated. One of them found the amulet and made off into the wood. Young Jadeance, second son of Taggard, made after him. A small boy, yet he runs as if he has befriended the very wind itself."

"Well, even a strong runner will never be a match for a Troll." Hesih said taking a drink. "Trolls are too fast."

"You don't know Jade," Tannis replied.

Hesih gave a slight grin. "That fast, is he?"

"Faster," Atrius replied. "He caught the Troll, but not before he had run into the midst of the army.

Cyres was fast on his heels, and managed to save his life. Noble as it was, they were both taken deep within the mountain. We have no real knowledge of where they are now."

"We must free them!" Hesih responded quickly.

"We can't cut them out of that hornets' nest," Warwick said softly. "They have escaped, and Cyres will find a way out."

"How do you know this?" Hesih asked.

"I have a certain connection with the boy," Warwick replied. "They will be alright as long as we can keep the attention of the army."

"What do you have in mind?" Hesih asked.

"We need to get through to Astrothen. The Trolls have us cut off," Atrius replied.

"Well, that is easily remedied. They have made slight attempts to get around my guard. We control the north road," Hesih said, as several large platters were brought in. "For now, let us eat and drink our fill."

"What news from Astrothen?" Samous asked.

Hesih looked slightly uncomfortable. "Not the good kind. There are troubling rumors that the King is losing control. From what I have been able to gather, the council is bidding for more and more power every day."

"The council has always been corrupt," Atrius

replied. "But what power can they have over the King?"

"Things have changed in the years you have been gone, Magistrate," Hesih replied.

"I have only been gone a few years," Atrius replied.

"No, you have been gone at least five years now," Wurwick replied.

"What can possibly go wrong in five short years?" Atrius asked, puzzled.

"More than you know," Tannis replied. "Five years ago, Jadeance spent his time running the fields of Windhold, and I had just started helping at Wagstaff, with never a thought to what lay to the north or what a Troll looked like."

"Five years ago I had a family," Brie replied softly.

"Clearly, I have taken much for granted," Atrius replied. "Whatever is going on in Astrothen, we will have to work it out when we arrive."

"Troubling times," Hesih replied, shaking his head. "You were right to go through the mountain. The Trolls completely control the north pass."

"Why haven't troops been dispatched to clear it?" Barvik asked.

"Snow is too deep," Hesih replied. "Or that's the report I got, at least."

"Hog dung," Barvik complained. "Never too

much snow to clear your own roads."

"We're not all half bear," Samous
replied mockingly

"Well, snow or not, the north pass is theirs. No
one will be going through anytime soon," Hesih said.

"Well that is another thing we'll have to deal with
when we arrive." Atrius replied.

"What about Jade?" Tannis asked. "He won't
know how to find the tunnels here, and the Trolls
will have their way blocked."

"Perhaps we can take a group of men to clear the
pass when we arrive," Atrius suggested with a light
smile. However the look on his face told all that he
didn't believe what he had just said.

"Wurwick, can't you clear the pass?" Brie asked.

"I'm afraid my power only goes so far," Wurwick
replied, looking at the small man that had been
carved into the head piece of his staff. "Do not worry
so much about young Jadeance."

"Well, can't you talk to him?" Tannis asked. "I
mean, he doesn't have to be right next to you to hear
you, does he?"

Wurwick relit his pipe. "I see where this is
going. Yes, there are several different ways of
communicating with other wizards over long
distances. Most however, require an object to channel
through. You are both missing the point. I could

run off and walk him back to Astrothen, but then how would he learn and grow? His life will be filled with great peril. Many men will be looking to him to find the way out, and if he is to have any chance of success, he needs to start in the right direction. If I came and provided him the means every time he was tested, he would inevitable fail. There will be a day when many will turn to him for answers. He will only be able to give them if he learns to think clearly in times of distress. He is far stronger than you can possibly imagine. How strong is up to him. I can tell you he has barely started to touch the fringes of what will someday be a formidable power. He will find a way back to us, and if I read the signs right, he will be the key for unlocking a great lost power."

"And if he doesn't?" Brie asked.

"We all fail," Kainan replied bluntly. "I agree with Wurwick. You underestimate him. I will do all in my power to clear the road for him when we reach Astrothen. The rest will be up to him."

"Did I miss something?" Tannis asked. "Not to be ungrateful, but why all the doomsday talk? Who is going to be looking to Jade for help? And why do we all fail if Jade fails? I think it's time you stopped lying to me."

There was a long awkward silence, finally broken by Atrius. "How much do you know about the

Karnation prophecies?"

"Never heard of it," Tannis admitted.

"Karnation was a great prophet. Many believe that he was the first to speak with the Divines. It's said the he brought their order to mankind. Whether he was the first to speak with the Divines or not, we don't really know. We do know he was the only man to have lived with the Divines. We have record of him being taken to the top of a great mountain where he lived with Thamis, himself. We don't know how long he was allowed to live with Thamis, but he was there long enough to be shown visions of the future. His writings of that time have been well preserved. It is believed that the culmination of the writings were about us, here in our day. For thousands of years, people have lived their lives without anything major happing. They were all waiting, waiting for us. In the years to come, all the powers that move and drive this great world will climax and the world as we know it will change. Excitement like this only comes around every Melina or so. Even then, to be one of the choice vessels, chosen to play an active role in the prophecy, it is very exciting."

"Are you saying that Jade is meant to do something important, something that has been prophesied for thousands of years?" Tannis asked shocked.

"You both have a role to play," Wurwick replied.

"Me and Jade? Are you sure you read that right? I mean are our names written?"

"Not in so many words, no," Atrius replied. "It's complicated."

"How complicated?" Tannis asked. "We have been taken from our home, thinking our part is to end in Astrothen."

"Things have changed slightly since we met," Atrius replied. "There is so much at stake here."

"You must understand we are not misleading you. You will have to choose your own path. A great crossroad will be placed in front of you when we reach Astrothen," Vel added. "We are merely your guides."

"Yes, listen to Vel," Kainan pleaded. "Has he ever given you reason to doubt?"

Tannis looked at the tall, silent man. Something inside him said he was being foolish, and he knew he needed to be reasonable.

"All will be made clear in Astrothen," Atrius replied.

"Yes, we'll want to make good time. Better turn in so that we can be ready at first light," Hesih replied.

"We?" Atrius asked.

"Yes, we," Hesih replied. "I can see that whatever this is, you might need me. I may still have some influence in Astrothen. Pathues will be able to handle things from here."

"Right, then," Atrius asked. "How long to reach Astrothen?"

"A week or better," Hesih replied.

"Better be off if we're going to make an early start," Kainan said, standing up.

"Right," Tannis replied looking at Brie. "It will be good to get some answers."

CHAPTER 15

ESCAPE

Jadeance sat in the dark, starring into the deep. The deep was ever pressing in, trying to crush him with its immensity; it took focus and concentration to keep in control of his emotions. If he allowed himself to drift, he found his breath coming in short gasps and his heart would start to race. Sleeping was difficult, to say the least. The most difficult part however, was that the Dwarves seemed unaffected by the pressing deep. In fact, they seemed as at home as a fish in the sea. The only thing that kept sanity within grasp was the fact that Cyres yearned for sunlight just as badly as he did. Time had lost all meaning. Jadeance had no idea whether it was night or day. He had no idea how many days he had been lost, wandering from tunnel to tunnel. At first the vast beauty of the galleries enchanted his imagination. Now the bright crystal formations stabbed painfully at his eyes. He tried to keep light in his life using his staff. Unfortunately it had pulled more than one group of wandering goblins upon them. Now he kept the light to a minimum.

Orin made his way to where Jadeance was sitting and asked, "Get any rest?"

"No, not really," Jadeance admitted. "No matter, I'll be ok."

"Not so, my young friend, you can only go for so long without sleep," Orin replied firmly.

"I'll be ok," Jadeance replied. "My staff feeds me in a way I can't really explain."

"I'm no fool," Orin said bluntly. "You're beginning to fade. You're not getting enough rest."

"I'll be able to rest when we make our way out of these caves."

"We have been approaching the surface for days now," Orin replied confidently.

"So you have said," Jadeance replied shortly. "I think you're just saying that to make me happy."

Orin smiled. "Is it working?"

"No, it's not," Jadeance grumbled.

Cyres stood up, "Let's be on the move." Orin grunted and awoke the others, and once again Jadeance was lost in thought as they moved quietly through the deep.

"Do you know where about this is leading us?"

Cyres asked

"There have been reports of cave openings in the mountains to the southeast of our own range," Grik replied. "I believe this to be one of the larger ones. Won't know until we make top side and have a look around."

"If this is one of those tunnels, what will be waiting for us?" Jadeance asked.

"Trolls most likely," Orin replied. "We had received reports of unusual Troll activity in our own range. My father did not see this as a threat. He felt that the Trolls could not gain access to our halls. I pleaded with Bolkun, my brother, to speak on my behalf to the Elders. Bolkun feels that the outside world does not affect us and should be ignored. He refused to plead on my behalf."

"Who are the Elders?" Jadeance asked curiously.

"Six Dwarves of great honor serve as my father's advisers. Unified, they have considerable pull on my father's mind. My father trusts them and their judgment." Orin replied.

"Why can't you speak to them?" Jadeance asked. "You are a prince, after all."

"A prince yes, not one bearing the birthright and therefore I have very little in the way of political influence. All that my father has is to fall to Bolkun. He and he alone can speak for our house. Only the head of each house and his eldest son may address the Elders, and even then the eldest must be of age. There are many rules involved when addressing the Court of Elders."

"I can see that," Jadeance complained. "Too many rules. Can't we get around that?"

"Tradition and honor mean more to my kind than the life blood that freely flows through our veins. That is our way," Orin replied solemnly.

"Will they not retaliate for your abduction?" Jadeance asked.

"Hard to say," Orin said as he sat back and looked into the darkness. "My brother will say I found what I went looking for."

"What do you mean?" Jadeance asked.

"One of my most trusted scouts came to me with a report of thousands of Trolls roaming our range. Bolkun denounced it as folly. Many Dwarves believe that the outside world is full of dishonor and deceit, self-righteous and foolhardy behavior, and unfit for our kind. My brother is one of the most outspoken of them. Bolkun doesn't consider them to be a threat. He doesn't believe them to have the power to take our halls. I convinced my father to allow me to take a small force and assess the danger. The Trolls fell on us in the night, while most were sleeping. Outnumbered and overwhelmed, our lookouts were killed before they were able to raise an alarm. By the time most of us realized what was happening, we had no chance. Two hundred Dwarves of honor followed me out of the halls of Zavan. Only two will return," Orin said looking broken hearted. "My brother will say I led them to defeat, maybe he is right."

"Don't be ridiculous," Jadeance scoffed. "You will return to your father and inform him they have slaughtered Dwarvin warriors, and that demands swift retribution."

"If only it were so easy," Orin replied, his face lost in sadness.

Borun approached quickly. "My lord we have reached the cave opening. It lays not two hundred paces around the bend. The way is unthinkable. I fear we have traveled in vain, for this is folly. We must return to the depths and find a smaller way out."

"Oh no, you don't," Jadeance protested. "I'm not going back inside this stupid mountain."

"How many guard the entrance?" Orin asked.

"A hundred strong," Borun replied. "They are camped in the mouth of the cave. It looks to be a way point. They have stores and weapons, and many large tents."

"Good," Cyres replied. "We need a good meal."

"A meal that you won't live to digest," Borun grated. "Big as you are even the blindest Troll archer can make you."

Cyres shrugged, "My blades are thirsty. And they have to sleep sometime."

"We must move," Borun urged. "It's only a matter of time before they smell us here."

Orin grunted, "He is right, we had better make our way back into the caves."

"No," Jadeance replied firmly. "We will walk right past them and they will never even know we were there."

"Oh, are you going to turn us into Trolls?" Orin asked with a chuckle.

"Just wait here," Jadeance replied.

"Just what are you going to do?" Cyres asked.

"I don't know, but I'm not going back. We need to get back to Tannis and Brie."

"You're being foolish," Cyres replied. "What are you going to do, kill an army? No one has that kind of power."

"I don't know what power I hold," Jadeance replied hotly. "I will find a way." With that Jadeance flew down the passage way, staff in hand. Peering around the corner, the passage way opened into a great cave, and Jadeance could see sunlight coming from the far end. The cave was filled with tents and fire pits. Shrewd fur shields and rusty mismatched swords lay strewn about. There were more Trolls than Jadeance had imagined. "What now?" he asked himself. Looking around, his mind raced from one bad idea to another. A small group of Trolls caught his attention. They seemed to be returning from patrol. Grumbling in a foul language, several of them sat on the ground and began tossing their armor about while others began cooking what looked like a fox. One of the smaller ones rested his head on his shield and fell asleep. A smile crept across Jadeance's lips. Sitting back, Jadeance smile grew bigger. "It's so simple," he told himself. Then his smile faded as he realized he had no idea how to do it. "Master I need you!" Jadeance pleaded into the depths of his mind. The staff in his hand began to tingle softly. As Jadeance watched in wonder, the tip of his staff began to shift and change, until the wonderfully carved little man that sat upon the tip of Wurwick's staff sat happily at the tip of his own staff.

"Why did you say that?" the little man asked.

Confused, Jadeance looked around and then replied, "Who are you?"

"You know who I am boy. Now, did you have a reason for bringing me here or is this a social visit?"

"But how are you...?" Jadeance wondered.

"That is not the lesson for today", Wurwick grumbled. "Why did you say that?"

"I feel overwhelmed and confused," Jadeance

replied softly. "Freedom is a few hundred yards away, and a small army stands in our way."

"But you already know what you're going to do." Wurwick replied. "So, what's so over whelming?"

"I don't think it can be done." Jadeance complained, feeling despair filling his mind.

"What is possible and impossible is completely dependent on our own mind. If you believe it, it is. If you don't, it isn't. You lack confidence boy. You have done well so far. Just because you aren't working directly with your element, doesn't mean you are any less powerful. Use your mind and heart, trust your feelings. Trust your intuition and rely on your power."

Jadeance smiled. "I seem to remember Meshire saying something like that once."

"Well, why didn't you listen to him then?" Wurwick demanded. "Look, our time is running short. You have met new friends, have you not?"

"Yes, we saved Orin and..."

"No time," Wurwick interrupted. "You must follow them to King Dimlun. There you must persuade them to send an ambassador to Astrothen. You must not fail in this. Swear to me Jadeance."

"I swear, Master. I'll bring them," Jadeance replied.

"Good, good. I'm very proud of you, my

apprentice. You will make a first rate wizard one day. That is, if you make it out of there in one piece."

Jadeance watched as the little man shimmered and faded until just the smooth tip of his staff remained. Without really thinking about it, he closed his eyes and pictured his brother's face. Holding his breath and concentrating as hard as he could, he began rubbing the end of his staff. After what seemed like an eternity he opened his eyes, and smiled. The tip of his staff now had a life-like resemblance of his brother looking up at him from a river bank. "There," Jadeance said softly. "It's easier with you here to help me." He again peered around the corner and looked at all the Trolls moving around. Gathering his energy, Jadeance closed his eyes and extended his staff. Even with his eyes closed, he could see the world as the elements began to flow and come to life. Jadeance began to pull the blue elemental lights towards the tip of his staff. With one burst of energy, the lights erupted from his staff and cascaded along the ground encompassing everything. "Sleep," Jadeance whispered over and over, as the lights flew and began to overtake the Trolls. As the Trolls were overcome, they fell hard to the ground right where they had been walking or sitting. Several were perched high atop ladders, keeping watch. Jadeance didn't bother to help them to the ground gently. In fact, he took a slight pleasure as they fell. Jadeance opened his eyes and began to walk around. With a shrug and a smile, Jadeance made his way back to where his friends were waiting for him.

"Well?" Cyres asked.

"We can go now," Jadeance replied.

"What about the Trolls?" Orin asked.

"They won't bother us," Jadeance replied, smiling at the thought of the sleeping Trolls.

"Oh, yea," Borun replied. "And why is that?"

"Because, they are all asleep," Jadeance replied with a shrug.

"Asleep?" Cyres replied. "You managed to put them all to sleep?"

"I said that I would find a way, and I did." Jadeance grunted. "Now let's be on our way."

They made their way into the cave and the Dwarves were astonished at the sight.

"Did you kill them?" Grik asked.

"No," Jadeance replied. "They are just sleeping."

"Why didn't you kill them?" Borun asked, his eyes filled with anger.

"I didn't think it was a good idea to use the elements at my control to commit mass murder," Jadeance replied a little heat.

"Murder," Borun scoffed. "They are monsters fit for death. They would not have spared you. And yet, here they are asleep before our very eyes, a chance to avenge our fallen brothers." Borun grabbed his axe and walked towards a sleeping Troll.

"No!" Jadeance yelled. "They need to live."

"If I didn't know any better, I'd think you a traitor," Borun yelled. "Sympathize with murdering Trolls."

"No," Jadeance replied. "This is clearly a way station. If the next caravan arrives and finds the place with nothing but the dead, the hills will be flowing with Trolls by nightfall. We don't want them to have any clues we were ever here at all."

"Jade is right," Cyres grunted. "If they think there may be a resistance, they will flood the surrounding hills. We'll be bogged down for weeks."

Orin grunted and agreed. "We will move through here quickly."

"No," Borun almost cried. "Go and leave them here to live?"

"We cannot make this our fight, not here," Grik replied. "Think boy, our duty is to return the prince to safety."

"And what of our fallen brothers?" Borun cried. "Brothers who fell defending the crown. Do we let them lay dead without the honor of avengement?"

"No," Orin replied. "We will visit these murdering Trolls with death. I vow to you here and now. No one will know our vengeance more firmly. I will not rest until it is done, my promise to Grungni."

"I will help you in this fight, if I have power left in me," Jadeance declared.

Borun looked at Jadeance, then to Orin. "It will be as my prince declares," Borun replied somewhat bitterly.

Orin grunted, "Let's move quickly. Grik, you and Borun visit the stores and take what we need."

"Right", Grik replied, and they shuffled off.

"Let's head to the mouth and get our bearings," Orin replied.

The sun was shining brightly, and there was a fresh snowfall. "Any idea of where we are?" Cyres asked.

Orin looked around, "No, not really. We'll head east and wait for nightfall."

"What happens at night?" Jadeance asked.

"The stars come out," Orin replied pointing to the sky.

"You know the stars so well?" Jadeance asked.

"You don't?" Orin asked back, his eye brows raised. "You will find that the stars make an excellent way to navigate this mountain range."

"I think I'll take your word for it," Jadeance replied.

Jadeance followed along quietly for the better part

of the morning until Grik called for a break.

"I need to rest for a moment," Grik said, sinking heavily into the snow.

"Hold in there, old friend," Borun replied, sitting down.

Grik grunted. "I'm not as young as I used to be."

"We could use a hot meal," Cyres said looking through a bag they had taken from the Trolls.

"Is there any meat in that sack?" Orin asked hopefully.

"Unfortunately, Trolls don't keep meat well." Cyres replied. "All we have is some roots and beans."

"That won't do," Jadeance replied. "We'll need some real food." Looking around, there were signs of animal life all around. "I'll go see what I can find. You guys wait here and get some rest."

"You can't go alone," Orin replied. "I'll go with you."

"I'll be all right," Jadeance assured him.

"Orin's right," Borun added. "You can't go by yourself. There may be Troll's moving about."

"Don't worry about me," Jadeance replied. "Besides, I can move faster alone. I won't be gone long."

"What do you mean to hunt with?" Cyres asked puzzled. "You don't have a bow."

"No, but I have my staff," Jadeance replied with a

big grin. "Get some rest. I'll be right back."

Jadeance ran off before they could reply. It felt good to run. The woods were so quiet that Jadeance felt peace for the first time in many days. The fresh snow seemed to muffle all noise. There were tracks all over but nothing seemed to be very large. "We could sure use a King boar now," Jadeance thought to himself. It had been days since they had any real meat. Although it's true you can live on roots, Jadeance knew they all needed some real food. Jadeance looked around and got an idea. Running towards a tree, he jumped and used his staff to spring himself to a low hanging branch. He then jumped and climbed up the tree. Sitting there patently, watching for something to cross his path, something small caught his eye. A squirrel jumped from one tree and seemed to float to the next. Jadeance watched this squirrel jump from tree to tree, amazed at how fast it was able to move. The morning was surreal, snow was softly falling from the trees, and the air was cold and crisp. Despite his hunger Jadeance felt calm and peaceful. Sitting there, he lost all sense of time. The forest itself seemed to be talking to him, everything coming to life all at once. Jadeance was so caught up with the beauty of the morning he nearly missed the two deer walking underneath him. Jadeance looked at them in wonder. He had never seen deer so small.

They appeared to be full grown, despite the fact that they were nearly half the size of the deer that are common to Tigman. With a shrug, Jadeance aimed his staff at the one on the left. With a searing surge both deer spun to the ground toppling head over heels. "That didn't go as planned," he thought to himself. "Now how am I going to get two deer back?" he wondered.

"Clumsy," Jadeance heard Wurwick's voice in his head.

"How did you...?" Jadeance asked.

"First things first, as my apprentice you must come to the understanding that I know everything you do."

"Do you really?" Jadeance asked.

Wurwick grunted, "I know you nearly knocked over the tree you're sitting in with that spat of clumsiness."

Jadeance could feel his temper rising, "I didn't want it to get away."

"Indeed not," Wurwick replied. "You did want to eat it when you're done right?"

"They are both perfectly edible still," Jadeance shot back.

"So they are," Wurwick replied with a deep chuckle. "Still, you need to be practicing. Concentration is just as important as strength.

You certainly have power. You need to learn some measure of control. As you make your way through the forest, seek out a single leaf, and using your mind knock it down without throwing the entire tree into the ocean."

"I'm not that bad," Jadeance complained.

"Tell that to the deer," Wurwick replied.

"How do you know I didn't mean to bring them both down?" Jadeance asked quickly. "Have you ever seen a Dwarf eat? I thought Barvik ate a lot."

"He eats more than you know. And as for the deer you wanted, it was the one on the left. Good thing for you, you missed it entirely. If you had been on target you would have most likely blown the poor thing in half. Work on it, is all I'm saying. You are growing more powerful by the day. It is not enough to use it in times of need. When you get excited, your power surges and that of course is completely normal. You are dangerous like that. Control can be difficult. For the sake of your companions you must work at it both night and day. Let all your thoughts navigate you to control. It might help if you weren't thinking of Brie all the time."

"I do not," Jadeance protested.

"You can't hide your thoughts from me," Wurwick replied with a laugh. "She is a fine girl to be sure. However, you seem to devote an unnecessary amount of your time thinking about her."

Blushing furiously, Jadeance shook his head. "Why don't you mind your own business and stay out of my head?"

"Presently, you are my business," Wurwick replied, laughing at Jadeance's frustration.

"Go away," Jadeance said aloud. Grumbling, Jadeance took out his knife and began to clean the deer. There was a fire going as Jadeance made his way back to camp. He could barely drag the two deer, and was grateful for Borun who ran up to help him.

"How in the name of Grungni did you get these?" Borun asked.

"I have my ways," Jadeance replied with a smile.

Borun looked Jadeance in the eyes for a moment. "I have underestimated you. Indeed you wield a power greater than I could have imagined. Forgive a foolish Dwarf too stubborn to see past his own pride."

"There is nothing to forgive. You have been a great companion and I will be forever grateful to call you friend," Jadeance replied clasping the Dwarf on the shoulder.

Borun grunted. "You are wrong there, and it is I that am grateful to call you friend. In fact, I can't wait to drink to your honor when we arrive at our great city. Come now, I'll take them from here."

"What are you doing?" Jadeance asked as Borun grabbed a deer in each hand.

"What?" Borun replied hefting both deer easily.

"You can carry both of them?" Jadeance asked shocked.

Borun turned, "Well," then his eyes widened and he dropped the deer. "Run! Jade, run!"

Jadeance wheeled to see two huge wolf like creatures running towards them. They were bigger than most men, long bodies covered in hair. Their teeth were huge. They had long snouts and tall ears. One was slightly smaller than the other and it was black as night. For Jadeance this moment seemed frozen in time. Jadeance recognized the creatures from Atrius's stories to be the dreaded Volkru. The moment seemed almost unreal. The snow covered ground harshly split by the deep black fur of the Volkru; far too close to have any hope of escape. Snow flew out behind the beasts, creating a thick mist. With teeth bearing, Jadeance could hear his heart beating as the Volkru lunged. Its eyes burned with an intensity that was forever burned into Jadeance's memories forever, eyes a deep yellow color that Jadeance had never before seen, almost as if it could only be a dream. Unable to move, Jadeance could only watch the Volkru as it sailed through the air. Just as Jadeance braced for impact, Borun slammed into the beast and together Dwarf and Volkru rolled through the snow. The sound of the impact snapped Jadeance back into reality. Borun rolled to his feet and gripped his axe, muttering in old Dwarvish tongue. The second Volkru which was larger than the first, and was approaching rapidly at Borun's unprotected back. It was nearly a foot taller and it had grey fur and black eyes. Just before it reached the raging Dwarf, Jadeance sent it reeling with a blast from his staff. Borun turned and threw his hand axe straight at the beast. With a rush of excitement Jadeance ducked under a slash from the Black Volkru and aimed his staff at the beast. With a growl, the Volkru sent the staff flying. Jadeance shook his hand to relieve the pain. One of the Volkru's claws had dug deep into Jadeance's flesh. In the distance, Jadeance could hear Borun cry in desperation, and then he seemed to hear a Dwarvish horn. Jadeance shook his head. The world was spinning slightly, and it was at that moment a new pain took a hold of him and he realized he was being hefted into the air by the Volkru. Its claws were digging deeply into his side. With his last deep breath, Jadeance drew his sword and with all the strength he could muster he swung at his attacker. Jadeance was shocked at how easily Tyuru bit through fur flesh and bone. Jadeance fell to the ground as he cleaved the Volkru's arm off. Jadeance sat for a moment lost in wonder. His sword looked so strange lying in the snow. The Volkru blood ran off its perfect surface, almost as if the sword rejected it for some reason Jadeance couldn't understand. The blood was soaked up by the snow, turning it to a red sludge. As Jadeance looked, he noticed that there was a great deal of red snow. Rolling over Jadeance was shocked to see the Volkru's still twitching hand clung deep inside of his side. The world was spinning; his head seemed too heavy to hold up.

"I've got you now," Cyres said as he laid Jadeance's head down.

"Cyres, the Volkru...," Jadeance began to ask, however he lost his breath.

"Hush now boy," Grik replied. "The beasts are all dead. You need to save your strength."

"The claws need to come out right now," Orin said.

"They may still have venom that hasn't been injected into the boy yet," Grik barked. "We need Nagguv."

"Nagguv was gutted buy the damn Trolls!" Borun replied.

"Yes, I was there too," Grik grunted.

"It's too late for that," Orin replied. "When he cut its hand off, the venom would have been released."

As Grik pulled the clawed hand out of Jadeance,

he began to convulse in pain. "Hold him down," Grik barked. And the old Dwarf ran off into the forest.

"What's happening to him?" Cyres shouted.

"The poison works fast," Orin replied, holding Jadeance's hands down. "We have two days to get to my father or he dies."

"Can it be done?" Cyres asked.

"Can you run for a long time?" Borun asked.

"All day, if I have a need to," Cyres replied.

"You have a need," Grik replied as he returned.

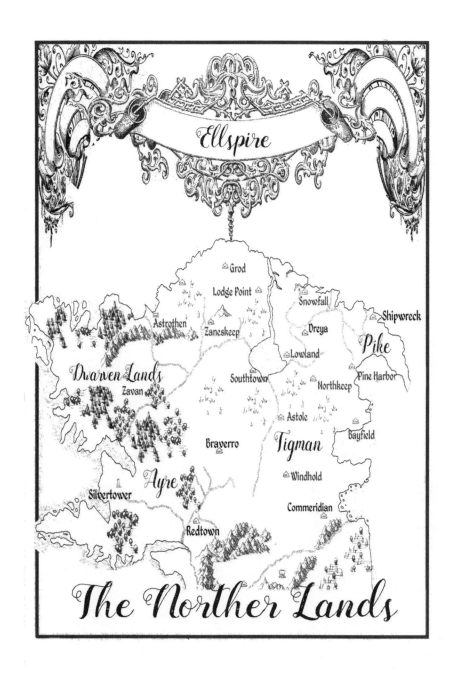

CHAPTER 16

ZAVAN

Jadeance was falling in and out of consciousness. The pain was searing and it felt like his skin was burning. Time seemed to fly and then creep. He felt as if he had been asleep for days. He had memories of Borun carrying him through the forest. Jadeance felt lost and confused as he slowly opened his eyes. He was in a strange dome shaped room, and there were small shelves cut into the room where small fires burned. The room was simple, with no bright colors and there was little in the room. Just a small table with two small yet stout chairs, and a small chest nestled into the corner. Jadeance found breathing to be difficult and his side hurt whenever he tried to move. Jadeance sat for a time wondering where he was when the door opened and a small girl entered the room. At first she seemed young, but as she approached Jadeance could tell she was older than he had thought. She had long dark hair that draped down most of her back. Her features were strange, thicker than he had ever seen before, however she was still very beautiful. She looked at him with her dark brown eyes.

"You have awakened," she said gently. "How do you feel?"

"Terrible," Jadeance replied, trying to sit up.

"Don't do that," she said as she rushed to him. "You are not strong enough to sit up yet."

"Where am I?" Jadeance asked.

"Zavan," she replied softly. "You were brought here by prince Orin nearly two weeks ago."

Jadeance grunted, "And Cyres?"

"He is here, too." She replied. "You were the only one wounded." Then her face saddened. "Well, the only one to return wounded, that is."

Jadeance closed his eyes as he teared up from pain.

"Your pain is great," she said softly. "Your wounds were deep. The poison is searing your body. I have never seen someone with wounds this grave recover. However, you are not a Dwarf and your body is fighting it in a way I have never seen before. Drink this, it will ease your pain and help you sleep."

Jadeance looked at the mug she handed him. "Haven't I slept enough?" Jadeance kidded.

"No, not yet," she replied. "This will hurt but you

must drink." She helped him into a sitting position and held him as he groaned in pain. Jadeance took a deep drink. It was awful and it made his mouth go numb almost instantly. Shaking his head, he tried to set the mug down.

"I'm sorry," she replied. "But you must drink. It won't be so bad this time. Your mouth will be mostly numb. It's best to just drink it down."

Jadeance sighed and closed his eyes as he downed the rest of his drink. Almost immediately, his eyes got foggy and the room began to spin slightly. He had a hard time focusing on the girl, then he realized he didn't ask her name. He tried to phrase, "What's your name?" as she laid him back down. However, because his mouth was numb all he managed to do was mumble incoherently and drool on himself.

She laughed as she tucked him in, "Don't try to talk." She giggled. "We will have time enough for that later." Then she stood and left as Jadeance drifted off again.

Jadeance was sitting at a table. As he looked around, he was on a granite platform in a field filled with flowers. The sun was warm and as Jadeance looked around he noticed that the platform was circular with twelve carved pillars surrounding it. Each of them had four linked faces, facing as best as Jadeance could tell, north, south, east and west. As

Jadeance looked at the face, he realized that he had seen it once before. It was the Divine Thamis.

"We meet again, my child." Jadeance turned around to see the saintly figure walking towards him.

"Have I died, my lord?" Jadeance asked.

"No, my child, you have not. You will yet see many days come and go. Far more than you might think."

As Jadeance looked at the figure, he felt a total peace come over him. "Where are we?" Jadeance asked in wonder.

"A shrine," Thamis replied, "A place where my voice may be heard by many, if they choose to listen."

"I didn't know that men were allowed to hear the Divines," Jadeance admitted.

"What are we without our children?" Thamis asked. "If you cannot hear us, then you are not listening. We speak to you in many ways. The wind whispers our names. The thunder shouts our praise. We are all around you, even when you think you are alone. I have been watching you from afar since the very day you were brought into this world."

"Why?" Jadeance asked. "What am I supposed to do?"

Thamis smiled, "You will do a great many things. You have been given a great power and it is my will that you use that power in my name to battle the evils of this world. You are growing fast and you have much to learn."

"What if I fail?" Jadeance asked.

"Many have set their hopes on you my child. Their prayers will not go unheard. As long as you strive to do what you feel is right, you have no need to worry about failure. What will be, will be. We are but vessels hoping to finish our tasks. My time grows short and I must soon depart. Know that I am well pleased with you, my son, and you will always have my love to guide you. For now, I grant you a blessing. The poison that sears in your veins is null and void. I do so to prove to all that you are my chosen vessel. Go forth and show the Dwarves around you your power."

Jadeance woke and looked around. He was still in the strange dome like room. The Dwarvin girl was sitting at the table reading from a large book.

"How are you feeling?" She asked, looking up from her book.

"Better," Jadeance replied sitting up slightly.

She smiled, "You cannot lie to your physician and hope to get away with it."

Jadeance smiled back, "Well, I am feeling a bit better."

"You will soon be strong enough to visit the sweat rooms," she replied as she poured some water into a mug."

"Sweat rooms?" Jadeance asked.

"The poison is relentless. The medicine will help, but we will have to sweat the rest out of you. It won't hurt."

Jadeance was confused but he didn't press the matter. "I meant to ask you your name the other day, however...," he began to blush.

"You're not the first one to try to speak after taking osment," she replied with a laugh. "My name is Kiasma."

"Have you decided to live yet?" Cyres asked, as he entered the room.

Jadeance tried to smile. However, he began to cough, his lungs burned and he closed his eyes.

"We can't wait any longer," a husky voice said.

Jadeance opened his eyes, and there was an older Dwarf standing in the doorway. He had a long graying beard, and a long silver robe.

"He isn't strong enough yet," Kiasma replied.

"He will have to be carried then," the old Dwarf grunted. "We are out of time. His lungs are receiving irreversible damage." The Dwarf walked up to the bed, "It time for you to join us or pass my young friend. The next two days will be very hard on you. I will provide you with the things your body needs to expel this evil from your body. The rest will be up to you. You have several friends who have volunteered to sit with you. The heat is going to get to you. Find the strength to sit it out."

Cyres looked over and smiled. "You're going to have to pull this one off Jade. I don't think Brie and Tannis will forgive me if I let you die here in this mountain."

"He is going to be fine," Bourn replied, as he entered the room. He was wearing a long robe and it appeared as if he were going to visit the bath house. "C'mon Jade, let's go." He made his way to the bed and lifted Jadeance up and carried him out of the room and down the passage way. Jadeance held his breath and closed his eyes to ward off the painful coughing fits that seemed to plague him. Suddenly the pain simply wasn't there. It took them half the morning to make their way deep inside the mountain, and Jadeance wondered at his side. He could tell the wound was healing much faster than everyone else thought. Unable to find the words to tell Bourn he was feeling better, he simply rode along the strange corridors.

Jadeance watched in wonder as guards opened a pair of massive doors and the smell of fire hit his nostrils. Jadeance had been in smithies before, but nothing he had ever seen nor heard of had prepared him for what he was now seeing. Huge double doors stood nearly fifty feet high, opened the way into a vast chamber so large that you could fit all of Wagstaff manor, the stables, bath house, and all the surrounding fields, gardens, and storehouses inside of it and still have room to spare. Along the walls, large fires burned in openings and there were hundreds of Dwarves moving around them. The sound of hammer to steel filled the air.

"This is the largest forge in the world," Bourn said as they walked through the masses. "The fires are fed by Griffbauck stone, which we mine here. It burns nearly two hundred times hotter than the coal mined and used by the elves and humans. With it, we can shape and fold metal in ways that other races can't even imagine. Here great masters are made; the best work is done to the south end of the cavern. One master will work with an entire team. The axe made for the king took nearly six months to forge, mold harden and shape. The fires run all day and night, and everything is crafted here. Tools, carts and track for the miners; armor and all sorts of weapons; anything and everything that can be dreamt up can be crafted within our halls. As you can feel, the fires create intense heat. That heat moves up the mountain to great chambers have been carved just above us."

"How do your men breathe down here?" Cyres complained.

"You get used to the heat," Bourn replied, as they started up a set of stairs.

Cyres opened a large wooden door and billows of steam erupted from the doorway. The chamber was round, with seating cut deep into the rock. The room was superheated by the fires down below, and the Dwarves had routed a slight spring into the ceiling, it was dripping all over like a slow rain. Bourn set Jadeance down, removed his robe and placed it down on the bench that had been cut out of the rock face.

"It's more comfortable this way," Bourn said sitting on his robe.

Weakly, Jadeance removed his robe and placed it on the rock. Sitting down, Jadeance was already sweating from head to toe. The air was thick, and Jadeance had a hard time breathing.

"It gets better the longer you are here," Bourn said as he sat back. "Your lungs need to adjust to all the moisture in the air."

Cyres grunted. "As much as I love sitting in a room filled with naked men, I think I'll take my leave."

Jadeance looked up.

"I'll be back," Cyres continued. "You need to stay in here for a while, so we will come and go in shifts."

As Jadeance sat back, the warmth seemed to sink deep into his very bones, and despite the discomforts of the intense heat, he felt good. Another Dwarf came in and handed him a drink.

"You must keep lots of fluids in you," Bourn told him. "We'll be sweating your poison out, and if you run out of water we'll be sitting here for nothing."

Jadeance took a deep drink from his mug and sat back and closed his eyes. The heat was searing and he lost track of time. After several hours, he opened his eyes, and Bourn was gone, and Grik was sitting there with several other Dwarves.

"Ha, he is awake! He needs water and medicine," Grik said, and he gestured to one of the younger Dwarves. He stood put his robe on and left the chamber. A moment later he returned with several large mugs. He sat them down next to Jadeance, and then returned to his seat next to Grik.

"My boy, you must drink them all down. You are too close to lose now. When we met, I had resigned myself that death was upon me, and that I had failed my King and my Prince. You saved us all with a power I had never before seen nor imagined. Take this moment and use that same power to deliver yourself."

"I am feeling much better now," Jadeance told the sweating Dwarf. "I don't think I am in any real danger anymore."

"Better to let the physicians make that decision.

For now, keep drinking and we will humor them."

Jadeance grunted, and picked up his mug and drank. This continued through the day and into the night. Jadeance opened his eyes. There was a commotion at the door. Orin walked through the door. Jadeance could barely recognize him. His beard and hair had been neatly braided and his robe was covered with golden embroidery. He was accompanied by a half dozen Dwarves who were clearly body guards. Jadeance sat up as Orin was getting situated. Jadeance couldn't believe how good he felt. His head felt clear, and his cold seemed to be gone. He looked down at his side. There were deep scars that still had the stitching holding the wounds together.

"A terrible sight," Orin said as he sat next to Jadeance. "It is clear to us all that you are very special. No one has ever recovered from such a wound. The Volkru are fearsome. In truth, Bourn's father, my uncle, was killed by one not two summers ago. That scar will be told in story and song for years. I have told my father all about you. Our travel home made for quite a telling. Cyres delivered the sacred sword and breastplate to my father. He has been given a great honor. My father is having a set of amour made just for Cyres. Our finest sword maker has agreed to forge him two new swords of a special magnificence. He will be the first human to be given a full set of armor in over a thousand years."

Jadeance smiled, "Were you able to talk to your father about the Trolls?"

Orin's face took on a look of anger. "It is still my father's position to hold fast here in our mountain." Then he shook his head, "Let's not worry about that now. Get healthy again and then we can talk."

"I wish Tannis was here," Jadeance complained.

"I am excited to meet your brother," Orin declared. "That will be a day of drink and song."

Jadeance closed his eyes, "I feel like a fool. So many people have had to care for me as if I were a cripple."

"Well, you were pretty bad off," Orin laughed. "Don't worry about it. You will find your wound will help you more than you can believe."

"Oh yea," Jadeance replied with a grunt. "Just how is my getting skewered by a giant ugly wolf a good thing?" Then he looked down at his side. "You see, I thought getting your guts pulled out was a bad thing."

Orin laughed, "You didn't have your guts pulled out, just rearranged slightly."

"Oh, you're right," Jadeance replied with heavy sarcasm. "That is much better, indeed."

"No, you must understand. Dwarves don't like

outsiders. That curse may have been a blessing in disguise. The brave young Magi saves the prince and is gravely wounded. That's the kind of thing that brings a man great honor, assuming you survive that is."

"Great," Jadeance replied. "So I did the right thing by being no match for the Volkru."

Orin shook his head, "All that matters is you live and we move forward. You still need rest. I will take my leave of you now, and we will talk again when you're well."

Jadeance leaned back and drifted off. The rest of the week came and went slowly. His recovery was considered to be a sign. Jadeance spent his days walking and stretching. Although the effects of the poison seemed to be completely gone, the wound in his side still caused him some discomfort. His strength had not yet completely returned to him. He spent the nights in his room with Kiasma, his head physician. She was only a few years older than he was and yet she seemed far older. For one thing, she had been in schooling since she was a young girl and she had proven to be very wise.

"Your strength returns," Kiasma said one morning as Jadeance was waking up.

Jadeance smiled. "Yes, I feel much better." And then he felt his side as he often did, "It still hurts a little, but I am dealing with it."

"Grandmaster Jingbuk says that your stitching worked flawlessly," Kiasma replied with a smile. "I have also been instructed to show you around a bit more today. You need to get on your feet for longer than a few minutes at a time. It is time that you gained your strength back. I have set clothes out for you."

Jadeance smiled, "Not to be offensive, however, I have a robe of my own I need to wear. It's a mark of my order, or something like that. I don't really get that into it, myself. Wurwick feels that it is important and he always seems to know when I am not doing as I should. All in all, I wear it and it is kind of growing on me."

"Are you really a slave to the tower?" Kiasma asked curiously.

"No, not a slave." Then Jadeance thought about that. "Well, I don't really know. I am supposed to call Wurwick Master. It's hard to say. I am bound to several rules, so you could say I am a slave to them and the order."

She looked concerned. "It is hard to believe someone with such power could be a slave."

"A poor choice of words," Jadeance replied. "I am bound by my beliefs. The same way a soldier is bound by his honor. I must obey my Master as he obeyed his. If I am to become something greater than I am, then I must believe in something greater than I."

"Spoken like a true man of honor," Kiasma replied with a smile. "Where would you go first?" Kiasma asked. "We have much to see."

Jadeance thought about it. "Show me your people. I have seen your great forge but I just want to see your people. We hear very little about the Dwarves and how they truly are."

"Well spoken," she replied. "I will give you a moment to change."

"No need," Jadeance replied. "Can you tell me where my staff is?"

"All your belongings are in this chest here," Kiasma said, pointing to the chest by the bed. "All but your robes, they had to be cut off you."

Jadeance grunted as he got out of bed. "No problem, I'll make due." Jadeance opened the chest and pulled his staff out. The likeness of Tannis that sat upon his staff seemed to be smiling up at him. It felt good to hold his staff after so long. He then looked down at the ragged hospital style robe he had on. Smiling, Jadeance had a thought.

"Have you ever seen Magic?" Jadeance asked Kiasma.

Her face lit up. "No. Well, I have seen the wonders of our enchanters, but they really only know a few tricks."

Jadeance smiled, "We might want to visit them, too." He laughed then, and placed the tip of his staff on his head and the cavern filled with beams of blue light. Kiasma made a shocked sound as Jadeance stood there in his Magi robes, clean and fresh as the first day Wurwick had given them to him.

"How is that possible?" she asked quietly, as she touched Jadeance's sleeve as if expecting it to be an illusion.

"I can do a great many things," Jadeance replied. "I'm supposed to practice and do more every day, for all the good that does."

"What do you mean?" Kiasma asked curiously.

"When I needed it the most, I was too slow. That Volkru knocked my staff away and nearly gutted me before I could do anything about it."

"You cut his hand off, didn't you?" Kiasma asked.

"Too little, too late, you might say," Jadeance replied gently touching his side.

"It is said that we learn the most from our failures," Kiasma said, looking at Jadeance's staff.

Jadeance smiled, "I think I have heard my uncle say something like that before."

"Will we go now?" Kiasma asked.

"Yes," Jadeance replied. "Lead on."

Jadeance followed Kiasma through hallways and

caverns. The Dwarves looked just like everyone else he had ever seen. They came and went from shop to shop. They lived in dome shaped rooms carved into the mountain. Jadeance couldn't understand their thick language. It seemed hard to pronounce and Jadeance was afraid that he would get all tongue tied if he were to attempt it. Language to the Dwarves was important and it was pointed out to Jadeance that Dwarves, like the Elves, are taught to speak many languages so to keep their honor no matter the company. The Dwarves were also master craftsmen. There were hundreds of tall pillars though out the mountain to support the different levels. So much detail went into every aspect of this city that Jadeance couldn't even imagine how long it must have taken to build it all. They went from area to area. Beautiful stones were cut into different shapes and placed in cookware, jewelry and weapons. Everywhere Jadeance went there seemed to be busy Dwarves.

"I hope you're hungry," Kiasma asked as they approached a tall set of beautifully carved heavy doors.

"I am," Jadeance replied.

Kiasma stopped and looked at Jadeance. "There are a few things I haven't told you," she said, looking up at the doors. "You have been invited to eat at my father's table. What you must understand is, you are an outsider and there are many here who...," she hesitated.

"Who what?" Jadeance asked.

"Who don't want you here." Kiasma said bluntly. "Mostly, the priests of Grungni. They believe themselves to be powerful Magicians. They say their power was given them by Grungni himself. I have never seen them do anything awe-inspiring myself, but they think of themselves as powerful and they see you to be a threat. They say you are a deceiver sent here to lead the people away from Grungni and to the heathen gods of man."

"That's ridiculous," Jadeance scoffed.

"Well, for the most part, they are nothing but ridiculous," Kiasma said, looking Jadeance in the eyes. "Please be careful. They can be dangerous and they will be attacking you with everything they can."

"I'll be careful," Jadeance promised. There was a loud crack and Jadeance turned to see the massive door swing open. Grik walked up and motioned to Jadeance. Jadeance walked up to meet Grik, with Kiasma right behind him. The King's main hall was vast, huge stone pillars stood every fifty feet or so. Jadeance looked up and couldn't even see the ceiling, the pillars disappeared into darkness. Great fires burned in huge open pits, and several large tables were set up facing towards the throne. There, at the head table, sat King Dimlun, with a huge crown upon his head. He was a solid looking Dwarf, with strong features. Deep black hair erupted from under his golden crown and his long black beard was neatly braded and held in tight with golden clips. There were several seats vacant on his table. Orin stood and smiled at Jadeance.

"Come, my friend, sit with me," Orin said, sliding the chair next to him out.

"Took you long enough," Cyres said, as Jadeance passed him. "Wait until I tell Brie about all the womanizing you have been up to."

Jadeance blushed. "I have been doing nothing like that at all! You just keep your mouth shut," Jadeance fired back.

Cyres laughed as Jadeance sat down next to Orin. Kiasma took the seat next to Jadeance and smiled at Orin.

"How are you feeling, dear Brother?" Kiasma asked.

Orin smiled, "Hungry. I thought for a moment that you had forgotten about dinner."

Two Dwarves on either side of the King stood, and the room fell silent. The King stood and spoke for a time in Dwarvesh, and then he turned and looked at Jadeance. "We welcome the powerful young Magi from the Silver Tower, sent to save our Prince."

There was a loud cheer from all the tables across the assembled hall, all the tables except one. The table closest to the King's table was full of scowling Dwarves, all wearing matching robes, a fact that was strange to Jadeance, as most Dwarves wore armor of some kind. The King raised his hands and the room fell silent. "We feast today in honor of the great Dwarves who have fallen, our friends, brothers, and fathers. May they be awaiting us in the Great Halls of Grungni, drinking and feasting. As our own feast begins, the mighty Priests of Grungni have prepared some entertainment, a demonstration of the power and might given them by Grungni, Himself." The King sat and servants brought out the biggest feast Jadeance had ever seen. There were whole pigs, platters of fried fish, and smoked venison. Barrels of fine ale were brought out and the room took on a happy atmosphere.

Jadeance head was spinning. He turned as his plate was being filled. "You didn't tell me you were Orin's sister," Jadeance said looking at Kiasma.

"Does that really matter?" she asked.

"Yes," Jadeance replied, "It does. You are a Princess, and I have not treated."

"I am a woman who needs friends," Kiasma interrupted. "Everyone wants to befriend a Princess. Not everyone wants to befriend a Healer." Kiasma looked down, "I like you, Jade, and I wanted to see how you would react to me, not my title. I'm sorry."

Jadeance took a drink of his ale. "I can understand that," he replied with a smile.

"I'm glad," Kiasma said with a smile of her own, her large eyes gave her a beauty Jadeance had never before seen.

The table of robed Dwarves had assembled in front of the other tables. They all carried long ceremonial staffs that had all sorts of hanging ordainments on them. A Dwarf with a short red beard walked forward and bowed deeply before the King.

"That's Hosbuk, the head priest of Grungni," Kiasma said. "He has evil in his heart."

"Mighty King, eat your fill, and enjoy. We will show to all true power, and prove to all that Grungni has greater power than all the Magi in the Silver Tower could ever begin to understand." The Dwarves began to beet on drums and dance, spinning their staffs as they moved. In turns, the robed Dwarves would point their staffs at the giant fire pits and they would flair and sparkle. Some of the Dwarves would reach into the fires and then remove their hands, showing all that they had not been burned.

Kiasma had a scowl on her face.

"Why so upset?" Jadeance asked. "They put on a good show."

"Are they using any real Magic to make the fire do that?" Kiasma asked.

"No," Jadeance replied. "I haven't felt any Magic at all."

Kiasma sat back, They do nothing but insult. This whole thing is a way of belittling you."

Jadeance laughed then he took another drink. "It doesn't upset me. Just enjoy the dancing."

"Too bad you're all banged up, Jade," Cyres said with a laugh. "You could show them some real acrobatics."

"Don't aggravate them, Cyres," Jadeance replied, his face taking on a frown at the thought of twisting and flipping.

"Are you an acrobat?" Kiasma asked, her eyes lighting up.

"Well, I have nimble feet," Jadeance replied. "Definitely not right now, though."

The dancing went on for the better part of an hour. The fires flared and sizzled, and the crowd cheered and laughed. The Dwarves ended by flaring all the fires and beating one loud drum beat. The King stood and cheered. The Dwarves all bowed, and the red bearded Dwarf came forward again.

"Well, how did the great Magi enjoy a show of true power?" Hosbuk asked, his eyes hard.

"Be careful," Kiasma warned quietly.

Jadeance stood, "I loved it. You all have a great talent. I'm sure Grungni is well pleased."

"Well spoken, young Magi, well-spoken indeed. It has been many generations since we have had a visitor from the Silver Tower. Tell us, can the Tower of legend compare to our great halls in any way?" Hosbuk asked with a mocking shrug.

Jadeance took a deep breath. "I have not yet had the pleasure of going to the Silver Tower, as at present I am an apprentice."

"An apprentice?" Hosbuk scoffed. "Have you any real power then? I had hoped to meet a true Magi."

Orin's face was beat red and he stood. "How dare you insult my guest in my father's hall!"

"You forget your place, Orin, second son of Dimlun. You have no place in this hall or at the great temple. Be mindful of what you do in the presence of this High Priest."

"It's all right Orin," Jadeance replied. "Great High Priest, I can assure you that I am a true Magi."

"Not possible," Hosbuk scoffed. "You are too young, and as an apprentice you do not bring the honor that others have declared you. You have no place at that seat so close to His Majesty."

"Perhaps you would care to see a demonstration?" Orin asked glaring at Hosbuk.

"If I have to remind you again that you have no

right to speak here..." Hosbuk began.

Kiasma stood, "if you dare insult my brother again, I'll have you muzzled!"

"I will forget your remarks," Hosbuk said looking at her with contempt. "As a woman, you have little experience with respecting a Priest of Grungni. Your brother has lost his honor with his army, returning defeated, and more than that he has defiled this great hall by inviting outsiders."

"Enough," the King declared. "You are High Priest. Speak so to my daughter in such a tone again, and that may change. You doubt the validity of our young Magi and his honor. Maybe you would see him in action? Will you give us a small demonstration of your power, my young Magi?"

Jadeance looked at the face of Orin, who looked as if he had been mortally injured. "I think that's a good idea," Jadeance replied with a bow. Jadeance walked around the table and stood before the King. "You seem to be fond of fire, Master Hosbuk. Not really my area of expertise, but I think I can improvise." Jadeance turned to face the King. "I am young, and I know little of the great Dwarvin song I have the pleasure of hearing in your hall. With your permission, I would like to offer you a song from my home land."

The King sat down and inclined his head. Jadeance

closed his eyes and took a deep breath. Holding his staff out in front of him, he smiled. All of the fires in the pits flared up ten feet high and turned into a deep blue color. The first thing to come from the flames was a likeness of the Dwarven solders he had seen lining the halls. They pulled large drums out of the floor and began taking a rhythm. The fires all split into two forms, a woman and a man, and together they began dancing in pairs around the hall. All the Dwarves sat in absolute wonder as the giant fire shapes danced around, rolling and flipping each other. Jadeance produced a ball of fire from his palm and sent it into the air. As it flew above their heads, it blew out in fantastic colors, relighting the fire pits. Smiling, Jadeance beckoned towards one of the giant flames and a stunning likeness of Nala emerged. She offered a slight curtsy and then began playing her lute. A song that Jadeance so loved, and it nearly brought tears of joy to his eyes. Turning, he again beckoned to a fire pit and Brie stepped out, an image of near perfection. She also took to the lute, and like they had so many times they began to play, finding a quick rhythm, their tones so closely entwined that the music carried with it an excitement. Smiling, Jadeance began to spin his staff, pointing the end to different fire couples and they instantly morphed and changed into different animals. There were deer running around being chased by flaming wolfs, and birds flew through the hall. Then Jadeance spun the tip of his staff to the floor and a bright blue light erupted from its end, flashing for a moment when the light faded. All the fires had returned to the fire pits and had returned to normal. The two likenesses of Brie and Nala bowed deeply before the King and burst into a thousand pieces, filling the room with bright sprinkles that slowly faded. Silence fell over the hall as the Dwarves sat in wonder.

"Well now, we got to see some real Magic tonight after all," Cyres said, taking a big drink.

Kiasma and Orin began to laugh. Hosbuk shot a look pure hate and rage at Jadeance. He stood and fled the hall with his followers close behind. Jadeance made his way back towards his seat.

"In all my days I have never imagined such a thing," King Dimlun said in awe. "You are truly a great Magi, as my son has said. You honor my table."

"Thank you great King, it is an honor to sit at your table," Jadeance replied, bowing deeply.

"Show off," Cyres said with a big smile.

Jadeance shrugged. "I have my moments." Then he sat heavily in his seat. His hands were shaking and his side ached. He was not strong enough to use so much Magic.

"What's wrong?" Kiasma asked.

"I may have over done myself a little bit there," Jadeance admitted.

"Are you ok?" Kiasma pressed, feeling his head.

"I just need to rest a bit," Jadeance replied taking a drink.

"Then let's get you back to bed," Kiasma replied, helping Jadeance to his feet.

"Leaving so soon?" Cyres asked.

"I may have overdone myself a bit," Jadeance replied. "I assume that you can get along without me."

Cyres smiled and looked at a fresh barrel of ale being brought in. "Oh, I think I'll make it."

Kiasma helped Jadeance down the series of hallways to his room. The pain in his side was over powering and Jadeance began to stumble. As they reached the door to Jadeance's room, Kiasma was all but carrying him. She smiled as she laid Jadeance in his bed.

"You rest now. I'll watch over you," Kiasma said sitting down.

"You don't have to sit here," Jadeance replied.

"Don't worry about me, I have my book. Sleep now, we can argue tomorrow if you like."

Jadeance closed his eyes. He felt a slight surge as if a breeze had entered the room.

"You almost broke the first and most important

rule," Wurwick's voice said, as if he were sitting right there in the room.

"What rule was that?" Jadeance asked, exhausted and confused.

"Absolutely no dying!" Wurwick replied. "You can't continue to give me scares like this. I'm not as young as I used to be."

"Oh," Jadeance replied. "It wasn't exactly my idea."

"No matter, how are you coming along?" Wurwick asked.

"I've been better," Jadeance replied. "I'll be ok as long as I can avoid any future meetings with the Volkru."

"Just avoid being skewered altogether, why don't you?" Wurwick suggested.

Jadeance shook his head, laughing slightly. "I'll remember that."

"Yes, write that down somewhere," Wurwick grunted. "Rest up and listen. Things are not good here in Astrothen. The King is weak and I fear he will topple. I have arranged a counsel to discuss the problems at hand. I need you to bring the Dwarves out of that cursed mountain. A task I feel will no doubt be complicated and possibly dangerous. You have until the New Year's celebrations in three weeks to get here. There is little time to waste."

"How am I supposed to bring the Dwarves with me?" Jadeance asked. "Most of them don't really like me."

"Well, you're going to have to make friends fast." Wurwick replied. "Everything is resting on this, boy! We must not fail. The Troll army is on the move and the Ulmichs will undoubtedly reach our shores next spring. Things are beginning to look bleak."

"I will bring them, Master," Jadeance replied. "I don't know how yet, but I will."

"I have every confidence in you, my boy. Don't keep us waiting."

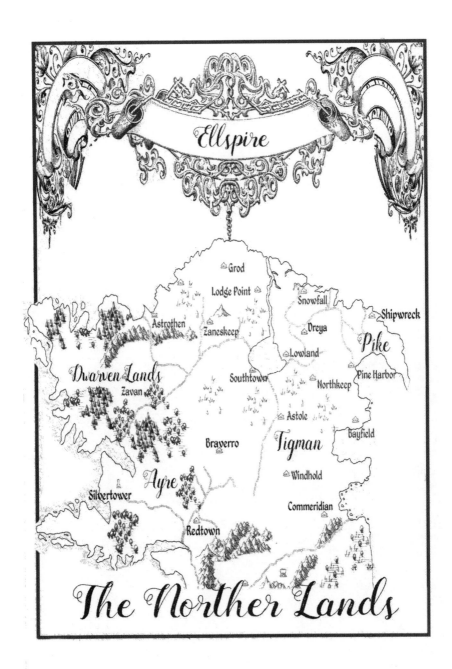

CHAPTER 17

GRUNGNI

Jadeance woke the next morning stiff and very sore. Holding his side, he sat up wincing in pain. The room was dark and quiet. Jadeance sat for a time, building up the strength to get moving. Fumbling for a moment, Jadeance found his staff and stood. "Could you give me some light?" he asked his staff. The likeness of Tannis began to glow. Jadeance made his way through the corridors and passageways quietly. Needing to think, Jadeance desperately wished he was healthy enough to go for a run. After knocking on the wrong door several times, Jadeance finally found Cyres, who didn't look very happy.

"Go back to bed Jade," Cyres said firmly.

"I can't," Jadeance replied as he slipped past Cyres and into his room.

"It's not a good morning for...," he hesitated holding his head. "Morning. Why don't we skip it and meet later, say tonight."

"Not a good morning for morning?" Jadeance laughed. "You had too much ale last night," Jadeance said, still smiling.

Cyres sat and held his head in between his hands. "Do you have to talk so loud?"

Jadeance sat in one of the small wooden chairs, grunting slightly as he felt his side. "We have to get to Astrothen by the New Year. There is going to be a great counsel and we, well I, have to bring the Dwarves or Wurwick is going to have my head."

"Bring the Dwarves to a counsel in Astrothen? And you only have three weeks?" Shaking his head, Cyres took a quick drink from a flask at his side.

"What is that?" Jadeance asked.

"You don't want to know," Cyres replied, shaking his head.

"More beer?" Jadeance asked.

"No, it's much better, or worse, depending on how you look at it. It's called white spice. It's a special Dwarvin drink. Not sure how it's made, but it is strong," Cyres said, handing the flask to Jadeance.

Jadeance took the flask and raised it to his nose.

"Don't do that!" Cyres shouted. "Don't smell it, just take a quick hit."

"Don't smell it?" Jadeance repeated with a laugh. "I don't think I want to drink something that I can't smell first."

Cyres shrugged and sat back. "You have been spoiled. Sometimes you need a good wakeup."

"I'll take your word for it," Jadeance replied, handing Cyres back the flask.

"What's your plan?" Cyres asked.

"I'm just going to ask the King to send Orin," Jadeance replied with a shrug.

Cyres walked over to the water basin and submersed his whole head.

Jadeance grabbed Cyres's shirt and tossed it to him. "We need to get moving. Put your clothes on."

Cyres groaned, "Can't you do it without me? I hear my bed calling."

"No," Jadeance replied firmly. "Let's go."

It took several minutes to get Cyres dressed and moving, and several minutes longer to locate Orin. Orin was sitting in a large room full of maps, tables, and important looking Dwarves. The walls were lined with tall bookshelves that seemed to overflow. What struck Jadeance the most was instead of colorful carpets or intricate paintings, there were assorted weapons' on the walls.

"Come in Jade," Orin bellowed warmly. "Can I offer you a drink?" Orin asked, pointing to a freshly opened keg.

"Not the time, I'm afraid." Jadeance replied. "I

have a bit of a problem," Jadeance hesitated, looking around at the assorted Dwarvin noblemen.

"Not to worry," Orin replied. "These are my clansmen. They are all of my house and will never betray any secrets offered within this room."

Jadeance nodded. "I had a vision last night. My master has beckoned me and I must return to him."

"Well," Orin replied with a smile, "Sad news for sure, but hardly a problem."

"I'm not done yet," Jadeance continued. "There will be a Great War Council in Astrothen. It will take place after the New Year celebrations, and it is meant to be a multinational conference. I have been tasked with bringing a Dwarvin representative from your father."

"Well now," Orin replied sitting back in his chair. "You do have a problem then, don't you."

"Will your father be willing to send someone to at least listen to what is said?" Jadeance asked.

"I doubt it," Orin replied. "And you are really asking for an ambassador, not a scribe. I can't see any member of the Great Council volunteering to travel so far from the King, not to mention the fact that most of them feel that men and Elves are inferior and not to be associated with."

"Well, I kind of had someone in mind," Jadeance replied with a slight smile.

"Did you now?" Orin replied, his smile fading from his face. "And here I thought this was a social call. I suppose I owe you though, don't I."

"You have shown me your home," Jadeance replied. "It would be nice to show you mine."

"You don't hail from Astrothen," Orin replied. "I thought you were from a small village in Tigman."

"I am," Jadeance replied, "but my father and mother were both from Astrothen, and so in a way it is my home. I am excited to see it, to be honest."

"My father will be in council until this afternoon," Orin replied. "Cyres, what is wrong with you?"

Cyres groaned and took a drink from his flask.

"Our good friend Cyres had a little too much to drink last night," Jadeance replied with a laugh. "He is feeling a little delicate this morning."

Orin began to laugh. "We have a way of fixing that here. Come on, let's go."

"Go?" Jadeance asked. "Where are we going?"

"To see Nogg," Orin replied.

"Who is Nogg?" Jadeance asked as he followed Orin into the passage way.

"Nogg is a bit of loon if you must know. He makes potions and whatnot. Grinds the rocks we find into powders, and mixes them in beer. He tries to get us to taste them and see if they work. I don't buy into it most the time, but he does have a way of making a headache go away."

Nogg was short, even for a Dwarf. His black beard was singed and matted, and he walked with a slight limp.

"Who are the outsiders?" Nogg asked Orin as they entered a somewhat smelly chamber. There were rock piles everywhere. Small workbenches were filled with small pots and assorted mortars.

"Friends," Orin replied. "We have need of your services."

"Obviously, everyone is in need of my services. I am the bitter glue holding sanity to our great halls."

"Not sure I would have put it that way," Orin replied glancing around.

"Well, are you going to stand there all day or are you going to tell me what the problem is? Has someone been poisoned? A fresh battle wound perhaps? Or have you..."

"It's a drinking situation," Orin interrupted. "Our friend here tried to consume several full barrels by himself last night."

"Did you now?" Nogg asked, interested. "Did you do it? You know I can make you a drink that will completely cure of the effects of beer."

"And with only minor side effects, I'll wager," Orin replied sitting down.

Nogg scowled in Orin's direction. "I'll have

you know some don't believe my gifts are entirely helpful," Nogg said as he pulled a chair over for Cyres. "I have a cure for every major ailment known. Sore muscles, the inability to sleep, maybe you need help with a certain lady in your life?"

"Let's stick to making him feel better," Jadeance suggested. "I don't think you are entirely prepared for the affect Cyres will have on the ladies around here. He tends to get around a bit."

"If you're done being useless, where is the rock I need to eat?" Cyres asked irritably.

Nogg shook his head and began to mumble in Dwarvish. "Drink this," he replied handing Cyres a small cup.

Cyres took a drink, and became violently sick all over the floor.

"Fascinating," Nogg replied casually, observing the heaving Cyres.

"What have you given him?" Orin asked shocked.

"Don't rightly know." Nogg admitted. "Must have been Hyncll." Nogg wandered to the far side of his little study and opened a new jar. "Red", Nogg marveled. "I thought it was red all along."

"Are you crazy?" Jadeance asked. "You could have just poisoned him and you're not sure what it is you're doing?"

"Well now, there's some gratitude for ya," Nogg

complained as he mixed the new powder into a cup. "This is a science, far too complicated for the likes of a young human boy to understand. Your friend here will be just fine." He walked back over to Cyres. "Sorry about that, my mistake entirely. You will want to pee as soon as you can and try to avoid apples."

"What the name of the twelve Divines is wrong with you?" Cyres grated.

"Me?" Nogg replied in a shocked voice. "I'm not the one vomiting all over my floors. Now no more nonsense, drink this."

"No way," Cyres replied pushing the cup back. "You first."

"Well that's some way to treat your physician," Nogg growled.

"You are no physician," Orin replied.

"Well now, did you come to me for healing or not?" Nogg asked pointedly.

"Yes, but you made him worse," Jadeance pointed out. "I have never had a physician make me worse."

"Well, you have been seeing the wrong kinds of physicians then," Nogg barked. "Science is a graceful balance of victories and failures. It is what we take from them that are important."

"And Cyres learned not to drink anything that you hand him," Jadeance laughed.

Nogg grunted and took a slight sip. "See, I'm not

dead. Your turn."

Cyres didn't look too convinced but he slowly drained the cup. It was a strange thing to witness. Cyres paled, his pupils grew and expanded, and then they slowly shrank back to normal.

"How do you feel now?" Nogg asked.

"I can't believe it," Cyres replied looking around.

"We have much to gain from the earth that the Divines have provided," Nogg replied with a smirk.

"Well, that was more fun than I thought it was going to be," Jadeance replied with a laugh. "But now it stinks in here. I say we be on our way."

"Oh, and leave me with a mess?" Nogg complained.

"I'll have it taken care of," Orin replied.

"Oh, and there is the cure. I'll make it easy and go half on the first one," Nogg replied with a smile.

"You don't think I'm going to pay you for poisoning the man, do you?" Orin demanded. "I'll be honest, I wasn't planning on paying you at all. It's bad business to poison the men I bring you to cure."

"Well, that is just the kind of thing I could expect of you," Nogg flared. "I demand fair compensation. You royal types are always trying to leave without paying your bills."

"I pay my way," Orin replied. "You need to keep in better practice if you expect me to pay you."

"This isn't over yet," Nogg growled.

"Would you like to clean your floors yourself?" Orin asked.

Nogg lowered his eyebrows. "No."

"Then I would just go have a drink and forget it," Orin replied as he led the way back to the great hall.

Jadeance followed Orin down one corridor after another. "Is it much farther?" Jadeance asked holding his side.

"Are you hurt?" Orin asked looking at Jadeance. "Why didn't you say something? Nogg may have had something to help."

"He didn't look too happy as we were leaving," Jadeance replied looking at Cyres. "Besides I don't enjoy being poisoned."

"Have you ever been poisoned?" Cyres asked with a smile.

"Oh yes, Brie is a fine cook. Nala however had a hard time learning the finer points and we had to put on a good face more than once." Jadeance hadn't thought of home in a while and his performance and the memory of Nala made him desperately homesick.

"It's not much farther," Orin replied. "Are you sure you're strong enough to do this today? We can speak to my father tomorrow."

"No," Jadeance replied. "It has to be today. Maybe we can get a bit of breakfast when we arrive, and it might help give me some strength."

"There you are, Great Prince," Grik said as they entered the massive great hall. "We need to talk."

"What is going on?" Orin asked as they made their way to a bench.

"Hosbuk and his priests are causing trouble, and lots of it. It feels like some bad things might happen if we don't get Jade and Cyres out of here and soon."

"Are they serious?" Orin asked.

"It seems like they have lost their greedy little heads," Grik replied. "I smell blood on the air. Something tells me something big is about to happen."

Orin looked around. "I think you're more right than you know. Gather your best men together and do it quietly. I want to have some dependable help in here tonight."

"What's going on?" Grik asked bluntly.

"I think I'm going to be leaving with Jade tonight. He has to get to Astrothen by the New Year," Orin said quietly.

"Looks like I'll be gathering more men than I thought," Grik replied getting up.

"Absolutely not," Orin replied. "I'm not taking an army to Astrothen. This must be low key."

"I'm not going to let you go alone," Grik replied stubbornly.

"Gather you're best and brightest," Orin said, looking down the table to Jadeance. "We follow Jade. Get ready, but keep it quiet."

"Right," Grik replied, and he made his way back down the hall.

"Have you given any thought as to a grand plan?" Cyres asked Jadeance.

Jadeance sat back, holding his side. "Not really, no. I'm afraid whatever I do I'll have to do it without any Magic. I won't be able to handle much."

"You're going to need a plan and it had better be a good one," Orin said seriously. "No King has sent an ambassador of any kind out of these halls in over a thousand years. I don't see this going your way, I'm afraid."

"It will be fine," Jadeance replied draining his mug.

"Just like that?" Cyres said with a laugh. "I think you're going to get turned into a frog when you tell Wurwick you didn't bring what he wanted."

"Magi don't turn people into toads or frogs." Jadeance replied shaking his head.

"Now you even sound like Wurwick." Cyres replied with a disapproving frown. "I thought it would take longer than that to drain all the fun from your soul."

"Orin!" Kiasma shouted. Jadeance turned to see Kiasma entering the great hall, and her face looked as if she were about to go to war. She began to berate him in Dwarvish. Orin tried helplessly to plead his case. Jadeance had a bad feeling that he was at the center of her anger.

"Is there something I can do to help?" Jadeance offered quietly.

Kiasma turned on Jadeance, her eyes hard as stones. "I haven't gotten to you yet," she flared. "You have got some gall if you think you're going to go off and leave me here, and I have to find out by cornering poor Bourn. I can't believe you two."

"Listen here Kiasma," Orin growled. "You have no place out there, this might be dangerous."

Kiasma spun like a snake ready to strike. "I can take care of myself, thank you! I'm going with you and if you think you can stop me..."

"Alright," Jadeance interrupted. "It has been my experience not to argue with a woman when she has her mind made up. You can come as long as you get your father's blessing."

"Are you getting his blessing?" she shot back, her eyebrows raised.

"I'm working on it," Jadeance complained.

"And if he refuses?" Kiasma asked.

"I haven't worked that part out yet," Jadeance confessed.

"If you go, I go," Kiasma replied stubbornly. "I

won't be left here like some child as you and my brother run off to have some great adventure."

"Orin is right. I don't know what will happen when we reach Astrothen. For me, I hope I can finally return home and tell my Aunt and Uncle that I won't be able to stay. They don't know that I have become an apprentice to Wurwick."

"I don't care what we find. You will need someone to set a good example. You will need me."

A pair of Dwarvin solders approached and bowed before Orin. "Great King Dimlun requests your presence at his table for this morning's feast. Your friends are invited as well."

Orin nodded and motioned to a sentry, who hurried over and bowed before Orin.

"What is your name solder?" Orin asked.

"Dofri, my Prince."

"Can I count on you Dofri?" Orin asked directly.

"Yes my Prince," Dofri replied, banging his fist to his armored chest.

"I need you to find Lord Grik as soon as possible. I need you to tell him that it's time. He will understand the meaning of the message."

"Yes, my Prince," Dofri replied as he rose.

"Dofri, it is important that you reach him and that you tell no one else that I need him. Avoid the Priests as if they have the plague. Do you understand?"

"Your will be done, my Prince," Dofri replied with a bow.

"Have you given him enough time to gather your men?" Cyres asked. "If we have to fight our way out of here tonight I would like some help."

"I hope so," Orin replied. "Grik has never failed me. We will be ok."

They followed Orin towards the King's throne room. Jadeance was struck by the vastness of the palace. The floor was a polished stone Jadeance didn't recognize, and the carving on all the giant pillars was almost lifelike.

"Orin," Jadeance asked, "How long did it take to carve this place out? Well, I mean, how long."

"It was nearly a thousand years in the making," Orin interrupted. "In truth, there is still work being done today. New halls are always under construction." They stopped in front of the King and Orin bowed deeply, "Father, young master Jadeance wishes to speak with you, if you will hear him."

King Dimlun sat up in his chair. "I will hear the boy after our feast. Now, we must eat and drink and give thanks to our fathers and our father's fathers! Thanks to Grungni, for the bounty of this feast!" Jadeance sat in between Orin and Kiasma. Cyres sat to the other side of Orin at the end of the table. There was a commotion and a cheerful atmosphere as large platters of food were brought in.

"Can we make it to Astrothen by the New Year?" Jadeance asked Orin.

"It will be tight," Orin replied. "The caverns under the mountain are extensive. We are still finding new ones. Grik will know which tunnels to take."

Jadeance groaned. "Do we have to travel under the mountain? I think I have had my share of caverns for a life time."

"It would take a month or more to go over the mountain," Orin replied. "We simply don't have time."

"Jade, I am so excited to meet your brother and sister," Kiasma said as she reached for her drink. "I'll be the first Dwarvin princess to ever leave Glorak-Arkul.

Jadeance choked on his ale, a multitude of questions coming quickly to mind. Coughing for a moment he cleared his throat. "The first one ever? Your father isn't going to let you leave, is he?"

"I'll be just fine, you will see," Kiasma replied with a smile.

"Kiasma," Jadeance said carefully. "I don't have any sisters. I have my brother Tannis, and my two cousins Nala and Saue. Brie is well," he hesitated. "She is complicated."

"Is she your betrothed?" Kiasma asked.

"Well no, she isn't," Jadeance replied.

"Does she love you?" Kiasma asked.

"Well, I think so," Jadeance replied. "But I guess you really never know, do you?"

"Men can be so impossible," Kiasma smiled. "Do you love her?"

"Well," Jadeance replied a little embarrassed.

"Stop playing," Kiasma chided. "She isn't here to hear you, so you can say it without any worries."

"It isn't that simple," Jadeance replied.

"Yes it is," Kiasma replied firmly. "Either you love her or you don't."

"Well if you put so bluntly," Jadeance said blushing, "I do love her. She is not like other girls."

"Was that so hard to say?" Kiasma asked, her eyes filled with curiosity.

"Well yes, you see I, well, I have this apprenticeship and..."

"Love holds many mysteries," Kiasma replied with a smile.

"Can we talk about something else?" Jadeance asked. "You said that you would be the first Dwarvin princess to leave Glorak-Arkul. I thought we were in Zavan."

"We are," She replied with a smile. "Glorak-Arkul is the palace that is the center of life in Zavan."

"Oh," Jadeance replied. Then, still feeling slightly

awkward he leaned in. "I hope I haven't upset you, but let's keep this whole love talk between us. I have to keep my head about me long enough to get to Astrothen."

"I will keep you in good working order," Kiasma replied with a smile.

"What about you?" Jadeance asked. "Do you have to marry a prince?"

"It is also complicated. A Dwarf's family has a lot to do with who you marry."

Grik made his way towards the table and nodded to Orin.

"Was that a good nod?" Cyres asked.

Orin smiled and drained his mug. "Grik has the men ready. He never fails to amaze me."

"Eat up boys, it may be a while before we eat good again." Cyres said as he hefted a huge portion of bear onto his plate. "Do we have a fresh barrel to open?"

Orin laughed, "No self-respecting Dwarf runs out of ale!"

"Orin!" The king bellowed. "Present your Magi before me. I am now ready to hear him."

"Good luck," Kiasma said, kissing Jadeance on the cheek.

Orin and Jadeance stood. The pain in Jadeance's side was nearly unbearable.

"Are you alright?" Orin asked.

"I'll be fine," Jadeance said holding his side. "I seem to be getting worse."

"Great King, may I present you master Jadeance, the great Magi that you have yourself beheld," Orin said, bowing before the King.

"I welcome you, young Magi. I see you have been enjoying the comforts of my hall. Let it be said that there is no limits to Dwarvin hospitality."

Jadeance took a deep breath, "I thank you for your hospitality. You have lent me your food, your physicians, and the love of your halls. I am truly in your debt. My Master has given me a message for you, and it is at his will that I beg your assistance. As you well know, there is a great disturbance in your woods. The Trolls are in an uproar and moving north. There are things in motion that I won't pretend to understand. The Great Council of Wizards has called a council of men and elves at my ancestral home of Astrothen. It is their hope that together we can discover what has caused this disturbance and heal it. We have been a divided people for eons. Yet I have discovered the great power and wonders of the Dwarvin people. I ask you to share that power with my people, to help us solve this problem that affects all of our lands. Your great son, Prince Orin, has proven to be a great face for the Dwarvin people, and a clear choice to be your voice before my Master. This council will have representation from most of the free peoples of our world. It is to be held just after the great New Year celebrations. I feel this to be a great opportunity to bring our peoples closer together and to begin healing the rift that has torn us apart for so long."

"This is a great thing you ask of me," King Dimlun replied gravely. "It has been the will of my fathers to keep our ways secret. Here we have kept our ways secret and secure for many generations. To send Orin to your Master could endanger the ideals that have kept this hall for near a Melina."

"Times are troubling to be sure," Jadeance replied carefully. "The things that are now in motion are far too important to be left to chance. This has already claimed many Dwarvin lives. You yourself sit atop a Council of your most trusted, to gain knowledge. Why then not lend some of your best to this one? We can learn from you and you will have the opportunity to learn from us."

King Dimlun sat back and looked around for a moment. "There is wisdom in your words, yet I feel this darkness will have a hard time reaching us here in this hall."

"That is true great King. However if that is true, that means you have sat back and watched as the free world falls. If it were your kingdom at the forefront, wouldn't you have wanted your neighbors to come to your aid? And if it does reach your door and all has been lost, what hope have you?"

"Father, if I may?" Orin asked.

"What have you to say on this?" King Dimlun asked.

"My men were taken and woefully slaughtered. I was tortured for many days. I feel as if I am already a part of this. Let me go and hear what they have to say."

The King sat silent for a moment, and Jadeance felt as if he was going to grin when there was a rush of commotion at the door as the priests of Grungni reentered the great hall. Hosbuk made his way to the King's table.

"Great King, I am little more than a humble servant," Hosbuk said with a great bow. "A servant of Grungni knows little of what it takes to run a kingdom, and I would never presume to tell you how to run your kingdom. However, I have been given the responsibility of maintaining the sanctity of these halls. I have not been given this responsibility lightly, and I won't pretend to fully understand the will of Grungni, but I have been given this ring of power to guide me." Hosbuk held his hand high to display the ring. "The ring has come to life, and its power has enlightened me. By the power granted me by Grungni himself, I declare these outsiders have poisoned the holiness and sanctity of our sacred halls. They have been allowed to move about freely, filling our halls with their stink. What will we have next? Elves? Trolls? We have to take a stand now." There was another large commotion and two lines of armed Dwarves marched into the throne room. They all wore the same emblems the priests wore on their robes. "Our halls need to be cleansed, and I demand retribution! They call for us to leave our halls! All they want is our blood to cleanse their lands!"

"I will not stand for this!" Orin declared.

Hosbuk pointed to Jadeance who was visibly shaking. "Take him."

"Yea, that's going to happen," Cyres said as he stood and drew his twin swords.

The priest's guards drew their weapons and began to fan out, as there was a rush of feet as Borun led a party of armed Dwarves in a side entrance. Borun and his guards took positions between Jadeance, and Hosbuk and his guards.

"What is the meaning of this?" Hosbuk demanded.

Orin stepped forward. "I brought him here, and he is under my personal protection."

"You dare to stand in my way? Dare to interfere with the will of Grungni? You who have lost your honor! You have no place in this hall! You have no place before me!" Hosbuk bellowed, his face beat red with anger.

"Bite your tongue!" Orin declared. "I was born on high, a Prince of Glorak-Arkul. I was taken, and I tell you now that I kept my honor as it was tested by the hands of my torturers! You will not take the means of my survival to your dungeons. If it is the will of Grungni that he leaves our great hall, which I doubt, then I will lead him safely to the outskirts of our lands and you will have no claim to him."

Hosbuk looked as if he had been mortally offended. Just before he could speak, there was a great rumble from deep within the mountain. The entire hall began to illuminate and great silver sparkles started to materialize, coming from the walls, the fire pits, and even the food on the tables.

"Jade?" Cyres asked concerned.

"It's not me," Jadeance replied, baffled by the beauty of the lights.

The lights all began to flow together. With a flash of light, the sparkles were gone and the timeless shape of Grungni stood before them. His face was flawless. He bore a light brown beard that reflected the light as he moved his head, as if his beard had thousands of sparkling diamonds woven in rows. Instead of armor, he had a thick golden robe that hung to the floor.

"Let your weapons rest this day, Lord Orin, son of Dimlun, of whom I am well pleased. Know this, I have a great plan for you and I will guide you and bless your companions, and curse your enemies as long as your heart and your prayers are ever in my name."

Orin fell on his face. "Thank you, my lord. I shall serve you until the end of my days," Orin declared.

"I have no doubt of this my son." Grungni replied with a smile. Then Grungni turned to face the shocked Hosbuk. "Of thee I am not well pleased. You have sought not but power and material gain with your calling. Your thoughts only dwell on how you might gain an advantage over your brothers. This is not my will. What have you done to help your people? Seeking to undermine the crown, do you not know that I bless the crown and the Priest? Know this, my brother has set this young Magi aside for a task, and any who would stand in his path need fear the wrath of both Thamis and Grungni. As for you, you have defiled the ring that was given you. Efi, step forward." A red headed Dwarf slowly made his way up towards Grungni.

"Yes, great lord?" Efi asked as he bowed.

"Will you pledge your life to me? Serve me and my children with all your power until the end of your days?"

"I will serve you with all my heart!" Efi declared.

"Then rise and go forth to my temple and clean it of the filth. Cast out any who would serve themselves, and fill it with humble servants."

Efi rose and looked at himself completely amazed. All his clothes had changed to the same style robes Hosbuk had worn, and on his finger was the ring that Hosbuk had worn. Hosbuk, who was now dressed in plain robes, looked as if he were a man on the headman's block.

"And what of me great master?" Hosbuk pleaded, sinking to his knees. "Don't cast me out, I can serve you still!"

"You have made this life of your own. You stopped serving me many years ago. It is my will that you are to be forbidden in my house. If you can prove to be a humble servant, you may yet prove to be useful." Then he turned to Jadeance. "You have had a long road that has not been of your choosing. You, like your father, have been chosen. Go your way with my blessing. Know that I, like my brother, am well pleased and you may draw strength from my sacred hall and places of worship. Go now! Take your path and prepare your soul for what must come to pass."

"What is that my lord?" Jadeance asked.

"This I cannot say, for it has not been set. Know that you will shape the world of tomorrow, just as the

Masters of my halls shape cold steel."

There was a great burst of light as the shape of Grungni burst back into thousands of tiny sparkles, falling about the great hall like the fiery sky at night. The hall was silent for a time as everyone took a moment to take in the feeling of what had just happened.

"Have you ever felt anything like that before?" Cyres asked quietly.

"Not in my lifetime," Orin replied as he rose to his feet. "Guards, will you remove this vile blasphemer from my sight," Orin said, pointing at the enraged Hosbuk. "He is unfit to stand in my father's presence."

"You haven't seen the last of me, Orin!" Hosbuk shouted, as two Dwarvin guards hauled him away.

"I see now that this is beyond me," King Dimlun said gravely, looking down at Orin. "It may be that this day will be remembered in song for generations. As for you, my son, you have my blessing. Take what men you need and make way. See that our people are not misrepresented."

Orin bowed deeply. "I will not fail you."

"Father," Kiasma said as she approached. "I too will travel with the Magi."

Dimlun took a deep sigh, "In a dream, I beheld you atop a white tower in the midst of the moonlight.

On your right stood a rose, a single solitary rose, a deep crimson such as I have never before beheld; To your left stood a great thorn, burnt and decayed. I have feared this now for many nights, yet I know not its meaning. Young Magi, might I ask a boon of you?"

Jadeance was having a hard time focusing. He had not expected to be hailed by one of the great Divines. More than that, as soon as Grungni gave him his blessing, he had felt completely healed. In fact, he had never felt better in his life. Jadeance shook his head and took a deep breath. "Anything, Great King."

"Will you use your not inconsiderable power to keep my children safe?"

"Father, I am not the young Dwarf of sixty anymore!" Orin flared.

"You are still my child, and as King of this land all who dwell and call Zavan home are also my children."

"I will guard them with my life." Jadeance declared.

"Then go, and take my blessing with you."

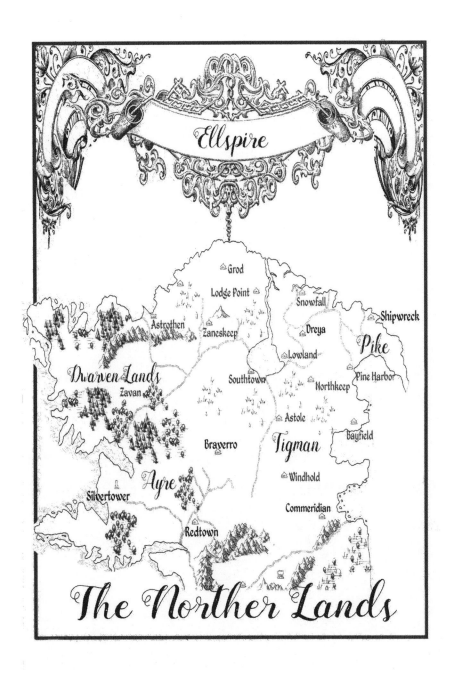

CHAPTER 18

ASTROTHEN

Tannis walked silently behind Brie. It had stopped snowing and the sky was clear. He had been in a somber mood since they had left Zane's Keep. The thought that he might have to take part in some strange prophesy scared him. He felt as if he may never see Wagstaff again.

"Why so somber?" Brie asked.

"I like being a bartender," Tannis replied. "I don't want to have any more adventures. That has always been Jade's dream, not mine."

"It will be all right," Brie said. "They say we'll reach Astrothen tomorrow."

"We'll see, I guess." Tannis shrugged. "Do you think we'll see Jade soon?"

"I hope so," Brie replied. "He needs me."

Tannis laughed, "I suppose so. I can't wait to hear his story. Of course he is going to embellish, Jade is never outdone."

"I miss him," Brie replied, "stories and all."

Kainan called a halt. "Let's stop here."

"Well reach Astrothen by high noon tomorrow," Hesih replied, sinking to the ground.

"Good," grumbled Wurwick. "I'm almost out of pipe weed."

"Can't you just wiggle your finger and fill your pot?" Samous asked as he rummaged through his pack.

Wurwick grunted, "Samous, a wizard doesn't wiggle anything. We use our connection with the elements that surround and bind us and this planet together to alter this reality as we know and see it. I pray this small bit of enlightenment may help you to stop saying the most ridiculous things imaginable. As for the pipe weed, I could of course create some but it is never as good as the real thing. It's a complicated bit."

"Oh," Samous replied with a smile. "Now I can see where I have been wrong all this time. It's the elements that wiggle their fingers to make stuff."

Wurwick took his pipe out of his mouth and pointed it at Samous. "Perhaps you would understand it a little better if you had a demonstration."

"Actually, I think I don't really care how it works," Samous replied quickly. Then Samous looked at the fire. "Looks like we are getting low on wood. I think I'll go find us some more."

Barvik began to laugh as Samous jumped up and hurried off into the woods.

"That little thief is going to be the death of me," Wurwick growled.

"Now you two," Atrius said, sitting down next to Tannis. "I think I have had more than enough doom and gloom. Astrothen is one of the oldest cities in the world. As such, it is large and beautiful. Stop worrying about what might or might not happen. It is time to trust in the Divines. They will help you on your path. It is up to us to turn to them. This is far greater than any of us. You should be feeling a great excitement. We will be in Astrothen for the New Year, and there is always a great celebration. And this year will be no exception."

"Atrius, the New Year is still a month away," Tannis replied. "Hardly time to get excited about it."

"If it will take your minds off your troubles, it is." Atrius replied with a smile. Then his face got serious. "Tannis, there is something else that has been troubling me. I know you bonded well with Cyres. But you have been slacking off on your training, and I have a feeling that you will need that more often than you might think. Kainan will help you, and that is a great honor. Men that have trained for years have paid greatly for the opportunity to train under him. Also, training will keep your mind focused."

"Alright Atrius." Tannis replied. "I'll go talk to Kainan."

There was a sudden flash of light? and then two men approached the encampment. Barvik jumped to his feet and drew his great axe.

"Hold your might, great Barvik," one of the men said aloud. Tannis could tell that the men were wizards due to the staffs that they carried.

"Sit down Barvik," Wurwick barked. "They are from the Silver Circle."

"How did you find us?" Kainan asked as he sat down next to Brie.

One of the men smiled. "In our travel form, you are easy to spot," one of the men replied.

"And what is your travel from?" Brie asked curiously.

The wizard smiled as he sat. "We travel as spotted falcons. It's hard to hide from a falcon."

"You can fly!" Brie exclaimed.

"We can do a great many things," The wizard replied.

"I'm not as concerned with how you found us, more why you did," Wurwick replied.

"We have been sent by the Circle to inform you that there is to be a Great Council of Men, Wizards,

Elves and Dwarves. It is to be held on the first day of the New Year in Astrothen. We will discuss how the conflict that faces us all will be dealt with."

"You are planning to gather the Elves and Dwarves in only a month?" Hesih replied shocked. "It cannot be done."

"Much must be done if we are to survive the years ahead," the wizard replied. "The evil that thrusts its will upon us is growing by the day. We will be no match for them if we do not do the same. We have everything in motion, everything but the Dwarves."

"The Dwarves haven't come out of their mountain in eons," Atrius replied. "In fact, they have been gone for so long that there is some debate as to their appearance. Some say they are small as frogs, others that they are quite large."

"They are not large," Wurwick replied. "About waist high is all, however they are incredibly strong. They can lift great weights, run long distances if they feel so inclined, albeit they don't get anywhere very fast. Short legs you understand."

"Have you met a Dwarf?" Atrius asked.

"Many years ago," Wurwick replied. "I'd say near five hundred years or so ago."

Tannis looked at the old man, shocked. "How old are you?"

"Old enough," Wurwick replied. "How old,

I couldn't say. I stopped counting a thousand years ago."

"Master Wurwick is known as a Zeta," the Wizard replied. "There have only been ten that we know of. They have the ability to connect themselves with the elements in a way that seems to prolong their life. It is said that only the most powerful of Wizards can do this. Currently there are only three in the world, and we only know where two of them are."

"I'm right here," Wurwick replied. "Now, what of the Dwarves?"

"We want your new apprentice to bring them to the Council." the wizard replied.

"Jade?" Brie asked. "How is Jade going to do that?"

"Apprentice Jadeance is in the Palace of Glorak–Arkul, in the keeping of Prince Orin himself."

"How?" Brie began, however she was cut short.

"Our time is spent," the wizard interrupted. "Relay the message and make haste to Astrothen. Many dangers lie in this forest." With that, the two stood and walked off.

"What do you make of that?" Atrius asked. "If young Jade can manage to bring the Dwarves out of that mountain it will be a momentous occasion."

"Can he do it?" Kainan asked.

Wurwick smiled. "I think it will be a good test

for the boy."

"How did Jade get to...," then Brie hesitated, "Where is he?"

"Glorak-Arkul," Wurwick replied. "It's the palace in Zavan, the greatest of the Dwarvin cities. It's the ancestral home of the Dwarvin royalty."

"Jade is with the Dwarves?" Tannis began to laugh. "He has always wanted to visit the far places of the world. I guess now he has. But how are we going to tell him?"

"I'll take care of that," Wurwick replied.

"Are you going to turn into a spotted pigeon and fly off to the great Dwarvin city?" Samous laughed.

Wurwick looked at Samous for a moment, and then he smiled. "No I think I'll send you instead."

Samous took a step back. "What? How, I mean no thank you."

"Don't you want to fly?" Brie teased.

Samous scurried back into the forest for another load of firewood.

Barvik was laughing and pounding his knee. "That little fool will have to cut down this entire forest before he learns to keep his mouth shut."

"How will you tell the boy?" Atrius asked.

"I have my ways," Wurwick replied with a smile.

"Well for now we need to get our plans straight," Kainan said. "We need some food and camp set."

"I'll find us something to eat," Tannis said, standing up.

"Good," Kainan replied. "Vel, go with him."

"I'll find some roots to stretch it," Brie said also standing up.

"What is your plan?" Vel asked Tannis as they started off through the wood.

"When we were coming up, I noticed fresh deer droppings," Tannis replied. "That would make us a good meal."

"Can you make one?" Vel asked. "The light is fading fast for your human eyes."

"Let's hope we can find something before the sun sets completely."

Vel put his hand up quickly and fell to his knees. "Look, there are a pair of rabbits. If you can make one of them we can at least get some stew."

"One of them?" Tannis laughed. "Both still won't start to feed a group this size." Tannis drew two arrows and set one of them point down in front of him.

"Let's get closer," Vel whispered. "They are too far away."

"No, I can get them," Tannis replied confidently. Drawing his bow, Tannis held his breath and let the arrow fly. What shocked Tannis was how slow the rabbits were moving. A strange feeling came over him, as if his mind were trying to tell him something that he was unwilling to hear. He had more than enough time to grab his second arrow and shoot the second rabbit.

"How did you do that?" Vel asked in shock.

"Do what?" Tannis asked. "That was a long shot but they were barely moving."

Vel didn't look very convinced. Tannis retrieved his arrows from the fallen rabbits and handed them to Vel. "Let's keep moving."

Vel took the rabbits and nodded. Tannis set another arrow and continued on. A large bird that looked like a pheasant took off from a tree fifty yards off, and Tannis made easy work of it.

Vel was looking at Tannis as he reached down to grab the pheasant.

"What?" Tannis asked.

"Nothing," Vel replied quietly.

"You are a terrible liar, Vel." Tannis replied.

"You are an uncanny shot," Vel replied carefully.

"You sound like Atrius when you talk like that," Tannis shot back with a laugh. "I have always been good with a bow. It's probably this bow," Tannis said holding the bow up. "It's Jade's."

"The Rymen make a fine bow, in the right hands that is," Vel replied, his eyes distant as if he was trying to see something within Tannis.

"Don't talk in riddles," Tannis groaned. "I hate that; just say what you are trying to hint at."

Vel closed his eyes. "There," he pointed, "there is something down that way."

"Don't change the subject," Tannis grunted. Then he looked down the way Vel had pointed. "How can you tell?"

"I can smell it," Vel replied.

Tannis re-notched his arrow and moved quietly. There, off in the distance was a large gray fox looking around as if he could feel the approach of strangers. Not wanting it to get away, Tannis let his arrow fly.

"That is not normal," Vel said as he passed Tannis. "That was too far to be a good shot. Tell me, did you feel anything different when you made that shot?"

"I don't see what is so strange about that, it seemed normal to me," Tannis replied puzzled. "I have seen much farther shots and at faster targets. Vel what are you getting at?"

"Nothing," Vel replied quickly as he turned and walked in silence back to camp.

"How did it go?" Kainan asked as they reentered the firelight.

"Young master Tannis may be the greatest bowman I have ever seen." Vel replied. Then he spoke to Kainan in a language that Tannis could only assume was his native Ulmich.

"We didn't find that much," Tannis apologized. "Two rabbits, one pheasant and a Gray fox."

"It will be just fine," Brie said with a smile.

"I can't tell you how happy I will be to see a full barrel of ale," Barvik said, looking around as if he were hoping to see a barrel sitting there.

"Yes, for you its ale. As for me, I can't wait to bath and shave," Atrius said with a laugh.

Kainan smiled as Vel whispered something into his ear.

"Tannis, it will be some time until supper. Care to dust off your blade?" Kainan asked standing.

"Yes," Tannis replied, also standing. As they moved back and forth, Tannis could tell that there was no nonsense to the way Kainan approached combat. Every move was timed and perfect. His movements were crisp and he moved with a rhythm that Tannis could not quite get the hang of. Tannis was near mesmerized; as he practiced, he noticed that he was at peace when he had a sword in his hands. He felt as if he were on top of the world. "I wonder if this is how Jade feels when he runs," Tannis thought to himself. Tannis kept that thought in his mind later that night as he laid his head down and pulled his blankets tightly around his shoulders.

They woke early and got on the road. As they

walked, the dirt faded into cobblestone. Then they topped a slight hill and all the trees faded. Ahead of them were miles of open farmland. Farms stretched out, with animals and horses ranging. Tannis felt as if for the first time since leaving Windhold that he was back into civilization.

"Ah, the low lands," Atrius said with a smile.

Several dozen men in well-kept uniforms were riding towards them on the road from Astrothen.

"Atrius, I'm new here, but is it standard procedure to have that many mounted men down this low?" Samous asked.

"No, not really," Atrius replied.

"Looks as if they are headed this way," Hesih said, moving to the front. "Let me handle this."

"Be my guest," Samous replied.

It didn't take long for the double column of mounted men to reach them. Hesih hailed the group as the approached.

"Good morning Coronel," one of the soldiers greeted loudly. "I have been sent to ensure your safe passage to the city."

"Thank you Captain," Hesih said with a salute.

Horses were brought up from the rear and Tannis was grateful to be back on horseback.

"We'll reach the gates by this afternoon," the captain said as they made their way towards the city.

"Captain, we have company that are about to have the pleasure to see Astrothen for the first time. When we crest Travelers Knoll, let's hold for a time," Hesih said with a smile.

"Yes sir," the captain replied and then he fell back a bit to confer with his men.

Tannis felt an excitement build inside of him as the day wore on. The people that they passed seemed happy; several stopped what they were doing to watch the column ride past. There was a pleasant breeze blowing and the sun was warm. Though Tannis didn't realize it at the time, this would be a moment that he would remember for the rest of his life; a rare perfect moment where everything seems to happen slower. As they crested a slight knoll, Astrothen came into view. The city was larger than anything Tannis had ever seen before. The sight took his breath; there were dozens of large pale towers reaching into the sky, tipped with flowing banners. The walls were huge and hundreds of whipping banners ran along its edge. The massive gates looked as if it would take fifty men to open.

"Welcome to Astrothen," Atrius said, "the greatest city in the world! Well, at least I like it. The towers are all hand crafted granite to give a show of beauty. There is an inner core of strong rock to give it strength. The walls stand nearly eighty feet tall and more than fifty feet thick. At any time, there are more than ten thousand armed soldiers poised to defend the city if need be. Astrothen is also the center of art and music, a truly magical place, and home to King Darius the IV."

"His Majesty has been awaiting your arrival for many days," The captain said.

"It's beautiful," Brie exclaimed.

"It will be my great pleasure to show you around," Atrius replied with a smile.

"I can't wait," Brie exclaimed.

The city grew as they rode closer. Tannis was not used to so many people. The road in and out of Astrothen was row upon row of neatly stacked stones, which were wide enough for several teams to pass at the same time with room to spare. Several armed guards stood and saluted as the party moved past the great gates. The city was bustling with people. The houses were packed tightly together and they all rose high and were several stories high. Bright colors adorned banners and carpets draped over the walls. The roads were lined with large flower beds that were full of bright decorations.

"What's with all the statues?" Samous asked.

"The city is gearing up for the Great New Year's celebrations," Atrius replied. "There is a great festival that lasts for several weeks. This year it's probably going to be extra special with this council meeting."

Tannis was reminded of how hungry he was as they passed a bakery. A quick glance, and he could tell that the wonderful smells coming from the bakery were having an impact on Barvik as well.

"We won't have to meet with the King immediately, will we?" Barvik asked his eyes still on the baker's window.

Samous laughed, "Smells good doesn't it?"

"I have sent word of our arrival," the captain said with a smile. "With any luck His Majesty may have extended his lunch."

"You didn't mention the fact that I am with you did you?" Kainan asked Hesih.

"No, I thought it best for you to tell him," Hesih replied hesitantly.

"Let's hold off on that as long as possible. In fact, maybe I had better stay here in town instead of following you to the palace," Kainan replied, looking up to the palace.

"Nonsense," Atrius said firmly. "You will stay in my chamber with me. You will be able to keep yourself hidden there for a time."

"How will you get into the palace without someone seeing you?" Samous asked. "You do stand out in a crowd."

"The thief's got a point," Barvik replied.

"I can get you in unnoticed, but we had better go off on our own for a bit," Samous said, looking around, a strange grin lighting up his face.

"How will you find my chamber?" Atrius asked.

"I know right where it is," Samous replied. "Not everyone has a two story flat in the palace."

"Have you been in my chamber, you sneak?" Atrius demanded.

"It was nothing personal, you understand," Samous replied quickly. "It's part of my job."

"We will talk about this later," Atrius said with a threatening look.

"Right then, let's be off," Samous said as he turned and rode away from the party with Kainan in tow.

"That could be trouble if someone has already seen him," Barvik said looking around.

"Who would have known who he was?" Hesih asked.

"A great many people," Wurwick growled. "I am losing my wit."

"You can't think of everything," Brie said smiling at the old man.

"I am supposed to," Wurwick replied.

"Why can't Kainan come with us?" Tannis asked.

"It's a long story," Atrius replied carefully.

"Sir Hesih, how long to the palace from here?" Tannis asked.

Hesih hung his head, "About a half hour or so. And it's just Hesih to my friends."

"I'm sorry, I was...," Tannis paused.

"No need," Hesih replied quickly. "There will come a day when I will have great honor in telling people that I was a friend to Tannis of Tigman."

"You're joking right?" Tannis replied confused.

"Hesih!" Atrius scolded. Hesih looked embarrassed for a moment, as if he had said something that he should not have said.

Tannis wanted to pound his fists on something. Normally he was slow tempered but he was feeling much like his younger brother just then. "I have had more than enough of you people treating me as if I am some child! Stop hiding everything from me! I don't want to hear you're not ready, or we can't tell you!"

"All right, calm down," Atrius replied quickly. "We don't have the time to tell you everything right now. Would you settle for understanding why Kainan had to leave?"

Tannis thought about it, his temper still raging. "Yes I suppose so."

"Please keep this knowledge to yourself," Atrius pleaded. "I don't think he would like to know I was talking about his past. Kainan was born to Magistrate Ristun, head of the Council of Chiefs in Astrothen. They serve the King in many respects. Kainan was an only child, and his father saw great things for his son. Kainan was enrolled in all the finest schools in Astrothen. It didn't take him long to set himself apart from everyone else. He was gifted, to say the least. His military skills emerged the fastest, a natural leader and a brilliant tactician. He was also larger than most of the boys his age. As you can tell, he is not a small man. He was sent to the military academy at the age of ten, unheard of to say the least. He moved right through the ranks and set new records in staged battles. When he finished his training at the Academy, he wasn't sent into a regular unit due to his age. Instead he was sent into a special forces training, where he met what he has said to be his two best friends, Cyres and Taggard. Again he rose to the top. His mind was able to see battles differently than other men did, and he was soon made a commander of his Mirrormen team. Now he had been gaining a lot of fame here in Astrothen, and his father being Magistrate, it's no surprise that he was introduced to Kathryn. Princess Kathryn was the oldest child of King Darius. The King was impressed with Kainan, and knowing the wealth of his family agreed to their union and they were married on

Kainan's fifteenth birthday as is the tradition here in Astrothen. Kainan became High General Leader of the armies of Ayre. He has never led a conflict that has not been victorious. He has fought on both of the great continents in dozens of great battles. Truth be told it was common knowledge that the King wanted Kainan to take the throne instead of his eldest son, for reasons I'll not delve into now. The trouble was Kathryn loved to be with him, so against the will of her father she traveled with him, and on such a trip she was tending wounded when a stray arrow struck her full in the chest. She died in his arms, a thing no man should ever have to endure. Everything changed that day for Kainan. The King blamed him for the death of his daughter, and dismissed his father and disgraced their name. Kainan was stripped of all his titles and cast from the palace. When Kainan left, half of the governing generals left with him. Taggard and Cyres to name a few."

"My father was a General in the Ayre army?" Tannis asked.

"That was no stray arrow," Barvik growled.

"What?" Tannis asked.

"I was there," Barvik replied. "She was too far behind our lines. Cyres thought he had made the assassin and chased him, but Neerings can be fast."

"We don't know it was a Neering," Atrius scolded.

"Don't play coy," Barvik replied. "You have three princes who were going to be passed by for the throne."

"Let's not speculate here," Wurwick said firmly. "This is going to be a difficult night as it is."

Barvik didn't look very happy but he rode on in silence. The wind was starting to pick up and Tannis could feel a chill in the air. The party passed through a large elaborate gate into the main courtyard of the royal palace. The palace was vast, however the impending storm had brought a mist of snow and Tannis could see very little of the palace. The party dismounted and hurried inside the protection of the palace. The palace entry was an enormous room with dozens of large fireplaces burning brightly. The floors were all tiled, and there were elaborate paintings and thick woven carpets hung on the walls. A mass of servants swarmed the group, taking their heavy winter cloaks.

"I must make my leave of you here," The captain said saluting to Hesih.

"Thank you Captain," Hesih replied also saluting.

"If I may, my lords?" A gentle old man asked softly.

"Ristmus, my old friend!" Atrius said as he embraced the old man.

"It is good to see you again," Ristmus replied

with a smile.

"It's good to be home," Atrius replied with a smile. "Everyone, this is Ristmus. He is the head steward of the King, the one who keeps the palace running from day to day."

The old man smiled, "We will have lots of time for introductions later. I have instructions to take to the King upon your arrival."

"Are things as bad as we have heard?" Atrius asked as they walked down a long hallway.

Ristmus looked uncomfortable, "It's not good to talk of such things here. Perhaps we can talk more later tonight in your chamber."

"Whatever you think is best," Atrius agreed.

The hallway opened into a large courtyard with several different pathways, the largest of which led to a pair of huge open doors flanked on either side by elaborately dressed guards. The throne room of King Darius was a large open room. The walls were covered with large windows stretching up to the ceiling. The room was full of people who appeared to be doing nothing at all. Some were talking lightly to themselves. What caught Tannis the most was how strangely they were dressed. They all had decorated themselves up with bright bits of clothing; large gold and silver necklaces adorned both the men and the women. King Darius was a sickly looking older man. His skin hung on him as if it he had lost a lot of weight. His eyes were dark and he seemed to be a man who cared little about what was going on around him.

Hesih made his way to the front and bowed deeply before the king. "Your Majesty, may I present you Lord Atrius."

"No introductions are necessary," the king replied in a near monotone voice. "I can recognize one who has betrayed me for a religious patronage."

Atrius moved forward and also bowed. "I do not enjoy the thought of all my years of service being cast away because I believe in something greater than myself," Atrius replied with a sternness Tannis was not used to.

The king's eyes flashed a slight anger. "What cause could you find that could possibly be greater than the service of your King and his people?"

"We did not come here to contest the practicing of a religion that your kingdom was founded upon," Wurwick intervened.

"What would you know of my kingdom?" the King spat. "There is only one power in Astrothen and that is my power."

"Yes, well like I said, we are not here for a contest," Wurwick continued as if the King had said nothing. "I am here to oversee the Council that will take place."

"This is my kingdom, and my palace. You meddling wizards may have arranged this foolhardy meeting, but I tell you now that I will oversee all proceedings that take place here. I and I alone will be recognized."

Wurwick's face hardened. "I was hoping to have a more pleasant stay. For your own reasons you have set your will against me. I hope you will listen carefully, for I will only say this once. We have obeyed your demands and held this council here on your soil. We have arranged for the Kings and Dignitaries from all parts of the world to travel at their own peril to your city. Rest assured that this will be easiest for you. For reasons unknown to me, you seem to have the idea that you are the most powerful and important man alive. You have cast the priests from your hall. You have elevated yourself in mind to heights your body will never fill. I will not stand here and be lectured by a fool on the ins and outs of this kingdom. I was there the day it was formed. I was there the day this city was born, and I was there the day your father's, father's father swore to the Twelve Divines to keep this kingdom in their names. You may not like that we are here, and you may not think this council is necessary. So I will give you this one chance. Say the word and we will leave and hold this council somewhere else, and Ayre can stand against the hordes alone. But know this; if we leave you will be cast on your own. No one will come to your aid, and when Astrothen is run asunder, we will come back and sift through the ashes and rebuild what can be salvaged."

King Darius stood his face livid. "Remember whom you address! I will not be disrespected in my own court! You will leave now! You will not return to my court until the day of this conference!"

"What has gotten into you?" Wurwick asked his old eyes searching. "This is not the mighty King I once knew."

Darius spun on the wizard. "Guards, shackle this foul wizard for his insolence and escort the rest of them from this palace."

Tannis thought his heart would stop as several guards set there arrows and drew their bows taut. The sharp sounds of the bow strings tightening seemed to vibrate in his mind. Brie screamed and Tannis reached for his sword. Guards began to pile in. It wasn't a sound or a flash of light that told Tannis something great was happening. It was a strange feeling that had completely taken Tannis over. Tannis looked over at Wurwick, who stood motionless. The arrows that had been drawn and aimed Wurwick simply vanished. Wurwick raised his staff above his head. The tip of his staff erupted into a bright green light that spread to fill the room. Every guard in the room toppled over and fell deeply asleep. The King went ridged and his eyes widened. No one said a word. The quiet was suddenly overwhelming. Then, the light faded and Wurwick approached the visibly shaking King. "Do we have an understanding?" Wurwick asked calmly.

King Darius looked as if he were going to faint. "We do," Darius replied in a light shaking voice.

"Good," Wurwick replied. Then he turned and started to walk back towards the party. "I trust we won't have any other problems like this. Next time I won't be as accommodating."

They all turned and followed Wurwick back down the hallway. "What was all that?" Brie asked.

"It's a problem with power," Wurwick replied. "Darius has all but convinced himself that he is the most powerful man on earth."

"Things aren't going very well are they?" Tannis asked.

"We will be ok," Atrius replied. "It might be a good idea to lay low for the next several days."

"Will we all fit at your...," Brie hesitated.

"It is a flat," Atrius replied. "My family has long worked in the palace. Long ago we were awarded a corner of the palace to live. As to your question, yes we will all be very comfortable there."

Tannis was slightly unprepared for Atrius's flat. It was about half the size of Wagstaff. One large common room was surrounded by ten comfortable rooms on two floors. As close as Tannis could tell Atrius was richer than the King himself. Gold and silver goblets and plates adorned the shelves. Elaborate carpets covered the tile floors and stone walls. Large upholstered couches filled the common room. A large decorated table filled the center of the room. As they entered, Barvik swore at the sight of the table. It was brimming from one side to the other with food. A boar sat at the center on a golden pallet. An elderly man in a long robe met them at the door.

"I got your message, Master." The old man said with a bow.

"Everyone, this is Accius, my dearest friend and housekeeper."

Kainan and Samous entered the room. "Now that we are all here, let's eat," Atrius announced with a smile.

Tannis was again amazed at the amount of food that Barvik was able to eat. The room was warm, and everyone's spirits were high. Atrius introduced everyone, one by one to Accius.

"Any news?" Atrius was asking Accius.

"The King is not himself. Over the last several

years he has been slipping fast. He gets lost in the hallways, and forgets people's names. I have seen it before, a condition of the mind."

"He has also lost weight," Atrius replied.

"His sons have felt his passing approaching fast. Achilles, His Majesty's youngest son, and his two bodyguards were killed by bandits last spring. No one at the palace knew why they had left the city. One of the Chair Holders had mentioned hearing Achilles and older brother Basilius arguing the morning they left. Unfortunately, he was found dead in his chamber, an apparent suicide."

"That sounds convenient," Barvik grunted.

"Many here feel as if something major is going to happen soon," Accius continued. "Basilius is the apparent heir but the best hope for the kingdom would be his last remaining brother, Nicomedes."

"Nicomedes is a good lad." Atrius agreed.

"I fear for his safety," Accius replied with a bowed head. "I see only death here in Astrothen."

"The darkness will not last forever," Atrius said with a small grin aimed at Tannis.

Tannis was about to ask Atrius why he looked his direction when he said that, but he was interrupted by a rush of footsteps and shouts from outside the entrance to Atrius's flat. The door burst open and a dozen armed soldiers forced their way inside. Right behind them came the King, who carried a sword that was so elaborately jeweled that it was clear that this sword was never meant for combat. Behind the King, there was a man who wore the same armor that Kainan wore. He was nearly a foot shorter than Kainan, yet he carried himself as if was the largest man alive.

"Your Majesty," Atrius began rising to his feet.

"It's true then," the King barked, his eyes flashing with hate. "You have betrayed me. You have brought this vile and soulless man into my palace, under my very nose!"

Kainan rose, his face emotionless. "If His Majesty will recall, I was banished from your sight, not your palace. In truth, Atrius has done nothing wrong."

The man behind the King moved toward Kainan, sword drawn. "How dare you speak! You have no honor! You have no place here! You should not have come back, Kainan."

Barvik was swearing furiously as he drew his axe. "You are a coward and a fool! I will not stand here and listen to you belittle your betters."

"That's enough, Barvik," Kainan said firmly. "Stand down."

"Not this time. I won't watch this again!" The giant bellowed.

"I will handle Paulinus," Kainan replied firmly.

"Yes, listen to your master you overgrown fool. That is, if you have brain enough to understand me," Paulinus said with heavy contempt.

"Enough of this, wearing that armor didn't increase your skills or grant you any magical aid. You are a snake and nothing more," Barvik spat.

Samous stepped in front of Kainan. "I'm sorry; I must have missed the first act. In what way can you even come close to meeting Kainan's many accolades? Perhaps it is that you feel an added strength from your position and bribed influence?"

"Shut your mouth!" Paulinus growled. "Arrest them all!" A soldier went to grab Samous. The little man slapped his arm down and spun into the man, kicking him solidly in the stomach. He then he flipped over the stricken man and ducked under a sword thrust. Spinning again, he laid an elbow to the inside of Paulinus's knee and then he leaped, kicking him several times as he spun backwards landing on his feet. Paulinus stumbled back from the attack, his knee giving way as he collapsed. Samous flung himself onto Paulinus faster than Tannis could believe. Before anyone could act, Samous had a long dagger pressed into Paulinus's throat.

"Call them off," Samous said in a calm voice.

"Back up!" Paulinus shrieked.

"Have you ever heard of Yeapst frogs?" Samous

asked in a calm voice.

Paulinus swallowed hard but said nothing, his face breaking out into a sweat.

"Of course not, how silly of me; allow me to explain. They are a small frog found in the forests of lower Ryman. They only grow to be about the size of the tip of your thumb, incredible little frogs. You see, their skin excretes this wonderful slime. It is among the world's most deadly poisons. This dagger is dipped in that selfsame poison. So far as I know there is no cure, and you die in the space of an hour. One little drop into the blood and it's all over. Now that I have your attention, I highly recommend that you stop making such a fool of yourself. It's unbecoming and all that."

"Samous let him go," Kainan replied. "If they want to arrest someone, they may take me."

"No one is under arrest," Wurwick growled. Then he turned on the now shaking King. "I thought we had an understanding. I guess I need to reaffirm to you our conditions." The King froze, his eyes were wide and there was a horror in his stare. "Kainan is here to advise me. He will be staying. Moreover, if you burst in on me again I will be forced to do something I may regret."

The king was convulsing. "I won't have him roaming my palace," the king stammered.

"If that is your wish, he will stay with me until we meet for council," Wurwick replied coolly.

"Take me away from this place," the King almost mumbled. The guards all looked confused but slowly made their withdrawal. Samous removed his blade from Paulinus's throat and moved away from the embarrassed man.

"We will meet again," Paulinus warned.

Samous laughed. "Yes," he agreed, "maybe you will do a little better next time."

Paulinus gave Samous a look of absolute hate as he left.

"Well that could have gone worse," Atrius said with a smile.

Kainan shook his head. "This is not going to be an easy stay."

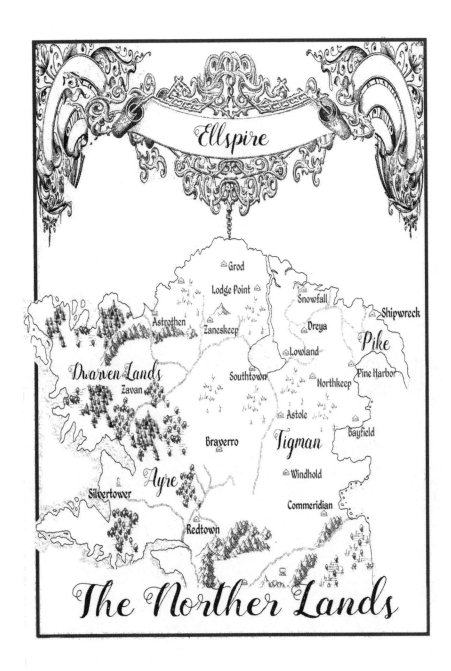

CHAPTER 19

THE REUNION

They stayed there for the next two weeks, enjoying the comforts of Astrothen. People started to arrive in greater numbers as the days grew closer to the New Year. A group of Elves arrived looking travel stained and weary. Tannis had never seen Elves before. They were slightly taller than the men of Windhold. Their long, pointed ears were much like Vel's. There was a beauty in them that Tannis could not even begin to understand. Their clothing was all very fine, in fact Tannis could hardly believe how intricate the gold and silver lacing was.

"The Elves are an immortal race," Kainan explained. "As you may expect, they have more patience than we do. Some of their clothing takes decades to make. They are a beautiful people and they take the time to present themselves." Tannis had spent most of his time with Kainan since they had arrived at Astrothen. In that time he had grown quite close to him. Kainan was not as good with a sword as Cyres, but he was a far better teacher. Tannis was improving faster than he ever could have imagined. Kainan taught him the sword one day, and the axe the next. He was taught how to throw knives and short spears. In all, Tannis felt his progress was nothing short of a miracle.

"It is not uncommon for some men to learn quickly," Kainan replied when Tannis brought this to his attention. "I was always moving faster than everyone around me."

"But what does it mean?" Tannis asked.

"It means you have a bright future," Kainan replied with a smile.

"You're not telling me something," Tannis complained bitterly.

Kainan only smiled and hefted his sword again.

A Chancellor and his staff arrived from Suil the same day that King Volugen of Pike arrived with his Guard. King Rosbin of Tigman arrived with King Adthan of Ryman. Everything was nearly ready. All that remained missing was Jadeance. Tannis was practicing with his sword as Wurwick entered the room. His beard was stuck full of snow.

"I haven't seen a storm like that in years," the old man complained, standing next to the fire.

"Why were you out in it then?" Samous asked with a smile.

Wurwick returned the smile with one of his own. "A friend of ours is trying to find his way to us in it. He is going to need some help", and then he paused slightly and struck a dramatic pose. "If only we had someone who was familiar with this land to guide him in."

Tannis felt a surge of excitement. "Jade is here?"

"He is close," the old man replied. "I thought he was going to be late."

"Late for what?" Tannis asked.

"The New Year," Wurwick laughed.

"I didn't know you liked to party that much," Samous laughed.

"This is going to be slightly different. Tomorrow will be a day to remember," Wurwick said looking into the fire. "That is neither here nor there. We have to go get him."

"I'll go wake Brie," Tannis said, sheathing his sword.

"Oh no, you don't," Wurwick replied. "It is very cold out there. She can wait a while longer."

"She isn't going to like that," Tannis said bluntly.

"She doesn't have to like it," the old man replied, shaking the snow from his long hat. "It is not good for her to go out in this weather."

...an and Barvik rose and started putting on ...ner clothing.

"Vel, you had better come too. We may need your eyes." The dark man nodded and also went for a thick woolen cloak.

"Well, there is no need for all of us to go," Samous said, looking at all the winter clothing that was being passed around. "One of us had better stay here and watch over the girl."

"I see," Wurwick replied with a disapproving look.

"It's not that I don't want to go and prance around in the snow," Samous protested.

Wurwick's answering scowl spoke volumes.

"You can see how one of us needs to keep her safe?" Samous asked Tannis innocently.

"I don't believe you either," Tannis replied.

"Nobody understands me," Samous complained.

"Oh, I think we do," Atrius replied. "I will try to conceal your whereabouts but I fear you are all in for trouble when you get back."

Wurwick shrugged. "I'm betting on her forgetting as soon as she sees him."

"We had better get moving," Kainan said, heading for the door.

####

The snow was blinding, Jadeance could hardly see the road in front of him.

"We can't continue like this," Orin yelled over the howling wind.

Jadeance could feel Wurwick getting closer. He was aware of a slight drumming sound that he could feel more than hear. "They are close!" Jadeance shouted back and he made his way to the front of the line. Holding his staff out in front of him, he focused his energy and a bright blue shield appeared. The defining sound of the wind faded considerably as Jadeance pushed on. He had no idea if he was even still on the road or not. The snow was knee deep and the only thing Jadeance could make out was the blizzard. The drumming grew louder and firmer in his mind until, through the snow Jadeance could make out the familiar shape of Tannis running towards him. They met in a fierce bear hug. Then the others were there, but the storm prevented any real conversations. They made brief introductions and started towards the city. Wurwick was able to find his way without any troubles, and though it took most of the day they finally made their way into the palace. As they made their way to Atrius's flat, Jadeance heard a slight squeal as Brie jumped into his arms. She kissed him soundly and for the first bit, he rather enjoyed the kiss. However he was very aware of the fact that they were not alone. Finally she released him, with tears streaming down her cheeks.

ʼt ever leave me again," she said as she
ʒd the tears from her cheeks.

Jadeance was more than a little embarrassed.
"Let me make the introductions," he rushed on to
cover his embarrassment. "May I present Prince
Orin of Glorak-Arkul. The lady at his side is Princess
Kiasma." They both inclined their heads. "This is
Grik," then Jadeance paused. "I don't really know
what your exact title is?"

Orin stepped forward, "He is my chief advisor on
this trip, among other things. I may assume this to
be your brother?"

"Yes," Jadeance replied.

Orin bowed before Tannis. "It gives me honor to
meet you. Your brother saved my life and is welcome
in my hall. You who are bound to him by the deepest
bond are also welcome in my hall. Know that Orin of
Glorak-Arkul is your friend."

Cyres who was toasting his return with Barvik,
Kainan, and Vel laughed out loud. "Come now, let's
drink now and talk later!"

Jadeance sat with Brie nestled in his arms telling
Tannis of his capture and escape and all the wonders
of the Dwarvin halls, as everyone else celebrated and
got to know each other.

Wurwick made his way over and sat next to
Jadeance. "Well boy, you have done a great deal of

growing in the short time we have been apart."

"Yes master," Jadeance agreed. "It has not been easy."

"I never said it would be. It was good for you though. I will not always be there to help you, and that can be a scary time for a young Magi. I have to say you handled yourself well enough. Well, except the business with the Volkru. That could have been done better."

Jadeance blushed. "I didn't plan on getting impaled."

"Try to avoid it in the future," Wurwick suggested with a smile. "You may not survive the next one."

"I wasn't planning on letting it happen again," Jadeance replied a bit hurt. He hadn't meant for it to happen in the first place, and it was his side that was hurt after all. Wurwick laughed and Brie held him tight. Her hair had a slight fragrance to it that Jadeance found to be quite pleasant. They all started towards the bed chambers as the fires began to fade. The next morning was like a dream for Jadeance. All his friends were close and they all sat around Atrius's table laughing and eating. Jadeance and Brie played for the group, as Samous and Atrius sang songs of old. Wurwick and Atrius left as Grik pulled out a strange looking set of pipes. They were nearly twice as long as the set Jadeance played, and the

ey produced was a rich set of low tones that
ed to fit the low majestic voices of the Dwarves.
ear midmorning Wurwick and Atrius returned.

"It is set," Wurwick said, as he motioned for
everyone's attention. "We will go to the Temple
of the Twelve tonight and meet with the high
priest. There, we will prepare for what is to happen
tomorrow at council."

"Why are we going to the temple?" Tannis asked.

"There we will find the answers you two have
so long desired," Atrius replied. "There you will
give up your responsibilities and be free to go back
to Tigman."

"You mean the business with him having the
birthright?" Jadeance asked.

"Yes," Atrius replied. "You will finish what your
father started and we will move forward." Tannis
smiled, however there was something in that look
that told Jadeance that it was far more for show than
anything else.

Tannis smiled. "It will be good to return to
Wagstaff after all this time." Then he looked down at
the chainmail he wore and his sword.

"The road home will be a long one," Vel said with
a slight smile, "and a dangerous one at that. You will
need that armor for a time longer."

Tannis flushed slightly, "I don't know why, but I

am not ready to give it all back yet."

"The amour and sword were gifts," Vel replied simply. "They are yours as long as you draw breath, or until you discard them."

Tannis looked grateful, as his fingers ran along the hilt of his sword.

"So you will answer all our questions tonight?" Jadeance asked.

"Yes child. We will tell you about your mother and father and why you needed to come here," Atrius said as he filled a crystal goblet with wine. "Your journey may very well be at an end."

Something deep inside of Jadeance told him that his journey was just beginning.

MORE BOOKS BY DAVID MUNSON

A NEW AWAKENING

A NEW ZEPHER

COMING SOON

A NEW CURSE